Bleeding Star Chronicles Collection 1

Ethan Russell Erway

CONTENTS

ACKNOWLEDGMENTS

Special thanks go to my wife Kara for her support and love. I'd also like to give a shout out to three of my favorite podcasts- The Sci-Fi Christian, Strangers and Aliens, and the Sci-Fi Diner.

Book 1

A Sort of Homecoming

From the bridge of the starship Katara, Galin Winchester and Jace Chang watched as the streaking pinpoints of light slowed to a halt all around them. They took stock of their surroundings. Nothing too unusual out there- just the black vastness of the void and a whole bunch of twinkling stars.

Galin stood up from his chair and twisted his torso from side to side in a satisfying stretch. He removed his faded leather duster and let it fall gently onto the back of the captain's chair. He straightened his vest, unfastened the top button of his navy blue shirt, and rolled up his sleeves.

"Alright, kid, here we are. These are the coordinates, so go ahead and scan the area. You remember what we're looking for?"

"This thing has a high amount of tritanium in it, right?"

"That's right. Crank up power on the short range scanners and see what you can come up with."

Galin watched as Jace worked the control panel at the co-pilot's station. The young man, a college drop out, had begged to come onboard as an intern. He had dreams in his head of fortune and glory, and wanted to learn the ropes of space travel. He'd tried to sign up for the Space Marine infantry but was turned away because of a knee injury he'd gotten while playing football in high school. At first Galin hadn't been sure that letting the young man come on with the crew was a good idea, but he was earning his keep. He was a hard worker and a fast learner, picking things up after seeing them done only once or twice.

This kind of life wasn't suited for everyone. Galin had met a lot of people who dreamed of doing what he and his crew did, at least until they got their feet wet. He'd learned over the years that either you're built for a life of traveling through space in an enclosed artificial environment- or you aren't. Most people were not. Galin, on the other hand, loved what he did. He seemed to be drawn to it, and couldn't imagine doing anything else. He loved exploring the stars, and he loved his ship.

The Katara was an old Dagger class starship, retired from military service years ago, but well taken care of.

What Galin and his crew lacked in expensive technology they made up for in experience and a lot of tender loving care.

Dagger class ships were so named not only because of their appearance- they actually looked like short, fat daggers, but also because of their function. They were designed to be stealthy fighters, relatively small and very fast, but large enough to perform rescue operations and haul supplies when the need arose.

When Galin Winchester had found the Katara, a little over ten years before, he knew she was the right ship for him; he knew she was exactly what he'd been looking for. He'd been dreaming of starting his own business, and rebuilding this ship had been the key to making that happen. Now they travelled through the constellations together, searching for treasures - both human and alien- that time had long forgotten.

"I've got something," Jace told him. He grinned and pulled the red baseball cap off his head, tossing it onto the floor beside him. "Looks like it's just up ahead."

"That was quick. Good work." Galin gave him a pat on the shoulder. "Looks like Starla really came through for us this time. That woman can be a real pain in the rear, but she sure knows her stuff."

"Hey Captain, you mind if I put the coordinates in and take us over?"

Galin raised an eyebrow. The kid had earned a little fun. He'd been willing to learn the ins and outs of running the ship, and hadn't complained once.

"Okay, take us in. But slow way down when we get close. We run into that thing, our deflector shield could fry its circuitry, or worse."

"I'll be careful," Jace said excitedly.

"Good man." Galin sat back down in the captain's chair. He was confident that the kid could pull the flight off without a hitch, but he needed a bit more practice before being left alone in the cockpit. "And don't get too comfortable in that seat, I don't think Peter is quite ready to give up his co-pilot chair."

He got on the com.

"Ulrick, report to the loading bay and suit up. We're approaching the artifact and preparing for pick-up."

Jace looked at him eagerly. "Hey Cap, I could go out there with you and help bring that thing in."

He shook his head. "Ulrick would thank you for that, but it's not going to happen. Not this time. You haven't had any training yet in the zero gravity suit. It's not as easy as it looks, believe me."

Galin looked at the young man and saw a little of himself when he'd been that age. There didn't seem to be anything Jace thought he couldn't do. That was admirable, a good trait, but it could also be dangerous. And the older he got, the more he realized it.

"So tell me, kid, how do you like it so far? Living on the ship, I mean?"

Jace smiled. "I'm loving it. It's not exactly what I

thought it would be though."

"Yeah? How so? More work than you'd planned on?"

"No, that's not it. I knew there would be a lot of work involved. I guess it's just...well it's a little hard to explain. Living in the ship for long periods of time- it feels a bit cramped, kinda stuffy, especially down in places like the engine room. But at the same time there's a tremendous sense of freedom. It's like we could go anywhere, do anything we wanted."

Galin looked at him thoughtfully. "I know exactly what you mean. I've always felt the same way."

He took in a deep breath. The kid was going to work out all right. He was right about the ship feeling cramped too; the air suddenly seemed a bit more stuffy than it had a few moments before.

"There's a small trading post on Omicron Five not too far from here. It's a really beautiful place. After making the pickup it'd be nice to stretch our legs there for a day or two."

Jace nodded enthusiastically. "Sounds good to me."

Galin looked around the small bridge of the Katara. He put his hand upon the cold metal hull. Even the most seasoned space travelers got cabin fever once in a while.

"Alright, that's the last clamp. Can we please get our tails back inside the loading bay now?"

"Stop being such a slaggin' baby. A large strapping guy like you shouldn't be whining all the time. Its unbecoming of your character."

Ulrick frowned at Galin's remark, although Galin couldn't see it. The dark, reflective visors worn by both men prevented that. Galin quickly rechecked that the straps and each of the three clamps were tightly secured. He'd learned that accidents happen when you least expect them to, and they all worked too hard to get lazy and complacent when handling their own pay dirt.

"You know how much I *hate* coming out in these zero-g suits? When's Joseph going to get the tractor-beam up and running again?"

"Fixed it this morning actually. We still need to conserve power though, and the winch is much more efficient. Once we get back to Earth with this here beauty I'll be able to take the old girl in for some long overdue maintenance, invest in some upgrades too. A new tractor beam is going to be one of the first things on the list."

Ulrick looked over their prize once again. It was a large rectangular steel crate, about twice the size of a coffin, with a small control panel on the side. It didn't strike him as an impressive thing, at least not compared to some of the other items that they'd brought in over the years.

"You really think this thing will fetch that kind of price? Looks like an old piece of junk to me."

"That's why I pay you for your muscles and not your brains."

Ulrick frowned again, and although Galin couldn't see the man's face, he knew from experience what kind of reaction the wisecrack would draw.

"Awe, don't take it personal-like. Truth be told I don't consider my own intellect vastly superior to yours. After all, that's what we brought the little girl along for. She's been working out pretty good for business so far."

Ulrick didn't say anything. He never was what Galin considered a talker, but he noticed that the man became even quieter when they ventured outside the ship like this. He knew that Ulrick was uncomfortable, maybe even scared. He sympathized, but didn't understand it. Galin knew they were securely attached, that they were nearly as safe out here as they were inside the ship. He always found it relaxing, peaceful even, to get away from everything for a while and come outside. He enjoyed gazing out into the vastness of space, and often liked to let himself simply float there and stare off at the stars. Out here, away from the crew, the ship noise, and the humming of the engine- it was just so peaceful.

Ulrick gave Galin's helmet a few sharp knocks with his fist. "Hello, anybody home in there? Can we please head back in now?"

"Sure, sorry about that. Let's get this thing loaded up."

Galin began to pull himself back toward the ship,

moving along the rope attached to his belt. Ulrick followed.

They got into the loading dock and flipped on their gravity boots, enabling them to walk in the depressurized bay. Galin started the winch and moved the load along slowly to prevent damage. They guided it in and set it down, adding pads and carefully chaining the box into place.

Galin's boots clanked with each step as he walked to a control panel on the nearby wall and closed the loading bay door. He re-pressurized the room and began to unfasten his helmet, but Ulrick had his off first.

The tall man inhaled deeply, like someone who had been underwater, seeing how long he could hold his breath. His large nose, chiseled chin, and shoulder-length blonde hair made him look like a Viking, and every time he had an angry look on his face like the one he currently wore, Galin half expected him to whip out some concealed battle-axe and start swinging.

"Don't worry about it big-boy," Galin said, slapping his friend on the shoulder. "With luck, that's the last time you'll ever have to do it."

The man sneered. "That's what you said the last time."

Galin smiled as he punched a few buttons on his wrist-com. "Starla, we've got it all loaded up, you want to come down to the bay and check it out?"

Immediately, the door a few feet away glided open.

There she stood.

"Did you really think I wouldn't be waiting right here for you guys to get it in?"

Galin gave her a knowing smile.

"So, let's take a look and make sure this thing is the real deal." She walked around the crate, examining it up and down- comparing the numbers and markings on its surface to those she had on her data-pad. Galin and Ulrick looked at each other, not needing to say what they both were thinking. Starla was a nerdy know it all at times, but she was a real looker. She had all the right things in all the right places, and enchanting brown eyes that could melt an iceberg. However, everyone on the crew knew that she and Galin had history, and they knew they needed to treat her right or they'd answer to him for it.

She whipped her long brown pony tail back behind her head and pushed her glasses further up her nose with one finger, and then stood up straight with her arms crossed in front.

"Well?" Galin asked. But he already knew the answer from the electrified smile painted across her face. She started to bounce in place. He hadn't seen her get this excited in a very long time.

"It's real, all right. I can't believe we've actually found it. I can't believe it's survived this long."

"Excellent. I've already had several buyers show some interest. Once word gets out there's no telling what it'll bring at auction."

Starla glared at him, her large, brown eyes spelling out her disapproval. "This thing *really* does belong in the World Space Museum. It's not just some common piece of space junk."

"No, its not. In fact it's a nearly invaluable piece of Earth's history, but it's *our* invaluable piece of history, and I aim to see just how valuable this invaluable thing is." He winked at her and she frowned back. "But, I'll tell you what, Princess, you're more than welcome to donate your share of the money to the space museum."

"And end up having to work for *you* for the rest of my life? I'll have to pass on that."

Galin gazed at her, and gave her what he considered his most charming smile. She smiled back despite herself. After all, he thought, she knew that the self-centered, male chauvinist jackass routine was all just an act. Well, most of it was. *Some* of it was anyway.

The truth however, was that they all had a good reason to be happy. This find was going to be the answer to a lot of problems for the whole crew.

Peter's voice suddenly rang out over the intercom. "Captain Winchester, please return to the bridge."

He opened the channel on his wrist-com. "What's going on, Peter?"

"Looks like we've drawn some attention. Three unidentified ships have approached. They're still hanging back a ways, but it looks like they could be trouble."

Galin let out a sigh of frustration.

Ulrick tossed his helmet and gravity boots into his locker, and threw the door shut with a clank. "Mama never said it was going to be easy."

Galin looked him up and down. "That's because she had to give birth to a big lug like you."

Peter opened up a hailing frequency and flipped on the universal translator. "Attention all ships, please identify yourselves. This is Peter Cervantes of the starship Katara."

Silence.

The three small ships had them surrounded and were slowly moving in.

Peter looked up at Galin, who had just come in behind him. "Looks like pirates, alright. They must have seen us lingering in the area and figured we were up to something. It's a good thing they didn't know what that was floating around out there. Probably just figured it was a common piece of space junk, not even worth using for target practice."

Galin moved past the captain's chair and into the gunner's pit. He got on the com. "Attention all ships, this is Captain Galin Winchester of the Katara. Identify yourselves immediately or we *will* open fire."

The ship suddenly rumbled from an incoming phaser

blast.

"Well, I guess there's our answer," Peter said with a sneer. "Shutting down all non-essential systems and re-routing power to the shields. Switching on internal battle-stations communication channel."

"Here we go again, let's keep these garbage-hoppers guessing." Galin looked at the battle display in front of him. "Are you thinking what I'm thinking?"

"Attack pattern Alpha- seven o'clock."

The Katara twirled around several times to port and then evened back out, flanking one of the small fighters. Galin squeezed the trigger, and the ship passing in front of them flickered as its shield absorbed the hits.

"That's what you suckers get for making my coffee run cold," Galin said angrily.

"Don't act like you don't love this. Evasive pattern Omega- nine o'clock." Peter steered the ship sharply to port again and pulled up, dropping into a flight pattern behind another of the enemy ships.

"Poor fools never see it coming do they?" Galin yelled happily.

"Nope. This old boat has a few good tricks left in her. Good thing she's so much faster than she looks."

"Sure is," Galin said, landing another series of shots, "But those little tubs are pretty quick themselves. They might actually give us a bit of a challenge. Their shields seem pretty tough too."

Suddenly three more ships popped onto the radar.

They were moving in fast.

"Uh oh," yelled Peter. "Looks like they're not alone. We've got three more unfriendlies coming in hot. Jace, report to the bridge immediately. Ulrick, get to the stern and hop on that phaser turret you and the Chief just put in."

"You really think we should trust the kid not to shoot our nose off?" Galin asked.

"Listen Ace, you're good, but not good enough to tackle all six of 'em. I've been spending some time with Jace on the guns, he's done okay so far."

"Good enough for me."

The bridge suddenly shook violently.

Now I know how a snow globe feels, Galin thought to himself.

"Ouch, that one's gonna leave a mark," said Peter. "Looks like that one at six o'clock launched an anti-matter torpedo. Good thing it wasn't a direct hit. These little suckers pack quite a punch, whatever they are."

"Looks to me like Kakon Vipers. I've never seen pirates with ships as fancy and mean as these before. They must have been pretty happy to get their hands on them."

"Well," Peter said with a frown, from what I've heard, it's a good thing for us they aren't trained like Kakon pilots."

The ship started rumbling, accompanied by a long series of ferocious booms.

"You'd better find some wood to knock on," Galin told him. "The shields aren't gonna hold up long if we keep letting them pound on us like this."

Ulrick's voice suddenly popped up on the com. "I'm manning the aft phaser turret. We haven't completed testing this thing yet, so keep your fingers crossed for me."

"Give em all you've got," Galin told him. "These guys aren't known for playing well with others." He took aim at a fighter that was blasting toward them. He squeezed the trigger, and several shots made contact on its port bow. Sparks flew, and something that looked like a ball of lightning engulfed the ship as its shields collapsed. It quickly pulled up and shot away in retreat.

"Hey, where you going," Galin yelled. "Things are just starting to get fun."

He saw an explosion out of the corner of his eye as Peter pulled the Katara around. A stream of incoming fire zipped over their heads, narrowly missing the ship.

From somewhere, they saw a flash.

"Got one!" Ulrick said excitedly over the com as they watched the ship disappear from the radar screen.

"Keep it up, big guy," Galin told him.

Jace had come in quietly behind them.

Peter pointed to the empty gun turret. "What are you waiting for young'un? Take the starboard repeater gun."

Galin looked over his shoulder. "And DON'T shoot our nose off, kid!"

He opened fire on another target. It's shields flickered as it returned the favor and landed several direct hits on the Katara. The cockpit shook as a series of sparks spat up at Peter from the communication control panel.

"I think we've made them angry," he yelled. "They don't seem to appreciate seeing their friends get greased."

"Yup," yelled Galin. "Now they're trying to kill us, not capture us. Jace, you've got one coming your way. Meet him at one o'clock and give him a good welcome."

Jace laughed gleefully as he tracked the viper with repeater gun fire.

Ulrick came through again. "Just got another one. What's that leave us, three?"

"Yup," responded Galin "Leave some for me, will ya?"

"Nope."

Galin locked on to another viper and opened up on it. The shields flickered and then dropped, and it exploded just seconds before the Katara shot through the debris like a gleaming silver bullet.

"Looks like the other two are retreating," Peter reported. "You want me to pursue?"

"Naw, we'd better quit while we're ahead. I know at least one of those two ships took some pretty heavy damage. I don't think they'll be coming back. All crew members please report your current status."

Peter looked down at the personnel screen for a few

moments. "All members have checked in. No injuries reported."

Chief Joseph, please generate a damage report."

"Already on it, Captain."

Galin stepped away from the gun turret and breathed a sigh of relief. Jayce climbed out of his as well, and moved back into the central cockpit.

"Well kid, did you hit anything?" Peter asked.

"Not sure. I think I might have gotten one a time or two."

"It's a lot harder than it looks when the adrenaline starts pumpin'," Galin told him with a slap on the back. "But, practice makes perfect. Hopefully we can find you some more junk to shoot at before we run across targets that fire back again."

Joseph's voice popped up on the com. "Sending that damage report through now. They hammered us pretty good, I'll just have to keep us patched up until we get back home."

"Copy that." He looked up at Jace. "You report to the chief and see what you can do to help. Tell him I'll be down in a bit."

Jace nodded and turned to leave.

Galin sat back down in the captain's chair and began to rub his temples. "That was a close one."

"Yeah," Peter grunted. "But we've had closer."

"Yes, we have. But, sure will be nice to upgrade some of these systems. Those filthy pirates won't want to mess with us once they see what I've got in store for the old girl."

"And that's only if they can catch us," added Peter.

Galin smiled. He loved the Katara. She was a clunky old boat, but she'd never let him down, and he'd tried to take good care of her, too.

"So what's the ETA back to Earth, about two weeks?"

Peter punched in a few numbers. "Well, it would be at maximum warp. Hopefully our engine didn't get banged up too bad. Everything's checking out okay from here, but that may not be the case from Joseph's end."

"Go ahead and set course for Omicron Five. It won't take us too far out of the way. I promised Jace a chance to stretch his legs before the flight back home."

Peter had already set the coordinates in to the navigational computer. "I don't think anybody will argue with you on the need for that. Are you thinking we can make a few repairs there and check for spare parts before getting too deep into space?"

Galin nodded. "You look really beat. Why don't you take a break while I cover things up here for a while. After that little scuffle, I don't want to leave her on autopilot too long without doing periodic system checks."

"Alright, I'm gonna try to get some proper sleep. Let me know if anything comes up."

"Will do," Galin said. "I think I'm going to get a little shut-eye too."

Peter retired to his quarters, and Galin ran another systems check before engaging the auto-pilot. The computer would alert him of anything unusual.

Reclining in his chair, he yawned and folded his arms across his chest. He had a pounding headache, but was only now realizing it. He gazed out into space, and watched the stars as they sped past. It made him think back to when he was a boy, lying on his back in the snow, and gazing up as the snowflakes dropped down around him. Back then he imagined they were stars. He thought of his children, and wondered what they were doing; he wondered if they were happy. He thought about Melissa. Would she ever be willing to take him back? Did he really want her to? His mind wandered through a hundred thoughts that faded slowly away as he drifted off into a peaceful sleep.

The Katara's hull gleamed as her landing gear touched down onto docking pad seven. Off the port side of the ship, Omicron Five's sun was just coming up over the ocean, and it was a warming and welcome sight after spending several unrelenting weeks in space.

The ship came to a rest, and the stairs had barely finished descending before Starla and Jace bounded down like a couple of kids who had just been let out for recess.

Galin laughed at them under his breath, and stepped

up to the hatch, letting the cool, refreshing air fill his lungs. He made a mental note that the ship's air filtration systems *were* going to need some attention. It just seemed to be getting too stuffy in there lately. Then again, maybe it was all in their heads.

Everyone else exited the ship, and Joseph punched in the security activation code.

A spry young man in a khaki uniform came up to greet them. "Welcome to Omicron Five," he told them, sounding like he meant it.

"Thanks. Galin Winchester. This here's my Engineer, Joseph Stormcrow. And that distinguished looking swarthy gentlemen over there..." he said while pointing at his unamused friend, "is the finest starship pilot in the quadrant- Peter Rodrigo Cervantes."

The young man, who was not quite used to getting such a wordy response, and wasn't entirely sure that Galin wasn't toying with him, smiled and nodded kindly.

"Wonderful," he said. "Well, my name is Buck. Can I be of any assistance getting you settled in?"

"No, we know the drill. But I appreciate the offer."

"Very good, sir. The offer stands if something comes up." He started off and gave them a wave, "Enjoy your stay."

"Thanks," Galin mumbled, as he looked up to the defense towers around the perimeter of the outpost grounds. This place was well protected. It would definitely not be a good place to come and start trouble, and the nearby pirates and outlaws knew it well, because- trying to make a name for themselves- some had done just that.

Out in this region of space you needed to look out for your own, if you got into trouble, you'd be waiting a long time for any form of help to arrive.

Galin scanned the landing pad and counted a few dozen other ships. It looked like the place was doing pretty good business. It made sense, as this was the only well stocked and well protected outpost in the sector.

The crew had already scattered, most making their way toward the main outpost building, but Galin noticed an outdoor picnic area. He wanted to enjoy the morning for a few minutes before going inside.

Galin looked around the place as he walked. The Safe Haven Trading Post was composed of three buildings. The center, and largest of them, contained the trading post. You could get just about anything you wanted as far as essential supplies. They even carried a few of the most common ship parts. On the top floor was a cantina. The building to the right was an inn. It wasn't nearly as high, but it extended much further back than the other two buildings. The third building was a restaurant with good, slightly overpriced food, but the portions were large and the staff was friendly.

The place had been built on a grassy mountainside above a section of steep gray crags that overlooked the ocean. It offered a breathtaking sight, and as he sat in a creaky wooden chair and put his feet up, Galin began to feel all the nervous energy inside him run out like water being released from a bath. The warm sunlight felt good upon his forearms and face, and the smell of the sea mist blowing up from the rocks far below was refreshing and exhilarating.

"You've been here before?" came Starla's voice from somewhere behind him. He hadn't seen her sitting there.

"Only once," he responded.

He got up and moved to the chair next to hers. "The thought of coming here to let everyone get some fresh air was just too good to pass up."

She nodded and smiled. "Thanks for letting us out of our cages. We all needed it. How long are we going to stay?"

"I figured today and tomorrow, then we'll leave the next morning, unless anyone has objections. The time difference is only two hours off our own, so it'll be a nice little rest without throwing off our sleeping patterns too much."

"Joseph told me that long range communications are down due to our skirmish with those pirates. I thought I could send a transmission from the trading post here to start generating some excitement about the T3038." She shook her head and formed a broad smile. "I still can't believe we found it, that it survived this long."

"I never doubted you for a second. When you said you thought we could track it down, well I could tell from the look in your eyes that you were sure about it."

She turned her head and looked off toward the ocean. They could see the large green waves crashing against the rocks far beneath them, sending up a large spray of salty mist. It was a violent scene, yet somehow it gave Galin a feeling of peace.

Starla blinked her eyes as the ocean wind blew a few strands of hair across her face.

"I'm glad you talked me into this, joining the crew I mean. At first I wasn't sure I could do it; live this kind of life. But it's been a wonderful ride."

"You talk about it like it's over. Are you still thinking about staying on Earth once we make it back?" Galin suddenly had a sinking feeling in his stomach.

"I haven't decided yet. It's possible. I'd miss the Katara, and the crew. I'd miss seeing new places like this, but I'm just not sure this is the life for me anymore."

Galin didn't know what to say. She had to know how he felt about her, no matter how much he'd tried to fight it over the years. She *had* to know.

"I didn't think you were serious about leaving. Listen, little girl—"

"Please stop calling me that."

"Sorry. Old habits die hard I guess. Listen, as long as I've known you, I've thought you were destined for a life like this. I knew you'd be out here somewhere, exploring an unknown corner of the galaxy, turning over some ancient cairn or ruins to see what was underneath."

He smiled warmly at her. "Your fascination with the unknown has always been a little...contagious. Heck, you and Jamie," his voice cracked, and for a moment he buried his face in his hands. Then he looked away from her. "Well, you're part of the reason why I got into all this in the first place."

They sat there in silence. Her eyes left him and turned once again to the furious crashing of waves down below.

Galin stood, and turned to walk away.

Starla grabbed his hand. "Her death...it wasn't *my* fault. And it damn sure wasn't yours. You've been punishing yourself long enough, you need to let it go."

He felt like she'd just stabbed him in the gut.

"I need to head inside and see about getting the crew some rooms," he said softly.

She let go of his hand, and watched as he walked back toward the front of the building and around the corner. She couldn't take this anymore. It wasn't just himself he was punishing, it was her too. It hadn't been easy, but she had moved on from the death of her best friend, Galin's sister, so many years ago.

She loved Galin, but couldn't go on like this any longer; being stuck in the past all the time was just too painful. When they got back to Earth she wasn't sure what she was going to do, she just knew that she *was* going to leave the Katara, and never look back again.

Jace Chang felt like a kid in a candy store. The glass display case in front of him had just about every kind of gun he'd ever seen, and many that he hadn't. He eagerly looked over each section, searching for something that he liked and could afford.

Earlier that morning, the captain had told him he needed to get his own sidearm, something he felt comfortable with. But he also said not to purchase anything before checking back first. He'd said in places like this it was easy to get ripped off if you didn't have a lot of experience with what you were buying.

Jace walked along in front of the display cases. It looked like the guns were arranged by firepower and type rather than place of origin. At first he gravitated toward the pieces that looked the biggest and baddest. He figured if he ever needed to slag somebody, he might as well do the job right.

Visions began to run through his head. There they were on some dark war torn planet, he and the crew. The captain and Joseph were lying wounded on the ground nearby. Starla, whose face was smudged and shirt torn to reveal her smooth stomach, clung to him tightly with both arms, squeezing her soft body against him. Ulrick cheered him on as they blasted their way back to the ship, dragging their wounded friends to safety.

"See anything you like?"

The voice startled him. He looked up to see a tall, fat Boreian standing behind the counter. He'd never met one in person, but recognized the race from pictures. The alien had dark crimson skin and a humongous, flat nose. He was bald, but had an impressive shaggy black beard and large sharp teeth.

"Let me know if you want to handle any of them."

Jace nodded. "I've shot plenty of guns, but I've never owned one of my own before. Got any recommendations?"

"Hmn," growled the Boreian as he scratched his hairy black chin. "All depends on your needs. And personal preference, of course. Are you partial to human weapons?"

"Uh, never really thought about it. Guess it doesn't matter really, so long as I only need five fingers to operate it." He chuckled at his own joke, but the Boreian just looked at him stupidly.

"Hey, you don't have any laser swords do you?" Jace asked him nervously.

"Laser swords?" he laughed. "Afraid not." His face grew serious again. "My brother-in-law cut his own arm off with one of those."

He stroked his beard and looked down into the case. "I don't think any of these would be right for you, come take a look over here." They moved about eight feet down the counter. "Yes, here's a nice model. Provides a lot of bang for the buck." He handed Jace the gun.

"This is a standard issue Galactic Confederation of Worlds phaser-pistol. It was brought in by a retired Star Marshal. It's got a lot of stories in it, that one does."

Jace weighed the gun in his hand. It felt good. "Stories? You mean it's seen a lot of action?"

"Oh yes. Just like people, all of these weapons have stories to tell. Some good ones, some bad. If you listen close enough they'll tell them to you."

Jace gave him a doubtful look. That sounded just a little bit crazy. Then again, it sounded like something Chief Joseph might say. He was always telling everyone old stories.

The Boreian held out his hand and took the phaser back. He set it gently down on the counter in case Jace wanted to look at it again.

"Look at this one over here." He took another weapon out and handed it over. "This is a heavy repeater pistol. It was confiscated from a notorious space pirate- a really bad character. He was wanted for multiple counts of rape, murder, heaven knows what else. How's that one feel to you?"

"Well, it sure is an impressive gun. I really like the way it looks. Feels pretty good, although it weighs twice as much as that other one." He considered it for a moment. "I don't know, I don't think this one's right for me." He handed it back.

"That one is full of bad stories," he agreed. "Let's see. Oh, these are very interesting. Some folks prefer black-powder firearms rather than energy-guns. Downside is ammunition can be harder to come by when you get in a jam. I'm a bit partial to this revolver here. It's another Earth model. Ancient design, they call it a .357 caliber. Lot's of fun to shoot."

Jace took the gun and looked at it. He liked this one too. But, he could already hear Captain Winchester's voice in his head, telling him how impractical something like that was for a young greenhorn like him. That's probably just what he'd say, and he'd be right.

"I like it. But…I think I'd rather go with an energy gun for now. Something I'm not going to have to constantly reload."

The clerk nodded and smiled. "A wise choice for a young man trying to make his way in the galaxy."

"What about one of these here?" Jace pointed down at two guns that looked the same.

"Ah, time for a test," the Boreian said with a smile, pulling both guns from the case. He set them side by side on the counter. "Standard issue Space Marine officer's service laser-pistol. These two are identical units. You think there's any difference between them?"

Jace picked up each one and examined them both thoroughly. He liked the way they felt in his hand. He liked the weight. Something about the way the guns looked really appealed to him. He couldn't see any differences between them. They were both slightly worn, a few little scratches here and there, but overall in about the same condition.

"Yeah. I think I'd like to get one of these."

"Good," said the salesman with a wide, toothy smile, "But which one?"

He looked at both guns again. Did it really matter? Could there actually be anything to what this guy was telling him? The whole thing sounded a little bit fantastic.

He picked up each gun once again, taking his time to look them over and holding each one in turn. After a few minutes, he realized that one of them did feel more comfortable than the other, which just felt wrong for him somehow. He set the gun he wanted down on the counter.

"This is the one I want," he said and gave it a loving tap. He handed the other gun back.

The Boreian laughed. It wasn't a patronizing or unkind laugh, but one that seemed to confirm something to him.

"The gun you selected," he said as he put the other away, "was owned by a highly decorated officer, who was loved and trusted by his men. In battle, he sacrificed his own life while creating a diversion so that his inferiors could fall back to safety. This gun has good stories to tell. Some of them sad, but they are good none the less."

Jace grinned at him. He never would have guessed that the gun was owned by a man like that, a hero. "And the one I gave back?"

"That one was owned by a Lieutenant who betrayed his own division. He fragged a superior officer with this very gun," he said tapping the glass. "He was a bad, bad man."

Jace thought about what the Boreian had just told him.

"So how do you know all this? Do people tell you these things when they bring in the guns?"

"Sometimes," the man nodded. "But it's like I said before, all you have to do is *listen*."

"So, if some of these guns have bad stories, bad vibes that is, why don't you just get rid of them? Why even take them in the first place?"

"Well, it's just like I said. Guns are a bit like people. You're a good person, I think. You wanted a piece with good stories. But not everyone has such noble intentions, you follow me?"

Jace did follow him. And he didn't like what he was hearing. How could anyone sell one of these things if they thought it would most likely be used to commit a crime? To rob someone, rape or even murder them? He didn't understand it. He wasn't so sure he liked this guy.

"Look, just set this aside for me and I'll be back a little later to pick it up, okay?"

"You got it," the Boreian said with a wink.

As Jace left, the salesman gave him another wide smile, revealing his large sharp teeth. He placed the gun on the shelf behind him.

The saloon on the upper floor was teeming with people, most of whom had popped in for a quick drink or game of chance before moving on with business. It was a good place to get the latest news and gossip from planets across the galaxy.

Peter and Joseph each pulled up a chair at the bar, and the bartender promptly appeared to take their orders.

"Give me a pint of ale," Peter told him.

He looked at Joseph.

"Firewater and I parted company a long time ago. I'll take a mug of your finest root beer." The man gave him a nod and set off to prepare their drinks.

They turned in their seats to get a better look at everyone. There were a few humans, but most of the clientele were alien races, including some that they'd never seen before. Ulrick was sitting off in the corner, surrounded by a small group of spectators, arm-wrestling a creature that reminded Peter of a pit-bull dressed in sweats. Ulrick waved enthusiastically when he saw them, breaking his concentration. His arm started to go down, but he quickly recovered and gave them a thumbs up.

At another table, a tall, skinny fellow stood up angrily and threw his cards down. His yellow fur bristled as he growled at the other members of his party. Before long a husky Boreian security guard grabbed him and escorted him into the back. The two creatures he had been playing with, who looked like four foot tall minotaurs, laughed gleefully like they'd just gotten away with something.

The bartender returned with their drinks. He shook his head and made a nod in the direction of the fight. "Some people just don't know how to act civilized," he said, blowing his nose into a dishrag on the bar before returned to his business.

Peter pointed to a man in a white long-sleeved shirt and black vest. "Hey, I think I know those guys." The man's companion was facing the other direction and wearing a hat, and they couldn't see his face.

"I'm gonna go say hello."

Joseph nodded and took a long draught of his root beer.

As Peter walked to the other side of the room, the man looked up and saw him. "Hey," he called out, giving his companion a thump on the shoulder. "Look who it is." The other man turned around to look, dropping his heavy cowboy boots down to the floor and pushing his new straw hat up out of his eyes. He smiled receptively.

"Howdy, gentlemen, haven't seen you guys for a while, what's it been, about three years?"

"Hey, Peter," said the vested man with a handshake. "Yeah, about three years now I think. Have a seat."

Peter sat down beside them, placing his ale on the table and calling Joseph over with a wave of his hand.

"What brings the two of you out to this corner of space?"

The man with the straw hat took a puff of his cigar. "Been running equipment to a dilithium mining crew stationed another two weeks out from here. Way out in the badlands. Boring as all get out but the pay makes up for it. I think they might be looking to contract another ship if you're interested. You still paired up with Winchester?"

"Yeah, I am. And I appreciate you thinking of us, but things have been going pretty well lately, looks like we might have a big payday coming up soon."

"I'm glad to hear that, you guys deserve it."

Joseph walked up and sat in the chair next to Peter.

"This is Joseph Stormcrow, he's the one that keeps the Katara glued together for us."

"So you're a hard working man," said the one in the vest. "Even if the Katara is twice the boat as *our* old clunker you've got your work cut out for you."

Peter laughed. This is Gabe and Caleb Russell. They're brothers. Used to serve under Captain O'Neil on the USTS Constitution."

They all shook hands and made their greeting.

Gabe snapped his fingers. "Hey, this reminds me. You'll never guess who we met just a few weeks back. Does the name Shinmen Musashi mean anything to you?"

"Sure," said Peter with a nod. "He's the man who designed the Katara, and a bunch of other UST ships."

"Yup. Well, we ran into his grandson- Kanbun Musashi. He was doing some design work out at the mine. The foreman we talked to said he's a genius. He came up with some new engine design for their drills that doubled productivity."

"Really? Did you ask him about his grandfather?"

"No, we only talked to him for about five minutes. He didn't even realize we knew who his grandfather was. Apparently the guy's a bit of a hermit. Doesn't like to be bothered much. Rumor is he lives out there all by himself in the badlands somewhere, experimenting on his own designs."

"Only comes in to find work when he needs cash for one of his projects," said Caleb. "I wonder what kind of things he's building out there?"

Peter smiled. "If he has half the brain his grandfather did it must be something interesting."

"So, you guys been back to Earth lately?" Caleb asked them, removing his hat and dropping it on the table.

"It's been about three months now, how about you."

"More like six for us," Gabe told them. "Spoke to our pa about a week ago. He said that peace talks with the Nazerazis are failing. You hear anything about that?"

"I've heard that they've been pestering the United

Earth Government to leave the Confederation and join the Nazerazi Alliance," Peter told them.

Joseph laughed. "That's never going to happen. Earth was one of the founding planets of the Galactic Confederation of Worlds. Why would we ever leave it?"

"Well," said Caleb as he tapped the ashes off the end of his cigar, "a couple years ago I would have agreed with you, but I'm not so sure anymore."

"Why do you say that?" Peter chuckled.

"Just look at what's being done with the fleet. They've been cutting the budget like crazy for the last few years ..."

Gabe cut in on him. "Not to mention the talk about retiring half the battleships currently in service."

Peter felt a little shocked. "I hadn't heard anything about *that*."

Gabe nodded. "And do you have any idea how powerful big the Nazerazi force is? Word is it's about twice the size of the current Galactic Confederation fleet."

"Actually, I have heard about that," Peter told them. "Our squadron actually ran into a few of their ships once. Scary suckers. Lot's of firepower."

"Well," said Gabe in a low voice, "a lot of this stuff is classified information. It's not been told to the civilian population yet."

Peter looked doubtful again. "I just don't know. I have all the confidence in the world in you guys, but I'm going to have to see some of this stuff before I believe it."

"Can't say I blame you. It *is* hard to believe. Heck, none of us have a crystal ball we can look into, but if you ask me, I don't like the way this whole thing seems to be playing out. I've never had a lot of confidence in the United Earth Government anyway. I'm not gonna depend on a bunch of frackin' politicians to look out for me. It's root-hog or die these days. That's why we're out here anyway though, I guess."

"Can't argue with you there," Joseph said. "I wouldn't put anything past the UEG anymore. I guess we'll just have to hope for the best."

Peter took a swig of his ale. "How long are you two going to be around? I'm sure Galin would love to catch up with you."

"Should have already been gone by now unfortunately." Caleb told them. "We're runnin' a bit behind as is. Couldn't pass up the temptation of stopping by for some fresh air and a drink."

Suddenly an odd green alien stormed up to the table. His gun was drawn and he pointed it right at Gabe's face.

"Alright, come with me. NOW," he said threatening.

Gabe discreetly raised his blaster pistol up underneath the table. "Uh, I don't think so. Look Mister, I don't know who you are but..."

"SHUT your mouth. You think you can just dump a whole load full of the boss's cargo at the first sign of

Confederation trouble and not have to answer for it. There's a bounty on your head, and I aim to collect it. Doesn't matter if you're alive or dead."

Gabe fired his blaster through the table and the alien collapsed down between them before he could get a shot off. Peter, Joseph and Gabe looked at each other with their mouths hanging open.

"I've never seen the guy before," Gabe pleaded. "I don't know what he was talking about, I swear."

The Boreian security guard ran up to them frantically.

"Hey, what's going on here. Who fired first?"

All four men pointed at the dead green alien. "He did," they said in unison.

Galin and Peter stood behind Jace. The captain placed his hand on the young man's shoulder and gave him a pat.

"Alright kid, let's see how your aim is with this new toy of yours, and just remember, you point it at me again and you're going to eat it; even if it *is* an accident."

Jace nodded and gave him a guilty grin. He aimed the laser pistol downrange at the target and squeezed off a few rounds. Two of the shots missed, but the third time was a charm. The black silhouette figure had a quarter sized, smoldering hole through its head."

"Not bad, not bad. Keep it up and remember to aim for the body next time."

"I *was* aiming for the body," he said. He shrugged his shoulders, turned back and began to fire again.

Galin and Peter walked a short distance up the hill to get away from the noise. It was a beautiful afternoon, just a little bit darker than the day before. It looked like the place might get some rain later that evening.

Heck, Galin thought to himself, *we could all be stuck in a blizzard and it would still be a nice change of scenery.*

Peter took a large swig of the Omicronian Lemonade he was holding.

"That stuff any good?" Galin asked him.

Peter shrugged. "Tastes a little like fermented garbage and cat urine." He took another drink. "Other than that it's great. Very refreshing. You know, it's too bad you didn't get a chance to talk to Gabe and Caleb yesterday before they were thrown out of here. You think there's anything to the things they said?"

"Who knows. The leaders of the United Earth Government are a lot of things, but they aren't stupid. I don't think they'd put us in a position of weakness while the Nazerazi Alliance poses any kind of threat."

"That's kind of what I was thinking." Peter took a deep breath and looked around. "This place reminds me a lot of Ireland."

"Never been there."

"It's worth a trip."

"I'll bet it is," Galin told him. "It's strange to think that I've been to dozens of other planets, but have never been to a place like Ireland."

"Yeah. It's funny to think about. I've been to parts of Asia, Europe once. Other than that I didn't stray too far from Texas."

"No need to," said Galin jokingly. "If it ain't in Texas, you don't need it."

Joseph walked up and gave them a nod.

"Any luck on the parts we need to patch up the ship?" Peter asked.

"Yes, on some of them. We can finish up this morning with the work needed on the outer hull. I got ahold of some things I needed for the engine too. She should do okay as long as we don't push her too hard. As far at the sub-space transceiver though, no luck there. I'll have to see what I can come up with going through the junk we've got on the ship."

"Blowing our engine out isn't going to do us any good, we'll just have to take her back home gently." Galin shook his head. "I'd hoped to have everyone back by Thanksgiving, but I guess we'll have to settle for Christmas. Either of you seen Starla around? I haven't seen her since yesterday morning."

They both shook their heads.

"I guess she decided to take a break from us all while she could," Galin said.

"Can't blame her for that," replied Peter. "It's got to be hard for her sometimes, being the only woman on the ship."

"Maybe," Joseph said. "I kind of think she likes it that way though. After all, she gets the attention of five pathetic slubs treating her like a princess all the time."

Peter laughed. "With all the scores she's made for us lately she deserves to be treated like a princess."

"That she does," Galin told them, his eyes seemed to have glazed over. "She deserves a lot better than what we're giving her. A lot more than what *I'm* giving her." He was silent for a few moments. "Well, I'm going to go check on some additional supplies; I wanna be able to leave first thing tomorrow morning. I'll meet you both back at the ship in an hour so we can finish up that work on the hull."

They agreed and Galin walked off, back toward the building.

Peter shook his head sadly and turned to Joseph. "So you think she's going to leave the ship? She's been talking about it for a while now."

"Wouldn't you?" Joseph asked him.

He nodded. "Well, it's probably for the best. She deserves to be happy. I don't know how he's going to take it though. He talks about it like it's a good thing, like it's what he wants for her." Peter glanced back over at Jace, who seemed to be landing the majority of his shots. "I think it'll only make Galin feel worse than he does already."

"It could," the chief agreed. "I've never seen anyone hold on to the past the way he does. He really loves that woman."

Peter nodded. "Problem is, sometimes it seems like he blames her as much as he blames himself."

Galin watched from the rear window of his quarters as Omicron Five grew smaller. It then disappeared completely as the ship went into warp.

He smiled as he looked at the Christmas presents he'd gotten for his kids back at the outpost. For Sarah, he'd bought a jewelry box, made of some kind of bluish wood the likes of which he'd never seen before. He wasn't an expert on the tastes of twelve-year-old girls, but thought she'd probably like it.

Choosing gifts for David had always been easier. He picked up the small robotic animal. It looked a bit like a dog. He flipped it on and the thing began to dance playfully on the floor. Taking control of it with the remote, he transformed it into a small saucer shaped ship and flew it around the room. He was almost tempted to keep the thing for himself.

He'd even picked up something for Melissa. He still couldn't believe he'd found it. It was a white and blue cameo engraved with the image of the moon. They'd seen one exactly like it years ago in San Antonio. He remembered that night well.

They had been strolling down the River Walk together. His wife had gotten a sitter and they were happy to have some time to themselves for a change. Melissa looked stunning. He didn't get many opportunities to take her out like this, and Galin had nearly forgotten how beautiful she was.

They were passing a group of street vendors. "Hey look at this," she said, picking up the cameo. "It's gorgeous. Reminds me of my dad." She held it up and examined it closely. "When I was a little girl he used to tell me stories while we sat out under the moon and stars, staring up into the night sky."

"You've told me," Galin said. He pointed into the darkness overhead. "I can *take* you up there you know."

"Are you kidding me? I just about die whenever I have to get on an *airplane*."

He took her hand and gave it a squeeze. "I really wish you and the kids would come with me next week."

"We've discussed this," she said with a sympathetic smile, putting the cameo back. "That's not the kind of life I want for myself…or the kids, you know that."

"I know. Every once in a while it wouldn't hurt for you all to come along though. I'm not asking you to pull stakes and move onto the ship."

"We'll always be here waiting when you get back. And when the kids get a little older maybe you can take them along sometimes, *when* it's safe."

He knew she wasn't going to budge. He'd been trying to get her on the Katara ever since he'd rebuilt the ship. She just wasn't interested, and sometimes she even seemed afraid of stepping foot onboard.

His phone rang, and he answered it. He listened for a moment, and then a smile spread across his face.

"Really? That's great. I can't wait to tell Pete and the others."

He looked at Melissa, his smile had been infectious, and she was excited because he was excited. But he knew she was wondering what was going on.

"Listen," Galin said into the phone, "I'll call you tomorrow morning so we can get together about all the details. Okay, talk to you then."

"Who was that?" She grinned at him enthusiastically.

"Uh, that was Starla." As soon as he said the name Melissa's smile faded into a hateful frown. "She's agreed to come on with the crew. Help us do research and track down artifacts."

"You've *got* to be kidding me," she told him. "You really think this is a good idea given the history you two have?"

"That's all in the past," he said, taking her by the shoulders and looking into her eyes. "She's more like a sister to me than anything. Besides, you know how smart she is. Just imagine how much money we can all make if she comes onboard."

"Money? Are you really trying to convince me that's the reason you're doing this?"

He didn't understand her, or maybe didn't want to.

"She's *not* your sister. Your sister is *dead*."

Rage welled up inside of him. He had to stop himself from smacking her.

"She's not your *wife* either. *I* am." Tears began to well up in her eyes.

Galin suddenly felt guilty. Felt almost as if he *had* hit her.

"Look, it's not like that. What have I been doing for the past two weeks? Begging you to come along!"

"I know that," she said. "Look, I love you so much. And I trust you, I do. It's just that... sometimes life doesn't take us where we expect it to. Life is hard enough without tempting fate."

"It'll all work out fine, I swear. Come with me if you're worried about it. What I really want is you by my side anyway. You *know* that."

"I know," she said, hanging her head. "But I just can't do it." She reached up and touched his cheek. "*You* go chase the stars, just come back to *me* between all your glorious little adventures."

He laughed. "I always have, haven't I?"

They kissed, and then continued walking along the river together looking for a nice place to eat.

It had been a good night.

He'd gone back to get that moon cameo for her the next day, but someone else had already bought it.

He looked down at the one he was holding, and wondered what she'd say when she saw it.

Galin had been thinking a lot about his family lately,

even more than usual. Maybe if he'd done things differently it all wouldn't have turned out like this.

As he put the presents away, he thought that lifting weights might help clear his head. He changed into some old work out clothes and headed for the small gym in the common area.

Joseph was making some coffee in the kitchen, and nodded as he walked to the refrigerator and grabbed a bottle of water.

"Coffee?" he offered.

"No thanks. I'm gonna go work out for a bit. Try to get a few things off my mind."

"Okay." He looked at Galin with something a bit too much like pity.

Galin sighed and sat down at the table. "What? What is it?"

"I didn't say anything."

"You don't have to. Come on, what's with these looks you've been giving me lately?"

Joseph sat down beside him and dumped some creamer into his cup. He was silent as he added sugar and stirred it all up.

"Did I ever tell you about the tale of two wolves?"

"Uh oh, is this another one of your grandpa's stories?"

Joseph ignored the snide comment. "It's an old Cherokee tale."

"I thought you were an Apache."

"You know I am. Are you going to listen to my story

so you can lift your rocks, or sit here and be a wise-guy all day?"

Galin just sat there and grinned at him.

"One night around the campfire an old man was talking to his grandchildren about life. He told them, 'A constant struggle is going on inside of me, its a terrible, vicious fight between two wolves.

One of the wolves is evil. He is made up of fear, hatred, sorrow, regret, greed, arrogance, self-pity, guilt, and lies.'"

"Sounds like a pretty bad wolf," Galin interrupted.

"Yes, he does," agreed the chief, taking a drink of his coffee. "But the other wolf- he is good. He is made up of joy, peace, love, hope, serenity, kindness, empathy, generosity, and faith."

Galin rubbed his nose and took a deep breath.

"The old man told his grandchildren, 'These same two wolves are fighting inside of you, and everyone else as well'.

They thought about it for a few moments and then one of the children asked his grandfather, 'Which wolf will win?'

He looked at Galin sternly.

"The old Cherokee simply replied: 'The one that you feed.'"

"And you think I've been feeding the evil wolf lately? Is that it?"

Joseph sat silently for a few moments.

He added some hot coffee to his cup and gave it a stir. "I think maybe you've been feeding both of those wolves more than they could eat for a long time now."

Galin frowned at him, and getting up from the table he left the room without saying a word. Maybe the old coot was right. Maybe he needed to stop feeding that evil wolf. Problem was, he wasn't sure he knew how.

He picked up some dumb-bells and sat down on the workbench. Clearing his mind as best he could, and taking in some long deep breaths, he started his routine.

Peter Cervantes set the large, steaming platter down in the center of the table. "Sorry about the bird everyone. It's the closest thing I could find to a turkey."

Ulrick eyed it suspiciously. It almost looked more like a skinned cat than it did a turkey. "What exactly is this thing anyway?"

"It's a Frommerian chicken. I picked it up from the butcher on New Japan when we stopped by for supplies last month." He carved the bird and began to dish it out.

When he finished he looked expectantly at Ulrick, who had already taken a large bite. "Well, how's the thing taste?"

"Tastes a lot like…chicken," Ulrick responded while stuffing another fork load into his mouth.

Peter shrugged.

"Well, I'd hoped to have you all home by

Thanksgiving, but I don't think any of us really has a reason to complain. Our hard work is finally going to pay off this time." Galin raised his wine glass in a toast, and everyone followed.

"Still," he said with a shrug. "I *was* hoping to be able to talk to my kids today. Fracking space pirates really gave the old girl a pounding this time. The damage to the engine turned out to be a little worse than we'd originally thought. I don't think she's ever taken a beating like this before. Not while I've had her anyway."

Starla shook her head. "I'm just happy we all made it through alive."

Ulrick raised his glass again. "You're right. We all have a lot to be thankful for this year."

Galin nodded. "Yes we do, but those pirates sure don't." The other men chuckled, but Starla felt a shiver run through her body. She didn't even want to think about the battle.

"Slaggin' no good thieves. Can't say Ulrick didn't earn his pay this time around." Galin held up his glass, toasting Ulrick and giving him an approving nod.

"I don't think they realized they'd be facing so much firepower from an old tub like this," Joseph said.

"Well, if it wasn't for Ulrick and that phaser turret the two of you installed they probably would have gotten the upper hand."

Starla eyed the meat on the end of her fork suspiciously. "We made the pickup and got out of there safely. As far as I'm concerned, you all did a great job."

"Wouldn't have even found that thing without you, sweetheart. You really came through for all of us this time."

She laughed in embarrassment, and shook some salt onto her chicken.

"Listen," Galin told her seriously. "I know I give you a hard time, but I want you to know what a valuable member of this crew you are. This ship wouldn't be the same without you."

"Thanks," she told him, knowing the wine was already starting to get to him.

"So what exactly is that thing again?" asked Jace as he adjusted his baseball cap. "The cargo I mean. Some kind of old robot or something, right?"

Starla winced. "Haven't you been paying attention to anything around here lately?" She thought she'd sounded a little harsh, so added more jokingly, "What cave have you been living in?"

"Actually, I feel like I *have* been living in a cave; I've been so busy over the past few weeks down in the engine room. It's a good thing we got that reprieve on Omicron Five, because Joseph is a slave driver, its not easy being his henchman."

Joseph gave him a sideways glance and smiled maniacally.

"So tell me about this robot of ours again. I promise I'll pay more attention this time."

Starla rolled her eyes. Everyone knew how much she enjoyed being placed on a soapbox, although she would never admit it.

"It's a T3038 Explorer. One of twelve that were deployed around the perimeter of our solar system in the year 2215. Its mission was to seek out inhabitable planets which were suitable for human colonization."

Joseph set his fork down next to his plate. "I remember reading about those. They were a technological breakthrough at the time."

"Yes," she responded. "They were constructed of crystalized tritanium, had highly advanced artificial brains, and utilized a compressed nuclear fusion power core. Even by today's standards, its pretty impressive stuff."

"So why'd they put these things together just to shoot them off into space?" asked Jace. "Seems like they'd be pretty expensive."

"They were extremely expensive. But at the time, the world's superpowers were desperate to get to other worlds, find resources. World War V had just decimated much of the planet; it was a pretty brutal time in Earth's history."

"The T3038s were built by the Chinese, right?" asked Joseph.

"The People's Democracy of West China, actually. They were allied with the United States of Texas. It was a joint effort. The United Socialist Democrat States of

America created a virus that was successful in preventing five of the bots from deploying. Our little friend in there is one of those. The only one left in existence. He'd been drifting through space until we stopped to give him a lift."

"Well," said Galin, "He has a new mission now, and that's to line my pockets with cash."

Ulrick and Jace laughed in agreement.

"You guys are such apes," Starla told them.

"That may be so, but we're *your* apes."

This got a reluctant chuckle out of her. It was impossible to not be in a good mood.

"So tell me what you've got planned for your cut of the money?" Galin asked Jace.

"Well, I've got some serious debts to pay off, you all know that. Whatever's left after that goes straight toward my laser-sword."

"Are you still going on about that?" Ulrick scoffed. "Kids these days. They don't want to listen to anybody! We've all told you how dangerous those things are, but you're still determined to get one?"

"Heck yeah I am. I've got a buddy on Mars who can get me hooked up with one, for a pretty good price too. Hopefully my cut will be enough to seal the deal."

"You're NUTS!" Starla told him. "There's a reason those things have been banned on just about every planet in the confederacy."

Joseph just looked at him and shook his head in

disapproval.

He looked at Galin pleadingly. "Come on Cap, you know how awesome those things are. Tell me *you* never wanted one?"

"Yeah, I wanted a laser-sword, until my uncle decapitated himself with one. I don't know of anyone- and I mean anyone- who has been using one of those things for any length of time and hasn't been seriously injured. How old are you greenhorn, twenty-one, twenty-two years old?"

"Nineteen."

"Well, you want to live a good long life with all your bits and pieces intact, I suggest you spend your money on something else."

It was obvious that Jace didn't like what they were saying, and Galin wondered if any of it was sinking in. Some people just had to learn the hard way.

"Just think about it, kid," Galin told him. He looked at Starla. "How about you, little girl? Got anything exciting planned?"

"Haven't made up my mind yet. I've been thinking about buying a house, it's always been a dream of mine. We'll see."

"Sounds great," Galin said. "How about you Chief?"

"Well," he said, taking a small sip of sparkling cider, "there's nothing I really need or want too bad right now. Probably just pump up some of my retirement savings. Maybe buy a few new tools."

"How about you Ulrick?" asked Starla. "Let me guess? It'll be something big, loud, and deadly."

Ulrick scratched the dome under his wavy blonde hair and shrugged. "There's always a bigger gun out there somewhere."

Jace pointed at Galin. "How about you, Captain? I know you've talked about fixing up the Katara, but what else have you got planned? Buy a small island on a nice quiet planet somewhere in the outback?"

"Well, I'm planning on sending a nice big bag of scratch to Melissa. She deserves it after everything I've put her through. Then there's college funds for the kids. As for the rest, I've got plenty of plans for the old girl here. She's been real good to me. I figure it's about time I gave her a makeover. She really needs it, especially after the last beating she took for us."

"Can't argue with you there," Joseph told him.

Galin knew the Chief was looking forward to playing with some of the new equipment they'd discussed putting in.

Ulrick took another big bite of the Frommerian chicken leg he was holding. "Well, everyone save a little money. If we're all together this time next year we need to pitch in for a real turkey."

Peter finished running his system diagnostics and put the ship back on autopilot. It was so frustrating to have to run the ship at half power like this. He just wanted to punch it and get back home. Of course, the bad thing about breaking down in the middle of space is you can't get out and push.

He got up to stretch his legs for a few minutes, and poured himself a fresh cup of coffee. It was time to settle in for another boring stretch of the trip. In times like this he wondered why he had never found a good woman and settled down. His mother had told him a million times if she'd told him once- family was the most important thing. He didn't disagree; maybe he'd just never grown up enough to follow through with it. How long would he be out here, traipsing through the stars with his friends? Forever, more than likely. His friends after all, had become his family.

Still, he did get lonely. He longed now more than ever to find a good woman. The right woman; maybe one crazy enough to live the same kind of life that he lived.

He sat back down in his chair and opened up his book- *Dracula* by Bram Stoker. Starla had teased him about it earlier, said that she liked old books too, but had never seen him read anything written within the last two hundred years.

Maybe she was right, thought Peter, but he'd always figured that if a book stood the test of time there must be something to it. Classics were always a safe way to go, not like some of this new-fangled sci-fi rubbish.

The console in front of him let out a soft ping. He lowered his book and saw that another ship had just come within range. It was flying along at a steady speed, going a little bit faster than they were, and would probably pass them up in about five minutes or so.

They were too close to home to be running into any more pirates, but it was a little unusual for another vessel to crowd them as closely as this one was, especially without hailing them.

He set down his book and stared at the screen. The ship sped up and after a minute passed them by.

We've been spending too much time in the outskirts lately, Peter thought to himself. I'm starting to get suspicious of everyone. He picked his book up and reclined back in his chair. At least he was a bit more awake than he had been before.

Galin landed with a clank as he jumped off of the final rung of the ladder leading down to the engine room.

Joseph had heard him coming and was waiting there at the bottom, arms crossed in front of him, with a whimsical look on his face. Jace, who was finishing up with the final turn of a torque wrench took off his cap and wiped a drop of sweat from his brow.

"So how are the repairs comin' along, Chief?"

"Not great. The neutron accelerator is just about shot, and the plasma injector has a hairline crack in it, could go anytime now. We've been pushing her way too hard lately, but I don't need to tell *you* that."

"Well, we haven't had much of a choice. Besides, I knew you could keep everything patched together for a while longer. Won't be long now till you have a whole mess of new toys to play with."

Joseph smiled. As much as he liked tinkering with the outdated components of the ship, some things were on the verge of being unsalvageable. It would be nice to have reliable systems for a change.

"Hey," said Joseph with a snap of his fingers, "there's something I've been meaning to show you."

Galin followed him over to a small storage closet in the corner of the room. "I've been meaning to clean this thing out for a while now," Joseph told him. "Haven't had the time yet. But a few days ago, I went in there and dug around to see if I could find a few dampening bolts, and this..." he carefully picked something up, "this was in the bottom of a box in the corner over there, buried under a bunch of old data cables."

"Hmn," Galin cocked his head and held the thing up closer to the light to get a better look. "Is this the original?"

"Original what?" asked Jace, who had come up behind them and stood leaning against the doorway.

"Yes, it is," Joseph said. He turned to Jace. "This here's the original processor and intelligence core for the ships computer, the one that was installed just before she was commissioned."

"Oh, okay," said Jace disinterestedly, as if he thought it might be something much more exciting.

Galin ignored him. "I can't believe this thing was overlooked. It was common procedure to download and then destroy these cores when they were replaced or when the ship was decommissioned." He scratched his head thoughtfully. "No, this couldn't have been overlooked. I'll bet you someone intentionally retrieved this thing and hid it back here in the ship."

Joseph looked a bit surprised. "Really? I wonder why. We might find some interesting data stored in its memory."

"You think it still works?" Galin asked.

"I don't see why not. It looks clean, undamaged. These things were built for durability."

Galin handed the processor back over. "Put it someplace safe until we can have a better look see at it."

He slipped out of the storage room and headed back toward the ladder. Jace followed.

"What kind of information do you think might be on that thing?" he asked, now seemingly intrigued.

Galin cracked a wry smile at him. "Nothing important, probably. The Katara was decommissioned from the Space Fleet over twenty-five years ago. Even if there was anything interesting on that core, its most likely outdated information by now."

Jace looked disappointed again, and Galin suddenly

had the urge to yank his chain.

"But who knows kid, this boat *was* once an elite fighter in the armada. God only knows what kind of classified info could be stored on there."

"Really? The Katara was an elite fighter? Hey, Chief Joe," he called over his shoulder, "is Captain Winchester messing with me or what?"

"Nope," replied Joseph, stepping out of the storage closet. "This ship was a force to be reckoned with in her heyday."

"Well, then *how* did she end up..." he seemed to be stumbling; Galin shot him a daring look.

"How did she end up, end up with you, I mean?" He made a nervous chuckle, not sure if it had come out as an insult.

"When the ship was taken out of service, she was stripped of all her advanced weaponry, shield systems, and various other system components. I picked her up from Bob's Salvage Yard out near the asteroid belt. When I started the antique business, Peter, Joseph and I got her up and runnin' again."

"Wow. How did you guys learn to work on a ship like this?"

Galin put his hand on the ladder. "We all served in the fleet together. Joseph was a ship mechanic, Peter was a pilot, and I—"

The ship suddenly shook violently. Sirens and red warning lights went off. A commanding female voice came over the com.

"RED ALERT! RED ALERT! ALL HANDS TO BATTLE STATIONS!"

Galin stormed onto the bridge as the door clanked shut behind him. Peter looked up at him angrily from the co-pilot's chair.

"It's *him* again."

"How does he KEEP tracking us down like this? He has to have a homing device planted on this ship somewhere." He gritted his teeth. "You talk to him?"

"Nope. He hasn't hailed us yet. Just been sitting out there giving us a mad-dog stare."

Galin recognized the ship on the view screen that hovered before them. It was called the Ravisher. He always thought it was an ugly, boxy thing. Its appearance was just as obnoxious as it's captain's character.

Galin sat down, gave Peter a disgusted glance, and opened up a hailing frequency.

"What can we do for you *this* time, Stringbean?"

The view screen in front of them popped on to display a scrappy man with a wide yellow-toothed grin. He wore a dusty black leather jacket and matching wide brimmed cowboy hat. His pointed eyes shimmered at them from beneath circular, crooked spectacles.

Not far behind him stood his companion- a Gray alien

with a slitted nose and a narrow mouth. He was shirtless, but wore blue, denim pants, and a red scarf was tied around his pencil-thin neck. A large caliber revolver hung from his gun belt. Humungous black eyes gazed out at them from beneath his dirty, brown Stetson.

Stringbean nodded. "Greetings, Captain Winchester. Greetings Cervantes." His big grimy teeth seemed to permeate his grin even while he was speaking.

"You wanna tell me why the hell you just fired on my ship?" Galin demanded.

"Captain, please," the man laughed. "We were just trying to get your attention. No harm was intended."

"Yeah, *right*. You've got a real strange sense of humor. One of these days its gonna get you slagged."

"Oh honestly, Winchester, always so dramatic."

The door suddenly opened and Starla came bursting in. Galin shot her a look of irritation, but didn't say anything. She looked back at him, nervous but determined. Putting her hands on her hips, she dug her feet into the floor as if she were daring him to try and kick her out.

Stringbean's companion, whose name was Dagget, gawked at her.

"Mmmm." He licked his lips with a thin purple tongue. "That is a *very* attractive female you have there, Captain Winchester. Would you care to sell her to me?" His voice was low and monotone, and ran up their spines like a cold set of fingers.

Starla huffed at him angrily and opened her mouth to speak, but no words came out.

"You couldn't afford her," Galin said shortly, then turned back to Stringbean. "Cut to the chase. What is it you want now?" He crossed his legs and began to tap the armrest of his chair in frustration. He knew that this man's ship was an even match for his own, and as much as he wanted to reduce it to space debris, would avoid a conflict if possible. You didn't make it long traveling around in space unless you could keep a cool head.

"Well, I thought we might finally be able to do some business together. After all, things *have* changed. Tell me, what are you doing in this sector? Up to anything I might find interesting?"

"NOTHING has changed. I've told you time and again that I'm not interested in working with you. We don't operate the way you do. We're all on the up and up, me and my crew."

"Oh don't be coy, Captain. What do you mean nothing has changed. *Everything* has changed." He suddenly sounded angry. "Besides, *nobody* who does what we do is on the 'up and up', is that how you put it? Come, there must be some way we can —."

"We *don't* do what you do. We run a salvage operation, you're nothing more than a slagging marauder. How many times are we going to have this conversation?"

Stringbean looked taken aback, but the Gray just

kept running his eyes up and down Starla, a thin line of drool escaping from his non-existent lips.

Galin looked at Stringbean's indignant expression; was this idiot for real? "Kindly stop following my ship around like a love sick teenager. We have real business to conduct back on Earth. So shove off before I call in and place a report with the authorities."

"The *authorities*, Captain? Surely you jest...." He slowly turned to Dagget in shock. "Wait a minute." He took a step toward his screen and squinted as if trying to get a better look at them. "You don't know yet, do you?" He stared at them piercingly. "No, they don't know yet, Dagget, I'm sure of it. What's the matter Winchester? Your sub-space communications system down again? Ha ha ha. Look at their faces Dagget. How delicious! They don't have a *clue*! Ha ha ha ha ha."

Peter shifted in his seat uncomfortably. "Stringbean, you lilly-livered tub-thumpin' fruitcake, what are you goin' on about now?"

"Oh nothing, gentlemen, nothing. Go back to Earth and conduct your precious "business". Sorry to have bothered you. Take care for now!"

He continued to laugh wildly as the view screen clicked off. They watched as his ship changed course. It gained speed before disappearing into a colorful warp stream off in the distance.

"What do you think he was talking about?" Starla asked feebly. "You think there was something *to* all of that?"

Galin got up and put his hand on her shoulder. "No, don't you listen to *anything* that nutcase has to say. He's always had a few screws loose."

He looked at Peter. Both could see hints of apprehension, bits of fear in the eyes of the other. Galin had a very bad feeling that something *had* happened. But what? Could war have broken out while they'd been gone? Stringbean had been a thorn in his side for years, but he'd never acted quite like this before.

He tapped his wrist-com. "Chief, you any closer to bringing long range communications back online?"

"Actually, I was just about to give you a call about that. The transceiver's completely shot, there's nothing we can do without picking up some parts."

"Alright. Thanks."

Galin looked off into the black distance before them. Things just kept getting better and better. "Lets punch it."

The next few days were very unpleasant. Every member of the crew was getting restless and frustrated, as the damaged engine had doubled the duration of the trip. To make things worse, everyone was uneasy. Nagging thoughts and questions plagued them about Stringbean's behavior. And then there was the information Gabe and Caleb Russell had relayed about the Nazerazi Alliance.

With his mind weighed down, Galin sat in the kitchen playing chess with Ulrick. Starla sat nearby reading a book.

Ulrick's eyes were glazed over as he sat looking off into the distance. It was his move, but the last time Galin had mentioned this he'd only gotten a mean growl as Ulrick contemplated the board, which ended with a frown as he hammered his giant fist down upon the table.

Galin sat back and closed his eyes. He couldn't remember ever being so frustrated. The Katara, which had always meant freedom and liberation to him, now felt like a prison cell. All they could do was wait. But, at least there was a light at the end of the tunnel. If the engine held up they would be arriving back to Earth in about ten hours.

Galin ran through it all again in his mind. The Galactic Confederation of Worlds had been at peace for many years, and although the Nazerazi Alliance had always been a concern, they'd never actually attacked. It was possible that Earth had been drawn in to war with them, it just seemed so unlikely.

Even if Earth was at war, Galin had complete confidence in her military forces. The United Earth Government however, well that was another story. For a long time now, he didn't agree with most of the decisions they'd been making, and if the rumors about retiring half the fleet were true it would erase any confidence he had left in them. He thought about his own service in the Galactic Navy, and looked at such a possibility as a betrayal.

Starla's voice came out of the blue. It startled him. "So have you ever met any of these Nazerazi characters?"

He opened his eyes and looked at her. She was trying to look brave, but he knew she was scared. They were all a little scared, concerned for friends and loved ones who they currently had no way of contacting.

"No, I've never met one or even seen one in person, just pictures. But, my squadron was once engaged in a skirmish with some of their ships. Peter was there, too."

She got up and leaned against the counter next to him. "What happened?"

He saw that Ulrick was suddenly sitting there looking at him expectantly as well.

"We were on patrol along the Nazerazi border when we received a distress call from a Pleiadian passenger vessel. It was en route to one of the Nordic colonies. The ship had run into some sort of trouble and was drifting helplessly along through space. By the time we got there, it had just gone over the Nazerazi border."

He could still see the images vividly in his mind.

"After several failed attempts at contacting the Alliance, our commander made the decision to cross the border and attempt a rescue. Well you can guess what happened next. A small group of Nazerazi fighters showed up to engage us, but we had 'em outnumbered five to one. When we told them why we'd crossed their border they responded by destroying the Pleiadian vessel. Frackin savages!

Well that didn't sit too well with the XO, whose mother was a half-blood Pleadian, so he told us to let 'em have it. We did, but they sure gave us a run for our money. We ended up destroying all their fighters, but it cost us a third of the squadron."

"Sounds like you were lucky they didn't show up with more ships," Starla said.

"We were. Their pilots weren't any more skilled than ours, but those ships sure packed one heck of a punch. If it is true that their fleet is twice the size of the Galactic Confederation's.... Well, I don't even want to think about the outcome of a full fledged war."

"Maybe we should change course," Ulrick grunted. "If Earth *is* at war, the Katara is in no condition to join the fight, not without making a few repairs first. If there really is a chance that the Nazerazis have attacked, wouldn't it be better to get more information and go in prepared for a fight."

Galin knew that Ulrick wasn't one to run from conflict. In fact, the opposite was usually true. And he was right, going in blind with the ship in this condition would be a foolish thing to do.

"You're absolutely right. But the truth is, we really don't have anywhere else to go. The only other planet we could get to in a reasonable amount of time is Necron, and I don't think any of us like the idea of landing there. Earth is our best chance by far; if we go anyplace else we risk pushing our engine too hard. As it stands we'll be lucky to get back home without a burn-out."

Ulrick nodded. "Well, we'll just have to see what happens when we get there. Once we land how long do you think it'll take to have the necessary repairs made?"

"Should only take about a day to repair the current damage. If we *are* at war, I'm sure the battle will wait for us. There's no sense in joining in on the fight until we can pull our own weight."

"Well you boys can go play war once you drop *me* off safely on the ground," Starla told them. "I think I've been shot at enough in the last month to last me for a while."

Galin gave her an assuring smile. "I know that getting shot up by pirates wasn't what you signed up for. But hopefully all this scuttlebutt about war is just wind in the sails. When we get back to Earth I'll bet the biggest thing we'll have to worry about is where to go for ice-cream while that fancy robot of yours makes us all rich."

Ulrick gave her an assuring nod and smile as well. She smiled back, and after a few moments returned to her book.

The tall warrior glanced back at Galin with a determined frown. He knew from the look in Ulrick's eyes that he too was expecting the worst.

The Katara dropped out of warp. Earth, about the size of a tennis ball, hung in space before them like a warm, blue Christmas ornament.

"There she is," Starla said with a smile, holding onto the back of Peter's chair. "It sure feels good to be home again."

"Sure does," agreed Galin. I don't see anything out of the ordinary, do you, Pete?"

"Nope," Peter responded. I'm not picking up anything unusual on the scanners. I guess we were all worried about nothing."

"Kinda looks that way, but we'd better keep everyone at battle stations just in case."

"Doesn't look like there's much traffic, I don't see any other ships coming in or out," Jace put in, who was manning the starboard gun turret.

Galin shrugged. "The kid has a point there, although I *have* seen things this quiet from time to time. Let's just keep our eyes open as we bring her in."

They flew the ship toward Earth, and Peter opened up a hailing frequency. "Earth Control, this is Peter Cervantes of the starship Katara requesting permission to approach."

They waited for a response, but heard only silence.

"Earth Control, Earth Control, this is Peter Cervantes

of the starship Katara, requesting clearance to approach Earth."

Silence.

Peter ran a diagnostic on the communication system. He looked at Galin with raised eyebrows.

"Joseph," said Galin over the battle com, "we're not getting any response from Earth Control, you aware of any problems with short-range communication systems?"

Joseph came on a few moments later. "No, everything looks good from where I'm sitting.

"This doesn't feel right at all," Galin said, "We'd better sneak in there and have a peak."

"You want me to take a detour around the moon?" Peter asked.

"Good idea. If anybody has their eyes on us that'll help get them off our trail."

Peter turned the ship and took them around the dark side of the moon. He moved in so close that for a moment Jace thought he was going to crash it right into the surface.

"Alright, this should do it. Initiate the camo shield."

"The Katara has a camo shield?" Jace asked in amazement. The stars in the view screen before them shimmered briefly before returning to normal. "I thought those things were illegal on civilian ships."

"I told you the old bird still had a few tricks up her sleeve. Alright Pete, take us back out and let's see what's going on around here."

The ship soared in a tight loop around the moon's surface until the Earth came back into view.

Jace pointed out into the distance. "I don't remember Luna Point looking like that when we left."

The four of them stared out as Peter flew along over the surface. The small moon colony, which was located on the outskirts of the Sea of Tranquility, had been decimated. Galin suddenly felt like he'd been punched in the stomach.

"I had a cousin who lived there," Starla said in a cracked voice.

Galin got on the intercom. "Joseph, Ulrick, if you two aren't seeing what we are you'd better flip your view screens on." He turned to Peter. "Take us over to the Galactic Confederation Navy base."

Peter guided the ship past the Earth and out toward the base's coordinates. He approached slowly to a point where they could get a good view, and magnified the screen in front of them.

There were gasps and shouts of anger as everyone took in the scene before them. Starla burst into tears, covered her mouth and staggered back, falling into a sitting position on the floor.

It looked as though the entire fleet had been destroyed. Charred debris and fragments of familiar vessels floated before them like common space junk.

The skeletal remains of the GCW Navy Earth Star-Base, which had been home to the largest fleet of ships in the confederation, drifted before them like some hanged prisoner that the executioner hadn't bothered to cut down.

"What happened?" Starla cried. "A Nazerazi attack?"

Ulrick's face held a look of barely-contained fury. "It had to be," he growled. "Who else would be powerful enough to take down Earth's defenses."

Galin's head was swimming. He didn't doubt that it was the Nazerazi, but how could they have done this so quickly? How was it even possible?

"I'm picking up two incoming vessels," Peter said. "Switching image to the main view screen."

Galin recognized the small ships moving toward them as Nazerazi fighters. They were hideous things, and looked more like dark clumps of broken glass than any kind of ship Galin had ever seen.

"You think they've detected us?" Jace asked.

"I don't know how they could have," Galin told him. "But… it does look like they're coming right for us."

Peter shifted in his seat uncomfortably. "Should I get us out of here?"

"Not just yet," Galin said. "Take us over into that debris field to give us some cover. Then we'll just hang back for a minute and see what happens. Joseph, do whatever you can to make sure we're ready to warp out of here in a hurry. Jace, you go down and try to help him out."

Jace left the bridge as Peter flew the Katara through

the debris. They held position behind the largest section of a destroyed battleship. If the Nazerazis *were* tracking them, now they'd be a little harder to get to.

The two fighters came to a halt a short distance from their position. They hung there as if they were waiting for something, looking like sentries - alert, unmoving, all seeing.

"Can you tell if they're trying to scan for us?" Ulrick asked over the com.

"Not that I can tell," Peter told him. "I'm not familiar with their technology though, I don't have any idea how advanced it is compared to ours."

"From what I've been told it's right on par with our own," Galin said. "Sure is weird that they're just sitting there. Maybe they're waiting for us to do something stupid."

Galin hadn't finished speaking before a humungous ship dropped out of warp behind the Nazerazi fighters. It was a GCW Nebula class Battleship."

"Hey, is that the Claymore?" Peter yelled excitedly.

"Yeah, I think it is! Those slaggin' Nazerazi's are going to get it now."

The battleship proceeded slowly forward, and Galin felt like he was going to jump out of his skin as he waited for it to open fire on the enemy ships.

But... it did not.

Much to Galin's shock the behemoth came to a resting position between the two Nazerazi fighters.

"We have an incoming transmission," Peter said, putting it on the view screen.

Galin recognized the bridge of the Claymore, as well as the man who stood in the center of the screen.

"Starship Katara, this is Admiral Winchester of the Nazerazi battleship Claymore. Please lower your shields and prepare for your ship to be impounded."

Galin glared at the man with water and fire in his eyes.

"Father," he growled, "what have you done?"

Book 2

Sins of the Father

—MEXICO CITY, TEXAS
A FEW WEEKS BEFORE—

Mrs. Ponte looked out over the nervous, puckered faces of her sixth grade class. Her bright, blue eyes, which appeared enormous through thick, round glasses-and were set off by her pale skin and snowy white hair-pierced every one of them in turn. She picked up the untidy heap of papers and dropped them gently through her gnarled fingers a few times to straighten the stack.

"All right, children," she said with a frown. "I've just finished grading the final quiz, and I really must say..." they twitched in their seats, "that I'm very pleased with the classroom's progress lately."

She smiled, and they all breathed a collective sigh of

relief. This would mean that the field trip to the zoo was back on, and Mrs. Ponte's good mood would be guaranteed for the next few weeks.

"However," she continued with a few shakes of her finger, "there are just a few things we need to review. On some of the questions there was a little bit of confusion."

A few scattered grunts of disapproval rose from the students.

"First of all, who can tell me why the United States of Texas was formed?"

At first everyone sat still, but then one of the young boys reluctantly raised his hand. The teacher nodded at him.

"Because they didn't wanna be a part of the United States of America no more?"

"Close, but not exactly. And mind your grammar, Mr. Ramirez. Anyone else?"

A young girl with short blonde hair raised her hand; Mrs. Ponte acknowledged her.

"The United States went through Civil War II, and Texas and some of the other states joined forces and broke off from the rest of the country."

"Very good. And why did Texas and those other states separate from the rest of the country? Anyone remember? How about you, Ms. Winchester?"

The girl lifted up her head and sighed, as if the effort bothered her. "Because," she said pointedly, "the country was being led by a bunch of *fracking* socialists."

The classroom roared with laughter.

"Ms. Winchester, *how* many times must I warn you about your language?" Mrs. Ponte reprimanded. *"Don't* make me tell you again. However, right you are, the country *was* being run by a bunch of frack—," her cheeks suddenly flushed as the children laughed again, "by a bunch of socialists."

She regained her composure and smiled warmly. "And the two countries which emerged after Civil War II were?"

The girl with short blonde hair raised her hand again. "The United States of Texas and the United Socialist Democrat States of America."

"Very good, Amy," Mrs. Ponte told her, giving her a pat on the head. "But remember to wait until I call on you next time."

"And who can tell me what led to the downfall of the USDSA?"

This time, every hand in class shot up. Mrs. Ponte chuckled to herself; she'd known that this question would draw some interest.

"Why don't *you* tell us Tommy."

"Because they tried to unleash a zombie virus on the Texans, but they all caught it themselves instead."

Again, the whole class laughed.

The old teacher nodded slowly. "Although, to be fair, there are some who claim that the virus was never developed to be used as a weapon. Under the leadership of a government scientist named Dr. Carl Mengele, a genetic modification was developed that would have given the USDSA soldiers the ability to regenerate. Whatever the reason for its creation, the virus actually attacked its host's body, causing severe brain damage and nearly destroying the host completely before the regeneration effect kicked in. From that point on the body was caught in a constant state of molecular warfare, the virus attacking and regenerating it at the same time."

She looked out at the children's faces again. Most of the boys had devilish smiles, but the majority of girls had disgusted, uncomfortable looks.

"But, as Tommy said," she continued, "the virus ended up spreading through the USDSA and bringing the country to the brink of utter destruction. The United States of Texas suffered many losses, but only a fraction of those suffered by the USDSA. Why was that?"

There were many scratched chins and fixed stares into the distance as the children searched for an answer. A few of the boys and little Amy, who looked ready to pop, had their hands up.

The old woman hobbled around to the side of her desk and moved her shawl away from the right side of her body, revealing a small, silver blaster pistol. She drew it from its holster and held it above her head before the class.

"This," she said cheerfully, "is why the UST survived

the breakout until a vaccine could be found."

Mrs. Ponte holstered the weapon and then turned to face a hanging skeleton located in the corner of the class by the window. She looked surprisingly like an old pale toad getting ready to leap, as her thin bent legs shook under the weight of her pudgy stomach and hunched back.

"You see, it's hard for a zombie to give you the virus," she drew the blaster with admirable speed, "if you blast his slagging head off before he can bite you." She shot the skull, which incinerated into a small shower of sparks and tiny molten bits of fiery plastic. The remaining pieces of the skeleton crashed to the floor.

She holstered the gun as cheers and applause erupted from the class, and began to hobble back over to her desk as the intercom popped on.

"Mrs. Ponte, this is Principal Smith, I just got a report of a laser bl—,"

"Everything's quiet all right, Mr. Smith. I was just conducting a little demonstration for the children. No need to fuss."

There were a few moments of silence.

"All right, Mrs. Ponte," he said in a slightly annoyed voice, "I wouldn't mind getting a heads up next time."

"Yes, yes, I'll try to remember. Goodbye."

She smiled at the class mischievously; as if that wasn't the first time she'd given poor Principal Smith a start.

"Just like you," she crowed, "he used to be a student

of mine. And as I recall, *he* was quiet impressed with my marksmanship too. Although I confess, I was a bit faster when he was in class."

She carefully eased down into her chair, holding her lower back with one hand and her desk with the other.

"Alright, let's everyone open up to page three hundred and fifty—, uh, yes Ms. Winchester?" She was surprised to see the girl, who never had much to say, raising her hand.

"Is it true that some of the zombies were exiled to the planet Necron, and that a colony of them still inhabit the place?"

Mrs. Ponte chuckled. "It is true that an infected cargo ship crew carried the virus to the planet Necron, which until that time had been called Bios. A population of the infected is still thought to inhabit the planet, so everyone stays clear of the place- if they have any sense, that is. As for zombies being exiled to the planet, this is certainly only a myth. Those infected by the virus became mindless, drooling killers. There would be no reason to exile them; destroying them was the only reasonable option."

She looked at the intrigued, spooked faces of her students.

"No need to worry, children. The virus has been eradicated on Earth. We now have a vaccine available as well. So unless your parents are planning their summer vacations on the planet Necron, none of you have any need to fear."

There were a few nervous chuckles.

"Now please open your books to page three hundred and fifty—,"

The whole room shook as an encompassing boom filled the air. Mrs. Ponte clung to her desk with both hands as the floor vibrated beneath her. A siren could be heard in the distance as the noise slowly faded.

"CHILDREN," she shouted. "REMEMBER THE EMERGENCY DRILL WE PRACTICED A FEW WEEKS AGO! YOU KNOW WHAT TO DO!"

Most of the children had already run to the windows, and were crowded around trying to get a good look outside. Explosions could be seen in the distance, but defensive fire from the ground was shooting up around them in all directions.

The room shook again, and dust fell down from the ceiling tiles like small heavy snowflakes. Mrs. Ponte began to fall back in her chair, but caught herself just in time. She struggled with all her might as her thin, white legs peddled through the air as if she were trying to swim.

She felt a small set of hands grasp her shoulders and push her back up to a sitting position, and let out something between a hoarse cough and a sigh of relief. Her chair spun around and the little hands again grabbed her shoulders, this time pulling her to a wobbly stand. It was little Sarah Winchester.

"Come on, Mrs. Ponte, we need to get you down to the basement."

She let the girl drag her along. "COME ON CHILDREN," she screeched over the noise. "REMEMBER THE DRILL! YOU KNOW WHAT TO DO!"

–NOW–

Galin glared at the man standing before him. He was seething inside. He was a volcano ready to erupt, his heart pumping boiling lava violently through his veins.

"Father, what have you done? WHAT HAVE YOU DONE!"

He couldn't contain his anger, his hatred at seeing this man standing before him unharmed, claiming that the Claymore was a Nazerazi ship, while the rest of Earth's fleet floated as charred pieces of garbage around them.

"What have *I* done? I've done what was necessary to secure Earth's future. You see, I've been passing information on to the Alliance for quite some time now. I've helped orchestrate Earth's surrender. It was necessary for humanity's survival, and in the end we will be stronger because of it."

Galin couldn't believe what he was hearing. He couldn't find any words. The rage within him turned into a heartbroken sadness. He hadn't spoken to his father much over the last few years. He was a hard man, unforgiving and at times downright mean, but Galin never expected this. He never expected his father to be a murderous traitor.

"Not that it's any of *your* concern," the Admiral continued. "Now, I'm only going to say this one more time. Turn off that illegal camo shield, come out of that debris field, and prepare to have your ship impounded."

"I'm not doing *any* such thing. But you already know that, don't you? What are you doing *dad*, going through the motions so you can murder me, just like you did everyone else in the fleet?"

For a split second, Admiral Winchester had a shocked, hurt look on his face, but was soon glaring back with a hatred that matched his son's. His crow's feet and widow's peak seemed to accentuate the squint of his black eyes.

"Don't be ridiculous. We've already locked onto your coordinates. Even with your camo shield you won't get far. That damaged engine of yours is leaving a nice little trail of hydrogen atoms for us to follow. How far do you think you can get flying a wreck like that? Are you willing to sacrifice the lives of everyone on board because of your stubbornness and pride?"

Galin suddenly felt like a snapped stick. Was this the man who had thrown a football to him when he was a boy? The man that taught him how to ride a bike? Growing up as a military brat meant that the man hadn't always been there for him, but he hadn't been a bad father. He'd been someone to look up to. Someone that Galin had aspired to be. It was only after the death of Jamie that they'd grown to detest one another.

Fear and doubt began to invade him. He'd been such a fool to bring his crew- his friends, back to Earth like this. The ship was heavily damaged and they hadn't known what they were going to find. He should have had another plan. Then again, how could he have ever expected this? How could he have known?

"What's going on down on the surface?" Galin demanded, looking up at his father. "What about Melissa and the kids? Do you have any idea what's happened to them?"

"Your family is not my concern right now. You can check on them after you've been processed and returned home."

A resurgence of anger flooded over him. The man couldn't even be bothered to look in on his own grandchildren? He needed to get back and make sure they were all right. Besides, resistance would just delay the inevitable. All he could do now was what was right for his crew and his family.

"I have your *word* that no one will be harmed?"

"Of course," the admiral said sternly. "You and your crew will be returned to the surface and the Katara will become the property of the Nazerazi Alliance." He stood there quietly for a moment and then sighed. "You have no choice, son."

Peter turned to Galin with determination in his eyes. "Whatever you decide, I'm with you. I'm sure everyone else feels the same way."

Galin nodded. Maybe the rest *were* with him, and maybe they weren't, but he didn't really care. They were his responsibility. Trying to fight their way out of this right now would be nothing more than suicide.

"Alright." He sat down into the captain's chair. If the Katara had to be surrendered, then he was going to be the one to fly it in.

"Turn off the shield," he said to Peter.

Peter gave him a nod and a sad smile, and then reached down and flipped the camo shield off. The Katara shimmered and came back into view. Galin took control and guided her slowly out of the debris field. He felt an overwhelming surge of sadness and betrayal as he handled the ship for what might be the last time. This wasn't how he expected it all to end; the Katara and her crew hobbling home like a beaten dog only to surrender to the enemy, to traitors.

He brought the ship to a halt in front of the Claymore, which loomed above them like a lion standing over a mouse. Galin felt naked, and for a moment thought that the Nazerazi ships might blow them into stardust, but a moment later everything shook as a tractor beam from the Claymore locked on, and began to pull them in toward whatever fate awaited.

Peter flipped off the view screen. "I guess that's it then. No way out of this now."

He was right. They were caught like a fish in a net. There was no turning back.

"What happens now?" Starla asked them. Her eyes were red and puffy, but she'd stopped crying. "Do you really think they'll return us all to the surface? What do you think things are like down *there*?"

"I guess we'll all find out soon enough," Peter said. He looked at Galin. "You want me to get everyone up here?"

Galin put down his head. There was no way out of this. Whatever would be would be. The entire fleet was gone and the Nazerazi had taken Earth. They were going to have to deal with their fate head on.

Then again, fate was a lady who loved to dance. An idea came to him. A twinkle of hope, a tiny pinpoint of light; it was a plan that just might work if everything fell into place. A plan that might save a few of his friends, if things took a turn for the worse.

"Yes," he said to Peter with a nod. Get everyone to the bridge, and tell them to hurry. We don't have much time."

Galin got up from his chair and pulled Starla to her feet. He threw his arms around her and squeezed her so hard that she let out a small gasp. He kissed her. "I love you," he said. "And I'm sorry. Sorry for everything."

—SAN ANTONIO, TEXAS FOURTEEN YEARS BEFORE—

Galin stood in front of the mirror, fixated on discovering every obscure flaw in his dress uniform. Any loose string, any speck of dust, any surviving wrinkle, would need to be found and eliminated. Tonight had to be perfect.

The doorbell rang. That had to be Jamie. Galin took one last look at himself, finally content.

He walked out of the bathroom and across the living room. He opened the front door, and there she was standing with her hands on her hips, in uniform. She looked like she'd just jogged over.

Jamie smiled at him. He staggered back as his little sister threw her arms around him and squeezed.

"Whoa, careful now, you're going to wrinkle me," he laughed.

"Sorry, I'm just so excited for you," she said, straightening him back out. "Congratulations."

"Congrats to you too. That uniform is impressive on you, Ensign. But what's with the new hot and bothered look? Somebody lock you in the trunk of your car or something?"

She moved passed him and went straight for the fridge, taking out a bottle of apple juice. "No, the stupid car went into the shop yesterday and I had to walk over here."

"What's wrong with it?" he asked.

"It's got a leaky flux capacitor."

"Very funny."

Galin got a glass from the cupboard and handed it to her.

"Why didn't you call me to come pick you up? It's a hot one out there today," he said.

She nodded while pouring. Galin didn't care much for apple juice, but his sister loved it. He'd picked up a few bottles to throw in the fridge for her.

"I need the exercise. Anyway, it isn't that far."

"Listen, I'm sorry I didn't make it back in time for your graduation ceremony. If it hadn't been for that scuffle with those slaggin' —"

"Look, it's okay. You don't need to apologize again. I know you'd have made it if you could."

"To be honest with you," he said, looking at her rank insignia, "I didn't know if you'd go through with it. Are you sure you didn't join just because it's what Dad and I wanted."

She emptied the glass and began to pour another. "I'm a *big* girl, you know," she said with a wink. "Capable of making my own choices in life, and all that stuff. I know what I want." She sounded a little irritated.

"I know that," he told her. "I just want you to be

happy. I've always wanted you to be happy."

"And *I* know *that,*" she said, smiling again. "But how did we get off and talking about me? Tonight we should be talking about *you*." She beamed at him. "Do you think Starla even knows what's coming?"

"You're her best friend. You tell me. I thought you were spying things out for me."

She strolled over and stood in front of a nearby air conditioning vent, letting out a big sigh of relief.

"Well," she said, looking up into the distance, as if to tease him, "I don't think she's expecting it tonight. She definitely wants you to ask her, she's told me that. But she doesn't think you're ready. It's going to be quite a surprise, I think."

Galin smiled. He was glad that Starla wasn't expecting anything.

"Are you sure you want me and the others there when you ask her? It's kind of a private moment isn't it?"

"Sure, but what better moment to share with your best friends and family? I talked to Peter this morning. He's going to be there too."

"Great, I haven't seen him in a while. How's he doing?"

"Just fine. Won't stop teasing me about getting hitched though. But he knows Starla's a great woman, he just likes to yank my chain."

"Everyone likes to yank *your* chain," she told him. "You're just a fun person to pick on." She took another drink and put the glass in the sink. "So, seven o'clock tonight, right?" she asked while heading back toward the door.

"Yup. Hey, where are you going? You just got here."

"I've got some shopping to do. I'll meet you at the restaurant in a few hours." She swung the door open and turned back, eying him sympathetically. "You look a little nervous. You gonna be okay?"

Galin nodded. He *was* a little nervous, but wasn't about to admit it, least of all to Jamie.

"I'm fine," he said. "You know how to find the place right?"

"Yeah, I've been there. Went there with mom a few years ago. It was just before she died."

Galin put his hand on her shoulder. "I didn't know that. We can go somewhere else if it's going to bother you."

She shook her head. "No. It's a good memory. I'm actually looking forward to going back."

She smiled as he kissed her on the forehead. "I'll see you in a few hours," she told him with a wave.

He closed the door behind her, and went back to the mirror.

—NOW—

Joseph stood at the hatch of the Shiv and handed

Ulrick the last two energy rifles. He leaned against the side, and could almost smell the fresh coat of black paint he and Jace had put on her only a month ago. This small shuttle, which had been designed as a short-range transport and doubled as an emergency escape vessel, didn't have as much firepower as Ulrick would have liked. Then again, Joseph knew that nothing had as much firepower as Ulrick liked. But if everything worked out the way they hoped, it wouldn't matter. Blasting their way past the Claymore and Nazerazi ships wasn't going to be an option. They were going to have to rely on their wits, something Joseph knew had always been Plan B for Ulrick.

"So you're sure you want to do this? It's going to be dangerous. If they detect your launch from the Katara they'll slag you for sure."

Ulrick smirked. "It'll work. If not, then my death probably won't be any worse than yours."

Joseph conceded with a shrug. "Here, take this with you too." He handed Ulrick an old, beat-up leather case.

"What is it?" he asked, taking it by the handle.

"The ship's old computer core. Probably just an old piece of junk, but someone went to the trouble of saving it once, and I have a feeling that we should try to keep it safe."

"You think the Shiv is going to be any safer than the Katara a few minutes from now?"

"No, but the Shiv won't be over-run and searched by

enemy soldiers."

"That's true," nodded Ulrick. He took Joseph's hand and they flexed their arms in a strong handshake. "Good luck, brother. Keep your fingers crossed. Wish everyone else good luck for me too."

Joseph nodded. "Be careful. Remember to stay clear of that tractor beam. If you get snagged it'll all be for nothing."

Ulrick closed the hatch and prepared the Shiv for launch. Joseph took a few steps back to the docking bay control panel to monitor its systems. Everything checked out. Her engine was purring like a kitten.

"Alright, Ulrick," he said over the com, "everything looks good. God speed!"

Joseph turned and jogged toward the loading bay door, nearly running into the large metal crate that contained the T3038. They'd all been so excited to have it a few days before, now it really *was* just a useless piece of space junk. He closed the door behind him, and turned to watch through the window as Ulrick depressurized the loading bay and opened the doors, which luckily were facing away from the Claymore, and the main stream of the tractor beam.

The Shiv shimmered and disappeared before him; Ulrick had activated its camo shield. Joseph grabbed the railing by the door. "Alright, hold on everybody," he said over the battle-com, "he's going for it."

A few moments later the Katara shook as Ulrick

attempted to punch through the surrounding grip generated by the Claymore's tractor beam.

"Did he make it?" came Galin's voice over the battle-com.

"I didn't see an explosion," said Joseph flatly. "He had to have made it."

They were only a minute or two away now. He needed to hurry. His boots clanked heavily through the passageway as he jogged toward the engine room. He was getting too old for this, had gotten too many banged knees and bruised shoulders over the past few years.

Joseph shot down the ladder to the engine room much faster than Jace had ever seen him do it, and the young man looked at him with wide eyes as he took a few deep breaths.

"All right, let's get you situated."

Jace tossed the last handful of wrenches into the cargo closet and shut the door. He hurried back and jumped down into the crawlspace beneath the floor that they'd been using as a storage compartment.

Joseph squatted down on one knee and looked him in the eye. "You sure you want to do this? It's not too late to opt out?"

Jace shook his head. "The Captain's right. If things go south on the Claymore, this could be a chance for us to escape with our lives, or at least cause some damage before they take us down."

Joseph put his hands on the young man's shoulders.

"Remember, if you don't hear anything from us within forty eight hours, it means we probably won't be coming back. You'll have to decide for yourself what to do. If you can escape somehow, do it. Otherwise, try to take a few of them with you for us." He handed down a few gallons of water and some rations.

Jace nodded. "It's been a pleasure, Chief. Thanks for everything you've done for me."

"You're a good man," Joseph told him. "Don't give up hope. We may get out of this yet."

Jace ducked down into the crawlspace, and the Chief slid the heavy, metal grate back into place. He looked around to make sure that nothing appeared out of the ordinary and headed back to the ladder.

The kid was in a safer place than the rest of them were about to be. Still, a part of him felt as though he were abandoning Jace. He hated to leave him there, crammed under the floor like a greasy old wrench.

Joseph made his way back up to the bridge, where Galin, Peter, and Starla were waiting for him.

"It's done," he told them.

"Are you sure this is a good idea?" Starla asked them. Tears had begun to run down her cheeks again.

"I'd be tucking *you* away someplace too if my father hadn't already seen you," he told her with a sad smile. "Jace will be fine. He can take care of himself."

"He'll be fine," Peter agreed, squeezing her hand. "So will Ulrick."

"I hope the two of you are right. I have a bad feeling about all of this."

"All right," Galin said, turning to Peter. "Erase all traces of Ulrick and Jace from the ship's computer."

—SAN ANTONIO, TEXAS FOURTEEN YEARS BEFORE—

The night air teemed with conversation at *Antonio's* restaurant. Even though the small group of friends was sitting outside, they had to raise their voices to be heard. Galin looked around the table. Starla was sitting to his right, and his sister was seated beside her, they were giggling quietly about something that he couldn't quite hear. Peter was sitting to his left, and his girlfriend Angelica was sitting beside him. Across from him was Clint, a friend that he and Peter had met at the academy, and his friend Jeff and his girlfriend Melissa.

Dinner was over and desert had been ordered, and Galin felt as though his stomach had been tied up in knots. It was time to do it. He was excited, but wanted to get it over with.

He pushed his chair back and got down to one knee, reaching into his pocket and taking out the small box. He opened it up to reveal the humble but charming ring he'd chosen for her, and gazed up into her eyes; she looked surprised and terrified.

Galin took Starla's hand in his, and opened his mouth to speak.

Please don't sound like an idiot, he told himself. This has to be perfect. She deserves it to be perfect.

"YES!" she shouted before he could say anything.

He looked at her in shock, not knowing what to do.

"Yes, I'll marry you," she told him as she slid off her chair to embrace him.

Before Galin knew what was happening, all the people sitting nearby were clapping and cheering, enthusiastically taking part in their happy moment.

They held the embrace for several moments. She kissed him all over the face and neck before letting him get back up to his feet.

"I love you," he whispered in her ear. He could tell that it tickled her.

He pulled out her chair and waved politely to some of the people nearby who were still clapping and giving congratulating nods.

Peter raised his glass for a toast.

"To Galin, the greatest friend I've ever had. And to Starla, the sweetest, most beautiful woman I have ever met, who sadly, to the dismay and grief of all free men, has been taken off the market."

Jamie touched her glass to his. "And to my best friend, who I'm convinced has always hung around so much not because of my delightful personality, but because of her crush on my big brother."

Starla's face grew red and she laughed under her breath, taking Galin's hand and shaking her head.

"I've known your plan from the start," Jamie smirked while pointing at her.

"So," Galin said, squeezing her hand, "are you sure you want to be a military wife? It's not always an easy life."

"I know that," she told him. "But I want you. I don't care what you do; I don't care if you're in the Space Navy or if you decide to open a carwash, all I want is *you*."

"Awe shucks," Clint said with a smile. "If I'd have known things were going to get this sweet I wouldn't have ordered any pie."

Starla stuck out her tongue at him.

"So how long have you two known each other?" Melissa asked them.

"A long time now," Galin said, gazing at Starla. "Jamie invited her over for a slumber party in third grade. They've been attached at the hip ever since."

"Well, back then he didn't even know I existed, but I suppose I've always had a bit of a crush on him."

"Oh, I knew you existed," Galin laughed. "And you annoyed me just as much as all the other little girls Jamie used to drag home. Sometimes it felt like I was living inside a fracking dollhouse."

His friends laughed as Starla punched him lightly in the shoulder.

"Are you *kidding* me?" Jamie shot at him. "Living at our house was more like being enlisted, even when Dad was away. I wish I could have bottled and sold the testosterone generated from the place."

Galin laughed. "I guess that's why you're dressed more like a GI-Joe now than a Barbie."

For a moment he thought the comment might have ticked her off, though it wasn't what he intended.

"I'm still a Barbie on the inside," she said.

"Hey, Jamie," Clint said to her, "what happened to that Allen guy you were going out with? Are you two still together?"

She shook her head. "No, he turned out to be a real jerk. He actually got violent with me, so we called it quits."

"Really?" Melissa asked. "He got violent? Did Galin slap him around for you?"

"No, I took care of him myself. Gave him a broken nose, actually. I don't think he'd ever been with a woman who knew how to fight back."

Melissa looked impressed. "Wow, good for you. So who was this joker? I mean, where'd you meet him?"

"He's a Navy guy actually. We met in the officers' club at the orbital base. He ended up stalking me for a couple of weeks after we broke up, but I haven't heard from him for about a month now."

"And you'd better not either, or I *will* get involved," said Galin with a threatening look in his eye.

He knew his sister thought she was tough, and she was- tough as nails actually. But he also knew she had a habit of attracting the wrong type of men. He couldn't remember her ever having a boyfriend who he genuinely liked, and it wasn't just because they were dating his baby sister. She had brought home some real winners over the years. Part of him wondered if it was all just to get a rise out of their father. He'd always been too overprotective of his daughter, even Galin could see that.

"I can take care of myself," she told him with a proud grin, "but thanks anyway."

"Yeah, I know. That's what you keep telling me," he muttered under his breath.

"Well," Clint said, "now that you've put that other guy out of his misery, I don't suppose you'd consider giving yours truly a shot?" He gave her a charming grin.

"That depends on how hard you're willing to fight for it, I guess," she said, smiling back.

Galin knew that she was just leading him on. A guy like Clint would never stand a chance with his sister. He was polite, honest, friendly, and kind. She probably wouldn't be interested.

The waitress arrived with desert. Galin took a few bites of cheesecake, and his mind wandered as everyone broke off into their own conversations. He was glad he'd proposed to Starla like this. It wasn't the most romantic way he could have done it, but he knew that she'd enjoy having their friends with them. He'd enjoyed it too, but now he just wanted to be alone with the woman he loved.

Galin thought about the girls he'd dated in high school and through college. Looking back on it all now, he'd loved Starla the whole time. Why had it taken him so long to realize it? Maybe it was because she was so close to his sister. Heck, he'd always thought of Starla a little like a sister. She and Jamie dressed alike, did their hair up the same way, and had always tried their best to look alike. It was a good thing *that* changed as they got older.

The girls' personalities however, couldn't be more different. Jamie was a tomboy. Their mother had been from a military family, and she was just as strict as their father. She never put up with any back talk, foolishness, or crying fits. Starla was definitely more of a girlie-girl. When they were all younger Galin thought she was a real crybaby, but now he knew that hadn't been the case; he'd just been used to his sister. The two girls had always gone together like salt and pepper, which was why they loved each other so much.

After a while, Clint, Jeff and Melissa congratulated them again and got up to leave. Peter and Angelica weren't far behind them, and soon Galin found himself alone with the two girls. He struggled to remain patient while Starla and Jamie finished up their chitchat.

"How'd you get here?" Galin asked his sister as they walked toward the front of the restaurant.

"I took a cab, but I think I'm going to walk back.

Like I told you earlier, I need the exercise."

Galin frowned at her. "You're going to walk home alone at ten o'clock at night? I don't think so. Why don't you let us give you a lift?"

She rolled her eyes. "I don't live that far away. It's not like this is a bad part of town or something; I'll be fine. If I didn't want to walk I'd take a cab."

"I just don't think it's a good idea. Especially since you're in uniform. You never know when somebody's gonna want to start trouble."

"Come on," she told him, getting a little frustrated. "You're starting to sound just like Dad. I'll be fine." She pursed her lips at him. "What are you going to do, stand here and argue with *me* all night? Get out of here, go spend some time alone together."

"Look, I just —"

"You're not going to change her mind, and you know it," Starla said, squeezing him. "You'll have to let her walk home or knock her out and drag her to the truck."

Galin was tempted to do just that.

Jamie smiled and nodded her head in satisfaction. "I love you guys, good night! I'll talk to you both tomorrow." She was waving and had already started to walk away.

"Good night, and be careful" Starla called after her. "You stubborn little..." she added under her breath.

"I swear," Galin grumbled, "sometimes I think she does this sort of thing specifically to piss me off. *'I need the exercise'*," he mocked. "Give me a break."

Starla pulled him in tightly. "I know. But it's just who she is, don't you know that by now?"

He opened the door for her. "Watch your dress," he said, and then shut it behind her. He walked around the front of the truck and jumped in.

"Let's just drive for a while," Starla said to him, placing her hand on his leg.

Galin started up the truck and started to drive. He listened to her talk about all the things she wanted to do for the wedding. He didn't find any of it too interesting, but he was excited because she was excited. He wanted her to be happy.

They drove for several hours before he pulled to a stop.

"Where the heck are we anyway?" Starla asked him. "Hey, is that the ocean?"

Galin laughed. She hadn't been paying attention at all to where they'd been going. She was just happy to be alone with him, to have time to talk.

"We're just outside of Corpus Christi. I thought it'd be fun to watch the sun come up over the ocean."

She giggled excitedly. One good thing about Starla, she was always up for a spontaneous adventure.

They got out and climbed into the bed of the truck. Galin reached up and placed something on the cab. He pushed the red button on top and a blue dome of energy shot out around them and disappeared.

"A force-field? Really? How romantic."

Galin just smiled at her.

He spread a blanket out over the top of them. It was a clear night, and the stars twinkled brightly overhead, almost like they were waving. They kissed, and he held her close. He could tell that she wanted him as much as he wanted her. She would probably give herself to him tonight if he asked. He pulled her in and held her in a tight squeeze. He respected her, loved her too much to dishonor her; they only needed to wait a little longer. She snuggled up close to him, resting her head upon his chest.

Starla fell asleep first, and Galin listened to the ocean and smelled her hair for a while before following her into the world of dreams.

—NOW—

Galin walked in front of the two armed guards who were escorting him to the bridge of the Claymore. He'd once worn a uniform just like theirs, but his had displayed the insignia of the Galactic Confederation of Worlds. These men's uniforms bore the symbol of the Nazerazi Alliance- a strange alien skull with an open mouth. Inside the mouth was a circle with lines projecting out like rays of light; a sun perhaps?

The steel guts and long metallic corridors of the ship

were all too familiar to Galin. He had once served on a ship just like this, but things felt different somehow. The people of earth may have built this ship, but it no longer belonged to them. It had been commandeered. It was a Nazerazi vessel now, and it seemed ugly and cold. The familiarity gave him no comfort.

Officers and enlisted men, and a few women, passed them as they walked. Most had looks of confusion or guilt on their faces; a few went about their business with blank, sad stares. He knew what they were all thinking, because he felt it too. They were broken, lost; wanting to grasp hold of some hope that none of them knew where to find.

"Where are the other members of my crew being taken?" he asked with a worn voice.

One of his escorts, a Petty Officer Third Class who was used to telling prisoners to shut up and keep moving, opened his mouth to yell, but stopped himself. "They're being taken to the brig," he said in a low voice. "They'll be safe. For a while, anyway."

Galin nearly stopped in his tracks, but thought better of it. "What exactly is *that* supposed to mean?"

The guard's partner gave him a scared look of warning, but said nothing.

"These Nazerazi characters don't seem to hold on to prisoners too long. Rumor is, they're shipping a lot of people off Earth. I don't know where they're taking them."

They stepped onto a turbolift.

"Bridge," ordered the quiet guard.

Galin hung his head. Had he let them all down? No, he couldn't second-guess himself now, it wouldn't do any good. There had been no other choice.

"Have you seen them yet?" he asked. "The Nazerazi I mean?"

"Yeah," the guard whispered. "There's a handful on the ship. They keep to themselves though. Most people onboard haven't seen them yet."

"What do they look like?" Galin asked.

"You'll see for yourself in a minute."

The turbolift came to a halt, and the door opened. Galin and the two guards stepped onto the bridge. It seemed humongous compared to the bridge of the Katara.

A dozen or so officers were present, trying to look busy and avoid eye contact, acting as if it was all business as usual. Admiral Winchester stood in front of the main view screen, gazing out into space, and discussing something that Galin couldn't quite hear with the large being next to him.

"Admiral," said the guard in a nervous voice, "we have brought the, er...prisoner."

Galin's father turned to face them, as did his companion, and they started toward them.

The alien was large- about seven and a half feet tall, Galin guessed. He was covered in a thick, crimson robe.

Only his clawed hands, the front of his face, and a thick tail could be seen protruding the folds. He had green scaly skin and a reptilian face. As he moved closer, his steps were quick and determined, and Galin got the feeling that he could have moved much, much faster if he'd wanted to.

"General Soth," said the admiral to his companion. "This is my son, Galin Winchester, Captain of the Katara.

The general nodded. Galin couldn't read his lizard-like face. It looked something like a smile, but was sinister and hungry.

"The Katara. Yes, I've heard of this ship. When your father told us you were its owner, I knew I had to meet you." Soth hissed out his words like an overzealous snake. His breath smelled disgustingly sweet and earthy.

Galin hadn't known what to expect from the creature, but an interest in his ship was definitely a surprise.

"The Katara?" He said insolently. "What do *you* know about the Katara?"

The general broadened his smile- if that was indeed what it was.

"Your ship is somewhat of a legend among the Nazerazi. It's something that they have greatly desired to get their hands on since learning of its existence. They will be most pleased with me for delivering it to them."

A legend? That didn't make any sense. The Alliance must have gotten their wires crossed somewhere.

"What do you mean *they*? Aren't you a Nazerazi?" Galin asked.

The general hissed in laughter. "Me? No. I am a member of the Alliance, but I am not a Nazerazi. I am Draconian. Like you, I am just a member of another conquered race. In the Nazerazi Alliance, there are many of those."

Galin nearly objected. He didn't take kindly to being called a 'member of a conquered race.' But now it appeared that this was exactly what he was. And if the General was a typical Draconian, he shuddered to think of what kind of beings could bring down and subdue such a race of brutes. If all his people were as intimidating, that couldn't have been an easy feat.

Admiral Winchester looked at his son with a grim smile. "He will make a valuable member of the Alliance," he told Soth. "He will be loyal."

"Yes, I hope he will," Soth said with a crooked head. He began to pick at something between his razor-like fangs, using one of his long fingernails like a toothpick. "Your father has told me about your contempt for the Galactic Confederation. How their weakness disgusted you, just as it did him. He has informed me about your receptiveness to joining with the Nazerazi."

Galin looked deep into the General's black, calculating eyes. He had no idea what the creature was talking about. He'd always been loyal to his country, his planet, and even the Confederation, even when he hadn't fully agreed with them. If his father had gotten another idea, he was sorely mistaken. Just because he'd left the Space Navy to get away from some things didn't make him a traitor too.

"But we shall see," Soth said softly. "We will soon allow him to test his loyalty." He looked at the Admiral, and then back at Galin. "Your father has been instrumental in helping the Nazerazi Alliance seize control of your planet. He has provided much information over the last few years, which has greatly expedited the invasion. I hope that we can look forward to such cooperation from you as well."

There were a number of things Galin *wanted* to say, but he wasn't about to argue with this creature, not while they had him by the short hairs. He needed to protect himself and his crew until the right opportunity arose. He forced himself to nod respectfully at the General's words.

Admiral Winchester motioned for the nearby guards. "Take him down to the brig. We need to keep him confined until we're assured of his loyalty."

Without another word, he turned, as did the Draconian, and they walked away toward the view screen.

The guards guided Galin back onto the turbolift. The door shut with a quiet whir.

"Who knew?" said the guard who'd talked to him before. "I thought *those* things were the Nazerazi."

"All of them on the Claymore," Galin said, "they're all Draconian?"

"The five that I've seen all look like Soth. Well, he's a bit more menacing than the rest." The guard shook his head "I guess he was right. We're nothing more than a conquered race now too."

The other guard nodded. "Only reason we were spared is because of Admiral Winchester's betra..., I mean, cooperation."

The words made Galin sick. He wasn't about to cave in to defeat; he didn't care if he died resisting. He'd find a way to hit the Nazerazi back, and he wanted to cause them as much grief as possible on the way out.

—CORPUS CHRISTI, TEXAS
FOURTEEN YEARS BEFORE—

Galin woke up to the sun shining brightly in his face. He felt hot and a bit sweaty beneath the blanket and the woman who lay upon his shoulder. She was still sleeping. There was a little wet spot on the right side of his chest from where she'd drooled on him. He laughed inside. It was cute and a little gross at the same time.

He tried to get up without waking her, but it didn't work. She sat up quickly and rubbed her eyes.

"What, what time is it?" she asked him.

He checked his watch. "Eight thirty. Looks like we

missed the sunrise. Sorry about that. I'll set my alarm next time."

She shook her head. "No, it's okay." She pulled the hair up out of her eyes and tied it behind her head. "We'll have plenty of sunrises to watch together."

He smiled at her and kissed her on the forehead.

Off in the distance, he could see a Beach Patrol vehicle coming toward them. He reached up and turned the force field off and put it under the blanket, hoping the officer hadn't seen it. Force fields weren't allowed on the beach- something about disturbing the wildlife or some such nonsense.

The patrolman waved as he passed by. They'd escaped a ticket.

"How about some breakfast?" he asked. "I know a great little mom-and-pop diner in town. If you're feeling up to it, we can take the pancake challenge."

"Uh, you don't think I keep my stomach looking like this," she said, giving herself a pat, "by doing things like the pancake challenge, do you?"

"Well listen to you," he said, helping her down from the side of the truck bed. "Just because I'm marrying a super-model doesn't mean *I* have to eat like one too, does it?"

"A super-model? I wish."

"I don't think you realize how beautiful you are." He shut the truck door behind her and handed her the blanket and pillows. "Which is a very good thing for me, by the way."

They drove into Corpus Christi and had breakfast. Galin couldn't believe how much this girl could talk about cake, flowers, and coordinating colors, but he managed to pay attention and even acted interested while she did it.

They were back on the road and headed for home by ten thirty. Now she was talking about bridesmaids' dresses.

Galin's phone rang.

"Hello."

"Galin, this is your father. Where are you?"

Galin didn't like his tone of voice. It just sounded...wrong.

"Starla and I are driving back up from Corpus Christi. What's going on?"

"You need to get back home as fast as you can, son. I'm on my way right now."

"What's wrong?" he pleaded. "What's happened?" He pulled the truck over to the side of the road. Starla gazed into his eyes. She looked scared.

The phone went silent.

"DAD?"

"...It's Jamie. She's dead, Son. They found her a few hours ago. Someone...raped her...and slit her throat."

Galin dropped the phone and began to sob. Starla, guessing what had happened, seized ahold of him. They sat there in each other's arms as cars continued to speed by, weeping bitterly together.

—NOW—

Jace clicked on his data-pad and scrolled through the menu to access the diagram of the Katara. It was the forth time he'd done it, but he thought that looking again might reveal something he hadn't seen before, might give him some new idea or plant the seed of some plan he had not yet considered. It was also nice to have a little more light; it made him feel less lonely.

He'd only been lying in the crawl space for about six hours, but it already felt like an eternity. *This is what it must feel like to be buried alive,* he thought. Then again, maybe he was just being dramatic. He could easily reach up with his hands or feet and push aside the grate that rested above him, but it wasn't worth the risk. He couldn't let himself be discovered- not just yet.

Only minutes after the ship had docked, he'd heard a group come in to take a look around, felt the vibrations as their boots clunked down with each footfall on the floor above him, but since they'd left everything had remained quiet.

"Come on, come on, *come on*. There has to be something here you can use," he whispered to himself, scanning the pad.

Off in the distance, he heard a swoosh and a clank. It

was one of the doors on the ship; someone had come back.

He turned off the data-pad and laid it on his chest. Then, interlocking his fingers and resting his hands on his stomach, he held very still, and listened.

Several minutes went by as he heard clanks and clunks. It sounded like someone was moving equipment around- probably taking things off the ship.

Jace's heart leapt when he realized that someone was coming back down the ladder into the engine room. There were voices.

"Alright," came a low, raspy hiss, "hand it down to me. Carefully. I SAID CAREFULLY, HUMAN."

There were a few more clanks as some things were set down on the floor.

"Hero, you lead the way. Surely you know more about human ships than we do." This voice was like the first- a low hiss, but more soft spoken.

Jace tried to see through the narrow slits in the floor grate as they walked over him and stopped in front of the engine. He could see a human form, it was small, probably a woman. The other two figures were significantly larger, but he couldn't see them very well. They had to be Nazerazi.

He slowly lowered his left hand to feel for the laser-pistol he'd placed on the floor. There it was. He carefully passed it over into his right hand.

"Icke, could you hand me that schematic over there?"

the female said politely.

"Get it yourself, lazy female," came the gruff voice.

"Here, let me get it for you," said the kinder voice.

"Mwaa ha ha. You weakling, Boreas. Allowing a female to dominate you? Perhaps we should find you a job tending hatchlings."

A threatening hiss came from the offended Boreas. "Watch your mouth, Icke, I've bested you in mache before and spared you. Next time you may not be so lucky."

There were hisses and growls from both of the aliens. It sounded like they were going to start scrapping right there in the engine room.

"I don't know how you Draconians get anything done," Hero told them. "All you seem to do is threaten and fight with each other."

"The female is right," said Boreas. "We need to get to work. Either help us with the repairs or report for reassignment."

"I'm not going anywhere," growled Icke. "I don't trust these humans, and I'm not so sure that I trust *you* either. Complete your repairs. I will observe to make sure that you don't do anything hsssss suspicious."

"ENOUGH of your insults," yelled Boreas.

Jace listened in confusion and awe as the two creatures began to struggle above him. He heard the smaller feet of Hero as she ran across the room, presumably to flee from danger.

The two large creatures crashed and thudded against the wall and side of the engine compartment, swearing at each other in words that even the universal translator in his ear was having a hard time deciphering.

Suddenly one of the creatures was thrown to the floor above him. He saw it's head slammed into the grate several times until it was held there, pressed firmly down by it's adversary.

A large reptilian eye peered down toward him into the darkness. It dilated surprisingly fast, and fixed on his face. Then it squinted. The thing saw him.

"WHAT?" it screeched. "Let me up, Boreas. Let me up! There is a *human* underneath this grate."

The creature was pulled to his feet.

"What are you talking about? Where?"

Jace got the laser-pistol ready, and listened to his heart pound within him as he waited for them to move the grate. He watched as long green fingers came down through the slits near his feet, and lifted up the end, setting it down gently to the side.

He lifted the pistol up and pointed it as the grate was thrust to the side. The shocked, scared face of a beautiful, young, blonde woman looked back at him.

"Don't shoot me," she gasped, staggering back and falling on her butt.

Two large, reptilian creatures stood there off to each side of her. They wore armor composed of large black and red scales, and each had a blaster rifle pointed right at him.

"Drop the gun, human. You will not be harmed." He recognized the voice as belonging to Boreas.

"At least not yet," sneered Icke. "Why is there no record of you in the ship's log, human? Are you a stowaway? I doubt it! Perhaps Winchester has put you up to something?"

Jace lowered his pistol.

"Hero," said Boreas. He nudged toward Jace, and she reached down and took the gun from him.

"I say we keep him for ourselves Boreas. Nobody knows he's here. We can make our own private feast of him." He licked his lips with a long, forked tongue.

Jace knew he couldn't escape, but he wasn't about to go out like some kind of weakling punk either. He sat up and got to one knee, preparing to spring. He looked at the blonde woman; she shook her head discreetly, as if to warn him not to do it. But why shouldn't he? He'd rather die like a man than wait around to be eaten by some large, ugly lizards.

Icke saw what he was doing and held up his rifle, taking aim.

"No," Boreas protested. "The human is unarmed. We will take him to the brig with the others."

"He's not going anywhere," Icke said with what could have been a smile. "I am hungry. We will taste his raw man-flesh before continuing our work—"

Suddenly, the loud sound of a blaster rifle pierced the

air. Jace instinctively closed his eyes and threw his hands in front of him. He felt something splatter across his arms and face, but where he'd expected to experience the fiery, burning pain of a laser bolt and the hot mist of his own blood, there was only coolness. It felt like someone had splashed him with cold, muddy water. The smell was sickening.

He wiped the goo from his eyes, and slowly reopened them. The large, headless form of Icke had just started to crumple above him. It crashed to the grate beside the engine, an arm swinging down and striking him sharply on the upper left leg, narrowly missing his groin.

Boreas walked up to where his companion had been standing and holstered his rifle. "Let's see him try to grow *that* back." He reached down and offered a hand to Jace, who moved away. "Do not fear, human. You will not be eaten today."

"We need to get started," Hero told the reptilian urgently. "We're never going to get this done in time."

Boreas followed the young woman to one of the nearby crates, which they opened and began to empty.

"Do not fear," Boreas told her in an assuring voice. "Remain calm. We will accomplish our goal." He looked back down at Jace. "Will you help us, human?"

Jace looked at the slimy, dark red blood that covered his arms and hands. "You wanna tell me what's going on here?"

"Look," Hero told him, "we really don't have much

time. We're going to fix this ship and get outta Dodge together. If that sounds like a good plan to you, I suggest you pull yourself out of that hole and give us a hand."

Jace climbed out of the floor. He was stiff, and the stench of the reptilian's blood was making him queasy. "What happened to the crew?" he demanded. "Are they safe?"

"I don't know," Hero said, her tone softening. "All I know is that this ship could be our only chance at getting out of here. If you want to help your friends, we need to get this engine up to snuff."

Jace stumbled to the small bathroom and washed the blood from his face and arms. This was not a turn of events he'd been expecting. He didn't know what to think, but he did know that these two strangers had not only spared his life, they'd saved it.

He emerged from the bathroom, noticing that the reptilian had been watching him, probably making sure that he wasn't going for a weapon.

"Alright," he said, walking up to Hero. "I'll do it. But why is a Nazerazi willing to help us?"

Boreas cocked his head. "I am not Nazerazi, human. I am Draconian. And like you, my world was invaded. I am only here to help."

Galin sat down on the bed in his new cell. The guards

stepped back out and activated the force field. It shimmered through the air before him, becoming an invisible wall to prevent his escape. He watched as the two men got some coffee and then left the room, presumably going back to guard's station.

"Galin? That you?" came a voice from the cell next to him. It was Peter.

"Yeah, it's me. They put the Chief in there with you?"

"I'm here too," Joseph responded. "They stuck us in a cell together. Guess they're not too worried about us collaborating about an escape plan."

"They must have figured that *that* ship's already sailed," Galin said. "If we haven't planned our escape by now, it's a worthless endeavor."

"Maybe, but these guys probably don't care if we escape or not," said Peter. "It's not like they're loyal to the Alliance. They're just going along with orders because they don't know what else to do. Most of the people on this ship are probably still in shock from what's happened."

Galin was silent. He knew Peter was right. The people here were just going through the motions, biding their time, trying to survive until they could work it all out. And yet, he wondered how many of them would end up conforming, settling in to a life shaped for them by their oppressors.

"Did they take Starla to another block?"

"They put her in your cell when we came in," said Joseph. "They came and took her away just a few minutes after we arrived. Told her they needed to question her about something."

"Has anyone questioned either of you?" Galin asked them.

"No," Peter said. "Not yet. I don't know what they wanted Starla for."

Galin looked around at the walls and ceiling. He knew from years of service on a ship just like this that there was no way to escape this cell, but for some reason he looked anyway, almost hoping to see some way out that he'd never noticed before. It was ridiculous, he thought to himself. The human mind- his own mind, never ceased to amaze him.

"So," Galin muttered, "I talked to my father. Turns out he *is* a traitor. He's been collaborating with the Alliance for years now."

"You sure about that?" Peter said. "I find that really hard to believe."

"He said it himself," Galin told them through the wall. "His new partner General Soth confirmed it."

"Look," Peter told him, "I don't know what he told you, and I know there's been bad blood between the two of you ever since…, well, for years now, but I can't imagine your father doing something like this. He's just not the kind of man who'd betray the Confederation, much less Earth."

"Maybe." Galin said. He never would have guessed that his own father was capable of such things, but the man *had* changed since his daughter's death. He'd become bitter, withdrawn, and full of contempt for himself and those around him. Galin had recognized some of these behaviors in himself, but he'd tried to let go of the past, forgive himself for what happened- but the pain was always there, he knew his wounds would never fully heal. The difference between him and his father, Galin thought, was that he'd actually been able to move on, to recover to some degree, but it seemed like his father had continually grown worse through the years. It seemed that he was more damaged now than he'd been the year after Jamie's death. The event had greatly changed him, changed them both. Before the two of them had stopped talking, there were a few times that Galin even thought the Admiral was losing his mind.

After a few minutes of silence, the guards came back in with two Draconian Soldiers. Galin watched helplessly as Peter and Joseph were removed from their cell.

"Where are you taking them?" Galin demanded, rising to his feet. Both of the Draconians hissed and eyed him meanly.

"There's a shuttle leaving for Earth," the friendly guard told him. "We were instructed to put these two on it."

"And what happens to them when they get to Earth?

Where exactly are they going?"

The guard just shrugged, and took a careful step back from the two Draconians, who were giving him threatening stares.

"I'll find you as soon as I can," Galin told them.

Peter turned to say something but one of the large lizard-men gave him a sharp jab with the butt of his rifle. Peter stumbled forward, but the quiet guard reached out and snatched the back of his shirt, pulling him back up to his feet.

Galin stood and watched as his friends were taken away, leaving him alone.

He stood there for a moment staring blankly out at the door they'd just gone through. He hadn't expected any of his crew to be taken back to the surface so soon. He was suddenly very worried about all of them, especially Starla. Why would she have been taken off for questioning while the others had been left, and where was she now? He sat back down on the bed in his cell. All he could do was hope they'd all be alright until he could catch up with them at the rendezvous point outside of Mexico City- if they all survived that long.

—SAN ANTONIO, TEXAS
FOURTEEN YEARS BEFORE—

The day was hot and humid, and the partially

overcast skies looked like they might bring forth some rain. Galin walked up the steps to the large church where his mother had brought them as children; it had looked so much bigger when he'd been a boy.

Just a few years before, they'd come here for his mother's funeral. He remembered walking up these steps, holding his sister's hand as they cried together, on their way to honor a woman who had been taken before her time. She had died too young, and both he and Jamie had felt robbed of her presence. Now here he was again; the thought had never crossed his mind that he'd be walking up these steps so soon for another funeral. His baby sister was gone- lost to him forever, and it was his fault.

Starla walked beside him. It seemed that she hadn't stopped weeping over the last few days. Galin's heart groaned for her. In a way, her presence made the entire thing worse. Not only had his own heart been broken by the loss of his sister, not only did he feel responsible, but now he had to suffer through Starla's grief as well, and he had no idea how to comfort her.

They walked into the church. People spoke to him, giving their condolences and offering other empty words of comfort. It all felt surreal, like a part of him was anchored to some horrible nightmare. He sat down in the front pew; the area reserved for family, where relatives he hadn't seen for years greeted him with tearful faces. His father, who was already seated there when they arrived, just stared ahead toward the casket that contained his daughter's lifeless corpse.

The service began, and Galin listened to the preacher and a few other loved ones who had been called upon to speak. Had he failed his sister a second time by declining to say something? He had been given the opportunity, but couldn't bring himself to do it. He had never been good in front of crowds, and doubted that he could keep his composure.

He looked between the casket and the large cross hanging a few dozen feet behind it. The cross was empty. Christ had risen from the dead, and by doing so gave hope and eternal life to all those who came penitently to the throne of God. That's what his mother had believed; that's what she'd taught them. But he'd never really been sure. He wanted to believe it, especially now.

He remembered the blank look on his dead sister's face when he'd identified the remains, imagined the pain and fury that she must have felt as her body was violated and her life taken. It hadn't looked like her anymore, he'd thought. She was no longer there.

The casket lying before them was closed. It, like the cross, could be empty, he thought longingly. It was a silly thought, and he pushed it out of his head. He continued to listen to the words, the verses of hope given by the preacher. Perhaps he *would* see Jamie again in the next life. Perhaps they could apologize to each other for this tragic loss, and find peace. No, this too was a ridiculous thought. Jamie would never apologize for her actions that night, nor would she hear an apology from him. She wouldn't admit that she'd been wrong, or that he'd been… what had he been? Weak? He could have stopped her. But maybe he was being too hard on himself. He had tried to talk her out of walking off through the night alone, pleaded with her, but she just wouldn't listen.

Galin's mind snapped out of these thoughts as the final prayer was given. Everyone rose and began to speak quietly to one another. Starla was touched on the shoulder by his aunt- his mother's sister, and the two embraced in a sad hug. Galin looked up to see his father standing near the casket, and walked over to join him.

For a few moments they stood there together, neither speaking.

His father suddenly looked up at him, tears streaming down his face. Galin had never seen his father cry, even when his mother had died.

"Where were you?" his father asked him.

"What?" Galin asked. He had heard the question, but wasn't sure what his father meant.

"Where were you when my little girl had her throat cut like some common street whore?"

Galin felt like the air had been sucked from his lungs. He stood there, staring into his father's eyes. His entire body began to shake.

"I told you to look after her. I've always told you to look after her. But I should have known you were too damned weak to do it." He looked back at his daughter's casket, raising his hands and resting them on top. "And now she's gone."

Galin stumbled away from the coffin, trying to get to the side door of the sanctuary. He nearly bowled over the preacher, who held out his arms in an attempt to steady him. His head was spinning; he knew he was going to be sick. He thrust himself out the door, hearing a few gasps and sounds of concern as he ran from the building and landed on his knees behind a shrub by the sidewalk, vomiting up what little food he'd managed to get down earlier that day.

Pulling himself back up to his feet, he staggered and then ran- ran away from the church, the crowd, his father, and his dead sister. He heard several people shouting his name, Starla calling out to him as he got further and further away. He felt as if his heart was going to explode from the fury and hopelessness within him. He wished it would.

–NOW–

Several hours passed as Galin lie on the bed in his cell. Everything had remained quiet since Peter and Joseph had been taken. Galin's ears became accustomed to the lack of noise, and he began to hear all those familiar sounds which emanate from the bones of a ship- the light hum and rumble of the systems that usually fade away into nothingness when anything else is going on.

He was just about to give in to exhaustion and had closed his eyes when he heard the door slide open. He sat up to see his father walking into the room, accompanied by a guard he didn't recognize.

"Leave us," the Admiral told the guard with a wave of his hand. The guard left and the door closed behind him.

Galin dropped back down on the bed and turned away from his father. The man would have nothing to say that he cared to hear.

The Admiral pulled up a nearby chair and sat just outside the force field.

"Listen to me, son. We don't have much time."

Galin didn't budge.

"There are some things you need to know. I didn't betray the Confederation. I'm innocent."

The Admiral had gotten his attention, he turned back around. "What do you mean? How am I supposed to believe that?"

"It's the truth. We were about a day's journey away when we received the distress call from Earth. When the Claymore arrived back in orbit, the entire fleet had already been destroyed." His eyes narrowed. "To our astonishment, General Soth greeted us as allies. Apparently someone, posing as me, has been in contact with the Nazerazi for several years now, supplying them with information. Our forces didn't have a chance when the enemy attacked; they had security access codes for every ship in the Armada. They remotely disabled the shields and injected a computer virus, which fried the navigational, and targeting systems. After that, every ship was a sitting duck. The Draconians picked them off one by one."

Galin sat up and crossed his arms, trying to digest what his father was saying.

"If *you* didn't betray the Confederation, then who did?"

The man sat silently for a moment, a dark frown spread across his face, which contorted and wrinkled, as his skin grew red. He looked as though he might break into a sob.

"I'm sorry, Galin. I blamed you when your sister died, but I knew all along it wasn't your fault." Tears began to stream down his face. It was only the second time in his life that Galin had seen his father cry. "Jamie was always a very strong-willed and self-reliant girl. But she had a habit of getting involved with the wrong people. I've held you responsible for what happened, but I've always known that if anyone is to blame for what happened to her, it was me."

Galin wanted to say something, but no words would come. He'd prepared himself for a fight when his father came in the room.

"I was so distraught, so broken when she died. I couldn't take it. You have to understand that I couldn't take it, seeing her lifeless and broken like that." Now he was shaking, sobbing as he spoke, tears and snot running down his face like some inconsolable child. "I was so wrong, so misguided in what I did. I wish I could take it all back, but at the time I thought that if there were a chance, any chance at all of making things right.... That's why I did it. Oh, God, I'm sorry. That's why I did it. How could I have known things would turn out like this? How could I have known?"

Galin shifted uncomfortably. What was his father saying? Had he betrayed the Confederation after all? He wasn't making any sense.

Suddenly the Admiral sprang to his feet. He wiped his face with his hands, and just as quickly as his hysterical fit had come, he pulled himself together. "As I said, there isn't much time. Listen, for some reason, the Alliance is very interested in that ship of yours. I don't know why, but you need to get it out of here, get that ship as far away as you can until we can figure this out. I'll continue to play along, pretend that I'm a loyal defector to the Alliance. Maybe I'll be able to do some good, redeem myself in some way."

He began to break down again, but quickly got himself under control.

My God, Galin thought, it's like he's got split personalities or something. Was the man a traitor? Was he nuts? Had the grief and sadness of Jamie's death finally driven him to the brink of insanity?

The Admiral walked over to the door leading to the guard station and opened it. "Sagan, could you come in here for a moment?"

The Admiral walked back over toward the cell and drew a blaster from his side.

"What are you—" Galin began.

"Quiet," his father commanded.

The guard walked into the room to meet a blaster bolt in the chest.

"NO," Galin yelled, seeing the innocent man crumple like a sack of potatoes.

The Admiral punched in the security code and dropped the holding cell's force field.

"I assume you have some sort of plan to get off this ship. Here's your chance." He adjusted the settings on the blaster pistol. "The engine on the Katara should be repaired by now, so if you can get off the Claymore, your camo shield will be able to conceal you. Get as far away from here as you can, and be careful."

He turned the blaster on himself, releasing a shot into his right shoulder. He staggered back, falling against the wall, teeth clenched in agony. The smell of burning flesh filled the room. He kicked the pistol, which was lying on the floor in front of him, toward his son.

"Go."

Galin had questions, but the Admiral was right, there

was no time. Another guard could arrive at any second. He stooped down over the dead guard and shook his head in disgust as he took the man's weapon. He turned once again to his estranged, presumably crazy father lying against the wall.

"Where's Starla? I need to save her."

"Already put her on a shuttle to Earth. I wanted to keep them all safe- in case things didn't work out."

Galin started toward him. He needed to do something to help.

"I'll be fine. Go."

He hesitated a moment longer, then turned to spring through the door. His father might be crazy, but he was right. He had to move fast. All he needed to do now was get to the landing bay without being shot.

It took Galin some time before he found a lone Spaceman in a uniform that he thought would fit. The poor guy never saw the stunning bolt coming, but Galin jumped from the shadows and caught his limp body, preventing a hard fall to the steel floor. He still felt disgusted at the way his father had shot the guard. It hadn't needed to go down like that. There must have been another way. He pushed the thought from his head, trying to focus on what needed to be done.

He dragged the unconscious young man, a Spaceman Apprentice, into an empty conference room and emerged a few minutes later. Hopefully nobody would notice the inconsistency between his age and rank.

It was an uneventful walk back to the landing bay. He was thankful that his nervousness and anxiety seemed to mesh perfectly with the feelings of almost every officer and enlisted person that he passed. Everyone seemed intent on going about with whatever business they had, and kept mostly to themselves.

Since Starla, Peter, and Joseph had all been returned to the surface, the plan hinged on Ulrick and Jace now. He had no doubt that they'd be ready, as long as neither of them had been discovered. His father had ordered the Katara's engine fixed, and all they needed to do was get the camo shield back up and get off the Claymore, then they could meet up with the others at the rendezvous point. From there they could regroup and figure things out. They could assess the situation and look for their families.

Galin arrived at the landing bay to find things relatively quiet. There were two men on duty in the control room and a few mechanics working on the hull of a nearby shuttle. He grabbed a clipboard hanging on the wall next to some lockers, and proceeded to walk casually along between two rows of fighters, making a beeline for the Katara.

He noticed out of the corner of his eye that the men in the control tower were watching him, but as he approached his ship they seemed to lose interest. They must have been informed that people would be coming and going to the Katara, getting it ready for transport back toward the heart of Nazerazi space.

He ascended the stairwell that led up into the corridor behind the bridge, then retracted the stairs and drew his blaster pistol. Someone else might be on the ship, and he needed to clear it before trying to contact Ulrick on the battle-com.

The door leading to the bridge slid open and his heart nearly stopped when he saw the large form of a Draconian step through.

"WAIT," hissed the reptilian as Galin raised his blaster and fired. The creature fell to the floor with a heavy thud.

"You didn't kill him, did you?" Jace asked, appearing at the other end of the passageway. He threw his arms up when Galin instinctively turned the gun on him.

"Unfortunately not, this thing was set to stun." He switched the setting to kill and pointed it back at the unconscious Draconian.

"No, don't," Jace pleaded. "He's on our side. His name's Boreas. He helped me fix the engine and wants to come with us when we escape."

Galin frowned. "Is that so? And you really think we can trust him?"

"He saved my life. Killed one of his own people to help me."

Galin's expression eased. "All right." He lowered the

blaster. "But we need to keep a close eye on him. I have a bad feeling about these guys. Give me a hand here."

Together they crouched down and dragged his heavy body over to the side of the passageway. It felt cool, and reminded Galin of the time the zookeeper had visited his elementary school. He'd reluctantly agreed to pet the boa constrictor, which promptly began to wrap itself around his arm. He'd hated snakes ever since.

Galin gave the creature's upper body a final heave. "Hopefully he's not too pissed when he wakes up." He stood back up and took a heavy breath. "You been in touch with Ulrick yet?"

Jace shook his head. "Everything's all set though. If he's out there, he should be ready for us. Doesn't look like we're going to have much resistance getting off the ship."

"No, my father actually helped set up the escape."

Jace nodded. "He's the one that sent Boreas and Hero to help us get out of here."

"Hero? Who's *that*?"

"She's down in the engine room. You're going to like her, she's hot."

Galin smirked at him.

"Just trying to ease the tension, Cap. Are we gonna do this or what?"

Galin nodded. "Let's do it. There's only a few mechanics in the bay right now. If we want to pull this off without anyone else being injured we need to move."

They sped into the cockpit. Jace manned the starboard gun turret while Galin jumped into the captain's chair. He opened up a secure channel on the battle-com. "Everyone, this is Winchester, it's time to make our move. Ulrick, I'm sure you see those three mechanics down at the far end of the bay. We need to scare them off before I blast the bay doors, but the EMP shockwave needs to penetrate that control room before they get the blast shields up, think you can handle that?"

"It's about time," came Ulrick's tired voice. "I'll be ready."

"Good," said Winchester. "As soon as the Katara fades out, you make your move. Hero, welcome aboard. Is everything set down there so that we can raise the camouflage-shields and punch it out of here in a hurry?"

"Everything looks good, Captain. Shield generators and the engine are running at one hundred percent and ready for go."

"Okay everyone, cross your fingers. Let's do this." Galin engaged the camo shield.

An instant later he watched from the view-screen as a stream of plasma bursts shot out from a supposedly empty spot in mid-air into the control room, shattering the window. Flashing red lights and an alarm went off. The two shell-shocked officers dove to the floor and headed for the door at the back of the room. The plasma burst was followed by a laser beam that ran through the room, surgically destroying panels of equipment.

Galin watched as the mechanics ran for the exit, wanting no part of what was happening. He waited until he thought everyone was out, and then prepared to launch the EMP torpedo. "Alright Ulrick, divert all power to your shields. Launching torpedo in five...four...three...two...."

The torpedo struck the wall just beneath the control room, sending a resounding shockwave throughout the entire bay. The place went dark as all unshielded circuitry was fried from the blast. The shields that protected the bay doors had dropped. The Katara's external lights flared up as the ship rose and retracted her landing gear. Galin guided her through the bay as Jace licked his lips in anticipation, eager to squeeze the trigger on his control stick.

Galin sped up. "You behind us Ulrick?"

"Right on your tail."

Jace opened up on the door with repeater gun fire, and Galin launched two rockets. The doors ripped apart, and the depressurization instantly began to suck out air and equipment.

The Katara's shields flickered briefly as she rammed through the remaining scraps of the bay doors and shot out into space among the debris.

Galin quickly shut off the external lights, and turned the ship toward Earth. They'd made it out.

"Alright people, good work. It's time to meet up with the rest of the crew and get some answers. It's time to go home." He looked at Jace and gave him a nod. The young man looked relieved, and grinned back at him weakly.

"I'm afraid, Captain," came a voice from behind them, "that you won't find the rest of your crew back on Earth."

It was the Draconian.

"What do you mean by that?" Winchester asked, annoyed with himself for letting the creature sneak up on him.

"I know what your father must have told you, that the prisoners were being shuttled back to Earth. But he was wrong. They wouldn't have been taken there."

"WELL?" he yelled impatiently. "If you know something then spit it out!"

"No humans would have been returned to Earth, because most of your race is being evacuated from the planet. The majority of survivors are being taken to the Zeta Reticuli system to be sold as slaves. Some are being shuttled to other destinations, but your father has not been made aware of all this. If your friends were taken from the Claymore on shuttles, they would have been picked up by slave ships."

Galin's heart sank. The feelings of victory he'd gotten from escaping the Claymore quickly drained from him. He once again felt beaten. What was he going to do now? All his plans, it seemed, were shattered once again. He couldn't abandon his friends, his loved ones, to some unknown fate as slaves- or worse. He *had* to help them.

Jace looked at him sadly. Galin knew that he must be feeling just as lost and broken. It somehow gave him a surge of determination, an injection of courage.

"Captain," said Boreas from behind him, "If I can get access to the Nazerazi mainframe, I can probably ascertain your crew members' destinations."

Galin looked back at him, wondering if he could really be trusted. Perhaps for now they had no other choice. He nodded to the Draconian.

"Alright," he said. "We'll get to Earth and head to the rendezvous point just in case. Besides, we need to find out what's happened back home, if we can." Images of his children and their mother flooded through his mind. He struggled to hold back his worry. "From there we'll figure out how to gain access to the Nazerazi systems, and go after our friends."

He stared into the reptilian's eyes. "Why are you willing to help us?"

"Because, Captain," he said, cocking his head to the side, "I had to watch as the Nazerazi Alliance invaded my own world, just as they have now conquered yours. But I have longed to find a way to avenge my planet and restore freedom to my people. I have waited many years for a chance at finding a weakness that might bring the Alliance down, looked for a chink in their armor, and now, there's a small chance I may have found it."

He beamed at Winchester, who guessed that the look

on his lizard-like face was a smile.

"And that weakness is?"

"I'm not altogether sure just yet, but I can tell you that the Alliance is very, *very* interested in *this* ship, and that greatly intrigues me. Perhaps if we find out why, we can discover this weakness together, and set in course a motion that will lead to regaining freedom for both our worlds."

Galin took a deep breath. Both his father and General Soth had mentioned that the Nazerazi had an interest in the Katara, but why? He looked over at Jace, who gave him a determined nod. It didn't need to be said aloud that this sounded like a job they were both very much interested in.

"Let's do it," he told Boreas.

Galin increased speed. The sun's rays shot out around the side of the blue, swelling planet, and the hum of the Katara's engine sang lightly as it soared once again toward home.

—THE PLANET NECRON FOURTEEN YEARS BEFORE—

A heavy rain had just finished bathing the tropical forest spread out before him, and Dr. Carl Mengele looked up into the dark, cloudy skies. He took a long draught of the cool air into his lungs. There might be more rain coming, but the clouds were moving fast and the sun was sporadically peaking through. It could go either way.

Off in the distant clouds there was an unfamiliar noise. It was a little like thunder, but started off as a soft rumble and was getting louder. Mengele hadn't heard such a noise in… many years. It was definitely a ship, coming down to land nearby, perhaps. He smiled. His children were in need of food. Their resources were getting low, and since the Galactic Confederation of Worlds had destroyed their only space-worthy vessels he hadn't been able to send his reapers out to collect. They were able to sustain themselves from some of the docile animal life that the GCW had placed on the planet after terraforming it, but his children greatly preferred human flesh. So did he.

The doctor looked down around the perimeter of his dilapidated fortress. Some of his children had already heard the noise and were beginning to gather from their wanderings in the forest.

He headed down the stairs, going carefully so as not to snap his rotting left leg. It had just begun to regenerate and he didn't fancy the thought of being in a wheelchair for the next few weeks. Reaching the bottom of the staircase, he picked up his sniper rifle and took the wide-brimmed hat off the hook by the door. He checked himself in the mirror; a bit more than half his face was rotted off. Not the best day for him to receive new visitors, but at least the food tasted better when it was scared. He put the hat on and twirled the rifle on his arm like some merry vaudeville actor.

He thrust the front door open, trudged out across the yard, and looked up to see a transport ship emerging from the dark clouds. Astonishing! It looked like the thing was heading right for the landing bay of his compound. Was it possible that someone was coming willingly to land among them? That didn't happen very often. He was intrigued.

Mengele hurried across the grounds to the landing pad as quickly as he dared with his bum leg, using the long sniper rifle as a cane. His children staggered toward the landing ship, but only one got onto the pad before he was able to close the gates. He escorted the excited creature, which protested loudly in grunts and moans, back to the gate and put him through, locking it behind him.

"It's for your own good, my son. It's not time just yet. Be patient."

He turned to face the ship once again. It looked like a Confederation transport ship, the kind that served as a short-range shuttle from one of the larger ships. Why would anyone from the Confederation be arriving in such a manner? They had occasionally come for bombing raids, or to drop off a load of criminals in the jungle, but they'd never *landed* at the compound before.

Four of his reapers arrived, fully armed and awaiting

his command.

"Were you expecting this ship, father?" came the raspy voice of one from beneath his filthy brown robes.

"No. But make no moves of aggression until I have a chance to speak to them." He gestured toward the gate. "You, Clinton, prepare to open the gate in case we need backup."

A few dozen of his mindless, beloved children had gathered and were now beating angrily against the fence, demanding to be fed. He wouldn't put them in danger unless it was absolutely necessary.

"The rest of you come with me. We must welcome our visitors."

Dr. Mengele approached the shuttle slowly, his three reapers moving closely behind him.

The hatch opened and a stairway descended. Two Space Marines in full battle armor stepped down, they took up position at each side of the stairs.

A moment later, a tall, grim faced man appeared. He was unarmed, yet his demeanor and impeccable black uniform somehow made him seem just as menacing as his guards. Two more space marines followed him down the stairs. Mengele swallowed nervously, knowing that the four Space Marines alone could easily wipe out his entire colony.

"Dr. Mengele?" asked the grim-faced man.

Mengele nodded, his eyes growing wide with curiosity and fear.

"My name is Admiral Sebastian Winchester. I've come to ask for your…assistance with something."

Mengele continued to stare at the stranger, carefully searching for the right words. He'd never been considered much of a people person.

"It's been a very long time since the Confederation sought *my* help with anything. Been at least a hundred years."

"This isn't exactly Confederation business," the Admiral told him. "This is something of a more…personal nature," he added quietly.

"I see," Mengele nodded thoughtfully. He breathed a small sigh of relief, not realizing how tense he'd been. Drawing the attention of the Confederation had always made him nervous, and he'd been trying to keep a low profile lately. "Tell me more," he said eagerly.

Winchester turned to the two Space Marines behind him. "Bring down the container."

The Marines acknowledged his command and stowed their weapons. They clanked back up into the shuttle and reappeared a few moments later carrying a large rectangular crate.

"Put it down over there," said the Admiral, pointing to a spot on the tarmac a short distance away.

The two men obeyed, and Dr. Mengele and the Admiral followed behind them, avoiding the larger areas of pooled up water.

"I assume you've heard the rumors, Doctor?"

Winchester asked him.

"Rumors?" he repeated. He thought he probably knew what the Admiral was alluding to, but wasn't in the practice of showing his hand so easily.

"Don't be coy, Doctor. Surely you've heard about the Confederation's intent to re-terraform this planet, which as you know would destroy every molecule of life that currently exists here."

"I've heard rumors, nothing more," he said dismissively. Mengele had always known that the only thing that prevented this from happening so far was the tremendous cost involved, but if the government had discovered the nature of some of his current experiments, it might be enough to push them into action.

"Some people believe that a re-terraform is the only answer. They believe that even if you and your people could be eradicated from the planet, the risk of re-contamination would remain. They believe you've been working on new strains of the virus that may not be affected by the vaccine."

"I've been doing no such thing," Mengele lied indignantly. "All I and my chil…, my people want is to live in peace. I've no interest in causing any trouble for Earth *or* the Galactic Confederation."

The Admiral nodded, his face full of doubt.

Reaching the spot that the admiral had indicated, the Marines got his acknowledgment and carefully set down the crate.

Winchester waved his men back toward the ship, and looked at the doctor with an unspoken request that he do the same.

"I'll be alright," he told his reapers. "You three head back toward the gate. Assist Clinton with the roamers."

The three reapers hesitated for a moment, but moved off when Mengele gave them an encouraging nod. He knew that they, like him, had no trust for anyone in a Confederation uniform.

"I have many contacts, many friends within the GCW government. I have no doubt that if I intercede, certain key people behind the idea of re-terraforming this planet can be, shall we say, dissuaded from their current positions."

"I see," Mengele said. His rotting face formed a toothy, grotesque smile. "But why would you be interested in helping us? What makes you care?"

"I don't," said the Admiral bluntly. "But perhaps we can help one another."

Winchester leaned over the crate and punched an access code into the control panel. The steel lid parted from the center, and the two sections retracted back into the crate. The sound of escaping air hissed as a dense cloud of mist appeared, obscuring the contents.

Mengele leaned over and squinted as the breeze cleared the mist, revealing a long block of something that resembled blue tinted glass. As he peered down, the form of a young woman materialized beneath it. She looked like a sleeping angel that someone had managed to freeze inside a large, dark ice cube. Mengele smiled. She was a real beauty, this one. Dead, but untainted with decay. He looked up and smiled at the Admiral, perhaps too eagerly, he thought suddenly. He reformed the smile into a more serious expression.

Winchester hadn't looked up at him anyway. His gaze was fixed on the girl entombed between them.

"This is my daughter," he said longingly. "She was murdered three weeks ago on Earth. Can you do anything for her?"

Mengele looked back down at the girl. "Perhaps," he said, running his fingers along the hard, blue substance. "What is this, cryotonium?"

"Yes," the Admiral nodded.

"And how long had she been dead before they froze her?"

"Approximately sixteen hours."

The doctor scratched at the intact half of his chin. "Yes. Yes I think perhaps I can help her." He looked at the Admiral with an interrogating squint. "And if I *can* help her, then you can ensure that our planet is spared from re-terraforming?"

The Admiral made a slow nod. His crossed arms and expressionless face made Mengele believe him.

"You understand," the doctor told him, "that she will not be like she was before. Not *exactly* like she was. At least, none of them have been so far."

The Admiral stood silently for a moment. Mengele wondered what exactly he was thinking. Would he have come all this way to reconsider the decision he'd made? Not likely. He must have already known the consequences for what he was asking. For some reason every person that sought him out for help wanted to believe that it would be different. For them, it would be different.

"I just want my daughter back."

Mengele waved his reapers back over.

"How long will it take?" asked the Admiral, resealing the container.

"Give me two days. After that, you *can* take her, but I strongly suggest you leave her in my care. She'll need a few months to recover fully from the process."

Winchester looked at the mindless brutes beating against the fence. They were making quite a racket.

He gazed up into the cloudy sky. It looked like the rain clouds might be clearing away. He suddenly remembered how Jamie had always loved the rain. He'd thought it a bit odd, how excited she'd get when the thunder and lightning started. But he hated storms, and lately he felt like he'd been caught in the midst of some great tempest.

"It looks like the storm's blowing through," he told Mengele. "Looks like it'll soon be over."

The Doctor pushed his hat back and looked up into the swirling sky.

"Oh, you don't know the weather here on Necron, Admiral," he said. "I think it may only be getting started."

Book 3

Albatross

Galin Winchester flipped down the blast shield and drew his phaser pistol. He took a long deep breath and aimed carefully, knowing that he had only one chance to get this right. He pulled the trigger and squinted as the beam burned through the rock. Pausing, he brushed the charred fragments away, and examined his work. It didn't look so bad, given the circumstances. That was one letter down. So far, so good. He continued the process, slowly inscribing each line and curve until the job was complete. Removing his helmet, he brushed away the remaining debris and took a step back. His work wasn't perfect, but it would have to make do for now.

Melissa Winchester
Beloved Wife and Mother
15 March 2355 - 28 Nov 2389

He nodded at Ulrick and the two men carefully slid the marble headstone onto the awaiting hover-cart.

"Careful," Galin urged him, pushing it along gently. He'd been lucky to get his hands on it, and doubted he'd be able to find another; there had been a lot of funerals lately. He needed to get Melissa buried quickly and continue the search for their children. Having to delay even for the few hours this task would take him was agonizing, but what was the alternative? Although their marriage hadn't worked out in the end, he'd loved Melissa, and the mother of his children deserved a proper burial.

The two men carefully guided the cart outside and up the winding, gravel path. Dozens of dark brown mounds of dirt dotted the hillside, marking fresh graves. A few had headstones, many had a simple wooden cross or some other makeshift marker, and even more were unmarked. In a way, those buried here were the lucky ones. At least they had someone to bury them. Galin had seen bodies- many bodies in the last few days that still rested where they'd fallen, rotting testimonials to the brutalities of war. He wondered how many of them might stay right where they were until eventually crumpling back into dust. The only burial that might be awaiting them was in the belly of a coyote or crow.

They followed the rough gravel path for a while before turning off toward a more secluded area where, not more than an hour before, Galin had buried his wife. Together, the two of them placed the headstone. When they were finished, Galin stood and wiped his brow, exhausted from rushing through such an arduous task.

Ulrick placed his hand on Galin's shoulder. "I'll be waiting for you back at the Shiv."

Galin nodded. "Thanks for your help." Ulrick handed him some wildflowers he'd picked while Galin was inscribing the headstone, then took the hover-cart and trudged off back down the hill toward the groundkeeper's shed.

Galin sat on the ground beside the grave.

"Well, Melissa, I guess you won't have to follow through with that divorce now." He closed his eyes, trying to picture his wife smiling and happy, eager to drive the image of the way he'd found her out of his mind. "I'm sorry we weren't able to work things out." A tear escaped and ran down his cheek. It felt like Melissa was out there somewhere, listening. "I think we both realized by the end that we were never meant to be together, but I'm so sorry things ended like this."

The breeze picked up and rustled the leaves of the nearby trees. The air was cold and fresh. It all reminded him of the long walks they used to take together. They'd both enjoyed those walks, and Galin had often found himself longing for them during some of his more tedious trips through space. He'd made a lot of great memories with Melissa. Of course, there were a lot of bad ones, too. All he could do now was try to honor her by focusing on the good times.

"You had a way of bringing out the worst in me, and I had a way of hurting and disappointing you, though I never meant to. But I want to thank you for being there when I needed you. I want to thank you for giving me the two most wonderful children a man could ever ask for."

He thought of Sarah and David, losing their mother too soon, just like he had. They were even younger than he'd been- much younger. It wasn't fair, and his heart broke for them.

"Maybe you weren't the perfect wife, I know I sure wasn't the perfect husband, but you were a great mother. I want you to know that I'm going to do whatever it takes to find our children, and keep them safe."

He got to his feet and wiped his face dry. "I guess this is goodbye. I love you, Melissa, and I'm truly sorry that things turned out this way."

He rested the flowers against the gravestone and headed back down the hill. There was no time to spare. He needed to find his kids, needed to make sure they were still alive, and get them someplace safe.

The Shiv emerged over the top of the tree line, and Galin pointed out the middle school and adjacent elementary school to Ulrick. The schools and surrounding area looked relatively unharmed. "That's the place. David and Sarah would have both been in school when the air raids started, so hopefully we can find some clues down there."

He flew around a few times, looking for a good place to land before setting down in the middle of an empty basketball court.

Both men armed themselves and stepped cautiously out of the shuttle. Galin made an X with scuffmarks on the concrete, so that they could more easily find the hatch, as the Shiv would be cloaked when they returned.

The entire area looked deserted, but they proceeded attentively toward the main entrance of the middle school, scurrying between trashcans, abandoned vehicles, shrubs, and any other piece of cover they could find, until they made it to the side of the building. The large double doors were locked. Ulrick activated the laser dagger that protruded from his right wristband and sliced through the lock as if he were running a hot knife through butter.

"Aren't those things illegal?" Galin asked him.

"I thought you said you were only going to start questioning me about the things you thought were legal," Ulrick reminded him.

"Oh yeah. That *would* be easier, wouldn't it? Cover me."

Ulrick nodded and knelt down beside the doors. Galin quietly opened up one side. He couldn't see anything unusual. An empty corridor ran along in front of them as far as the eye could see. They moved inside and began to clear the building. Every room they visited was empty; the gym, the cafeteria, all the classrooms-there were no signs of life. The place appeared to be abandoned. They looked for evidence of an evacuation, or notes or signs that might be left for anyone who came searching for their children, but found nothing.

"I don't get it," Galin told his friend. "I thought there'd be something around here, someone we could talk to, some indication or sign of where everyone went."

Ulrick ran his fingers through his wavy blonde hair. "Looks like everyone just picked up and left. Can't imagine where they would have gone. Seems like they would have held up here during the invasion."

"That was the plan," came a shrill old voice. The two men whipped around to see a short old woman aiming a blaster rifle at them.

"Don't try it, Goldilocks," she warned Ulrick, who was in the process of raising his own gun.

"I've taken out bigger sewer rats than you. Why don't you tell me what it is you fellows are looking for? And don't do anything funny unless you want me to paint that wall with whatever brains you've got in that pretty head of yours."

Galin suddenly recognized her. She'd been in one of Sarah's school photos.

"Are you…are you Mrs. Ponte?" he stuttered.

"Yes, that's me. And you are?"

Galin waved his hand to tell Ulrick to lower his weapon.

"I'm Galin Winchester, Sarah Winchester's father. This is my friend, Ulrick."

"Oh, little Sarah Winchester's father, huh?" she smiled. "The treasure hunter. Yes, she's told me all about *you*."

Galin couldn't tell from her tone if that was a good thing or not. He just smiled.

"I'm looking for Sarah and her little brother, David. Can you tell me what happened here?"

"Of course," she said, as if one of her students had just asked her to explain a test question. "Follow me."

She led them through a nearby door, which led into the teachers' lounge.

"As you can tell, our neighborhood didn't take much damage, I'd assume that's true for the majority of suburban areas. But from what I've heard, the big cities didn't fair so well. Have a seat, have a seat. I just made some coffee." Without asking she poured them each a cup and set it on the table. "We lost power a few days ago, but one of the maintenance guys restored it this morning. It's running off emergency generators, so who knows how long that's going to last."

Galin opened his mouth to speak, but Mrs. Ponte cut him off.

"I know," she said, "you want to know what happened to your daughter and son. Well, I'll tell you, but I don't think you're going to like it." She plopped down in a seat across from them and took a deep breath.

"When the air attacks started, we could see the city being bombed, so we all evacuated to the basement. We had assumed, of course, that this was the right thing to do." She took a long sip of coffee. Her arm was trembling, whether from age or from the distress of telling the story Galin couldn't tell.

"It's all right, Mrs. Ponte, this has been hard on all of us," Galin assured her. "Tell us what happened."

"Well, once all the children and staff were down there, we began to take roll. Quite a few children were missing, so several of the teachers and staff were sent to sweep the building again, but they didn't find anyone, and by the time they got back even more children were gone. It turned out that children were disappearing *from* the basement."

Mrs. Ponte looked up from her coffee to examine the looks on her guests' faces.

"I know what this sounds like, dammit, but I'm not some crazy old woman," she barked. "Everyone was getting frantic. We couldn't figure out what was happening. Teachers were posted at each of the exits and there was no other way to get out, yet children kept vanishing. And then..." she began to tear up, "and then we noticed that some of the teachers were missing as well. It was all very confusing, very disorienting. It was all happening so fast you see, but none of us knew what *it* was!" Ulrick reached for a box of tissues on the nearby counter, and offered it to her. She nodded her thanks, and continued.

"Eventually, nobody was left, except for myself, some of the other teachers, and the janitor. After a while those of us who remained realized that the disappearances had stopped. Only the old people were left, every one else was gone."

Galin shook his head. "Unbelievable. And the elementary school next door? My son was enrolled there."

"Same exact thing happened over there. Everyone disappeared and only the old people were left behind. After we figured it was safe, we came out and everyone went back home, or off somewhere else to look for family."

"Why are you still here?" Ulrick asked her. "Why haven't you left?"

"Oh, I leave every night, dear. But I come back each day just in case...just in case some of the children were to show up. They'd be so lost on their own, poor things."

Galin stood up and held out his hand to her. "Mrs. Ponte, I know this isn't easy, but we need to take a look down in that basement. Could you show us?"

"Of course I can. I'm not scared of the place, not for myself anyway. But to lose all those children, not to mention my friends...." She took Galin's hand and let him help her up. As they exited the room she let out an unexpected chuckle.

"What is it?" Ulrick asked her.

"What?" she said, looking up at him. "Oh, I just had a ridiculous thought. Maybe the Lizard-People did it."

"What do you mean by that?" Galin asked.

"Oh, it's nothing, dear," she giggled. "When I was a little girl I had a crazy uncle that everybody called Weed Whacker Tom. He was always running around with his trimmer cutting down weeds. He hated the things, but who can blame him for that? Anyway he was a real piece of work, had all kinds of conspiracy theories about government plots and alien invasions. He used to tell us kids stories about the Lizard-People, who lived in an elaborate cave and tunnel system beneath the earth's surface. Said he'd been down spelunking in a cave in the Superstition Mountains of Arizona when he ran across a group of these creatures. Isn't that the most unbelievable thing you'd never heard?"

Galin laughed nervously. "And what did Uncle Weed Eater say these things looked like? Exactly?"

"That's Weed Whacker Tom," she corrected him. "He said they were large, had sharp teeth and clawed hands, thick tails, and generally looked something like a cross between a lizard and a mythological dragon, but they were bipedal. He actually drew us some pictures. He was quite the artist. We were fascinated by it all as children, as you can imagine."

They arrived at the double doors that led down to the basement.

"Have you been down there since the day of the disappearances?" Ulrick asked, seeing that Mrs. Ponte had her blaster rifle ready.

"Oh, I go down there *every* day, but I haven't seen anything unusual yet."

Ulrick pulled open the door, and together they advanced down the stairwell. The place was lit up, and quiet except for the electrical buzzing of an overhead light and the movement of air through nearby ducts. The basement was comprised of a few small storage rooms, an electrical room, and two larger rooms that had been reserved primarily as an emergency bunker. Nothing appeared to be out of place, at least as far as they could tell. Galin couldn't see anything that indicated a hidden exit or other means of escape. He walked along examining the brick walls, which looked quite solid.

"Come look at this," Ulrick told them. He was squatting at the wall across from the electrical room door.

"I see it," Galin nodded as he walked up.

Mrs. Ponte looked confused. "See what?"

"Here," Ulrick pointed to the floor near the wall.

"The dust against the wall has been disturbed. And here. Look at all these scuffmarks, like people might have been dragged."

Galin nodded, but Mrs. Ponte still looked confused. "Dragged? Dragged where?"

Ulrich pulled a high power phaser gun off his belt and aimed at the bricks above the scuffmarks. He motioned for Galin to join him, and fired an energy stream at the wall. Mrs. Ponte shot continuous rounds from her blaster rifle.

Instead of damaging the brick, the wall seemed to be absorbing the energy, but after a few long moments, it began to flicker, and then disappeared completely with a sharp electrical crack.

The three of them stood looking into a large, roundish hole about eight feet wide. A tunnel disappeared into the blackness ahead, and a small control panel on the side of the cave wall was sparking and smoking. It had been a holographic force field, one of the more convincing ones that Galin had ever seen.

He frowned and put his hand on Mrs. Ponte's shoulder. "Looks like your uncle was right about those Lizard-People after all."

"Let's get moving," Ulrick grunted, taking a step into the cave.

"Wait," Galin said through clenched teeth. "That may

not be the smartest thing to do just yet." It almost pained him to say it. There was nothing he wanted more at that moment than to run into the blackness of that cave after his children, but if he wanted to save them he knew he needed to keep a clear head.

"Why not?" Ulrick asked defiantly. "What else are we supposed to do?"

"Listen to your friend, Goliath," the old woman said with a wag of her finger. "You have no idea where that tunnel goes. Whoever came from down there took over eight hundred people from this basement, and didn't manage to get caught in the process. Do you really think the two of you could manage to run off down there, guns blazing, and take them on? And that's assuming you don't get yourselves lost in the process."

Galin frowned. "She's right. This is going to take some planning. Some strategy. We need to talk to Boreas and find out what he knows about these tunnels." He looked at Mrs. Ponte. "You say your uncle talked about how elaborate this tunnel system was?"

"I guess he wasn't so crazy after all," she said, scratching her head and looking down into the dark passageway. Then she gasped. "I wonder how much of the other stuff he said..., oh, sorry, dear, yes. He said the tunnels went on for thousands of miles, connecting caves and making an underground system of roads that led around the whole North American continent."

Galin began walking toward the stairs and the others

followed. "Believe me, every bone in my body is calling out to run off down that tunnel, but we've got some important things to do first." He knew that Ulrick understood it too; the man wasn't stupid, just really hotheaded. He couldn't stand the thought of having to wait around when there were enemies to be shot.

They climbed the stairs, which took Mrs. Ponte some time, and she was breathing hard when they finally got to the top.

"I want to thank you for everything you've done. If you hadn't come back here, we might never have found out what happened." Galin took a mobile communicator out of his pocket and handed it to her. "I don't know what our next move is going to be, we may or may not be back, but I'll keep you informed of what we find, and please give me a call if you need to. It's an encrypted channel."

She walked them to the door and led them outside. Ulrick scanned the area, ready to spring at the first sign of trouble.

"What are you going to do now?" Galin asked the old woman.

"Exactly what I've been doing," she said. "What else is there to do? Don't worry about me, there are still a few of us old timers around to look out for each other." She looked up at Ulrick. "Besides, I got the drop on the two of you, didn't I?"

Galin smiled. "Yes, you did."

Mrs. Ponte crept back inside as the men moved swiftly but cautiously back toward the Shiv.

Ulrick covered Galin as he entered the shuttle's security code into the control pad on his wrist. "You think it's a good idea to tell Boreas about that tunnel? I still don't trust him."

"Neither do I, at least not completely. But, he *is* our best chance at finding out where the children and the rest of the crew have been taken. We need to take care of business as quick as we can and get the Katara out of here. There must be a pretty good reason that the Nazerazi want our ship, but I'm not about to abandon my family or my crew." He opened up the shuttle door; it looked like a portal hanging in midair. "I just pray I don't have to bury anyone else before this is over."

Jace sat leaning back in his chair with his feet up on the table, looking at the tablet upon his knees in exasperation.

"I can't believe you went back to Earth! Who goes back to a planet that's been invaded and occupied by an enemy army? I told you that Winchester friend of yours was off in the head. There's something wrong with that guy."

"Mom, give it a rest. Please! I told you our communication systems were down. We didn't know Earth had been invaded! Even if we had, some of the crew has family to find, not everyone was as lucky as I was. I would have come back for you and Dad."

She pursed her lips at him, searching for some witty comeback.

"I'm just glad you got off the planet safely," he told her. "And as soon as we wrap up our business we'll be getting out of here too. Besides, we've barely seen any signs of the Nazerazi since we've been here."

"Oh, they're there. Those Draconians are just like any other lizards. They're crawling around under the rocks even when you can't see them."

"We're being careful, Mom. The Katara has a camo shield. It's not like we're flying around in plain sight."

His father's head popped into the background. "Camo shield? Those illegal on civilian ships! That Winchester a shady character. I told you that already, Son. You listen to your father, you live longer."

His mother put her hand to the man's face and pushed him back off-screen. "Listen to me, Jace, I want you to meet us in New Lanzhou as quickly as you can. Do you hear me? Get away from those *crazy* people and come back to your family! You hear?"

"Alright, Mom, we'll see. I love you. Say goodbye to Dad for me."

"Don't you hang up on me young m—"

Jace placed the tablet down on the table and hopped up. He stretched his arms and took in a long deep breath, letting it out slowly. He was glad to know that his parents were all right. They should be safe on the planet Klo, at least for now.

He wondered how the captain was doing, and if he'd been able to get ahold of his wife and kids. Did Ulrick have any family to track down? He couldn't remember him speaking of anyone. What about Joseph and Peter? They'd mentioned family members here and there, but no wives or kids. There was really a lot he didn't know about these people who had, in a way, become a new family for him. He'd take more time to find out some of these things, he thought, that is if he ever got the chance.

Maybe Boreas was making some progress trying to hack into the Nazerazi database. Jace didn't know all that much about computers, but decided he'd see if there was anything he could do to help. He picked up his things and headed for the door, just in time to dodge Hero as she burst through.

She looked upset, but didn't say anything as she hurried past, apparently heading for her quarters.

"Hey, are you okay?" he called after her, but she didn't respond.

He made his way up to the bridge, where he found the Draconian sitting in the co-pilot's chair, working away busily on a data pad.

"Any luck?" Jace asked him.

"No, not yet. I don't believe I'm going to be able to do this remotely. To tell the truth I never thought there was much of a chance, but had it worked, this certainly would have been the easier option."

"So, what happens now?"

Boreas set the tablet down on his lap. "It means I'm going to have to get live access to a Nazerazi computer station."

"Why didn't you just bring one of their computers with you from the Claymore?"

Boreas shook his head. "They could have used it to track our location. I need to get to a workstation on one of the mother ships, which should present some very interesting challenges."

Would the captain really go along with a plan like that? He probably would if it meant tracking down his family and crewmembers. Maybe his mother was right, maybe the captain was a little crazy. But then again, maybe that wasn't so bad.

"Hey, do you know what's wrong with Hero? She almost ran me over a few minutes ago."

Boreas looked at him for a moment, trying to work out what he meant by '*she almost ran me over*'.

"Oh yes," he chuckled. "I see what you mean. Very witty. Hero's mate had been serving on one of the Earth Space Navy ships, the Axalon, I believe, which was destroyed when the Alliance fleet arrived. Perhaps she is grieving for her mate. In addition, they had a two year old hatchling, who was staying with her parents in a city called Phoenix down on Earth, but she has not been able to contact them or discover the child's whereabouts."

"From what I've heard, Phoenix was hit pretty hard during the invasion. No wonder she was so upset. That's a lot to deal with."

"Yes," agreed Boreas. "But, as I've gotten to know Hero over the past few weeks, I've come to respect her. She is strong."

The communicator on the control panel began to bleep. Jace turned the captain's chair and dropped into it, spinning back and flipping on the view screen. Captain Winchester and Ulrick looked back at them.

"Gentlemen, how are things going on your end? Any luck hacking into the Alliance's network?"

"I'm afraid not, Captain," Boreas answered. "It's just like we discussed, I'm going to need to get access from one of the Nazerazi ships. It won't be easy, but I'm willing to try if it moves our mission forward."

Galin nodded. "And what about your family, Jace? Were you able to get ahold of them?"

"They were able to escape on a shuttle. They're doing fine. Hero hasn't been able to get any news on her family, though. She had a two year old son staying in Phoenix with her parents when the attack came."

Galin sighed. "I'm sorry to hear that. How's she doing?"

"Not great. I'll go and check on her when we're through talking."

"We'll do whatever we can to help her. It's the right thing to do. Besides, we owe her one."

Jace hesitated. He was afraid to ask the next question. "Were you able to find *your* family, Captain?"

Galin was expecting the question. It had to be asked, but it still stung.

"Melissa's dead," he said, holding back his tears. "I have a lead on the kids, though. Boreas, I'm hoping you can help me out with that. We'll be arriving back at the Katara in about fifteen minutes."

Boreas nodded. "I am at your service, and will help in any way I can."

"I'm sorry to hear about your wife, Captain," Jace told him.

"Thanks. We'll see you guys in a few minutes."

The view screen switched off, and the clear blue sky spread out across the Sonoran Desert in front of them. A small, green lizard had somehow managed to crawl up onto the invisible ship and was making his way across the front window. Boreas looked at Jace and smiled.

"I'm going to check on Hero." He left the bridge as Boreas continued to poke on his data pad.

Jace wondered what he might say to Hero as he made his way to her quarters. It was hard to imagine what she might be going through. It might be better to let her have some time alone, but the least he could do was let her know she wasn't alone. Arriving at the door of Starla's quarters, he knocked, but there was no answer. Maybe Hero didn't feel quite at home in someone else's room. Jace knew almost immediately where she'd probably gone. He went down to the engine room to find her tinkering with the shield generators. She looked up to see him and wiped away tears on the sleeve of her grey jump suit.

"Hey, how ya holding up?" he asked.

She shrugged. "Just trying to keep my mind off things. Trying to keep busy."

"Boreas told me about your husband. I'm really sorry you lost him."

"Thanks," she said softly, continuing to wipe her eyes. "He was a good man. He didn't deserve to die like that." She sunk to the floor and leaned up against an electrical panel. Jace sat down beside her.

"We were planning a trip to Egypt for our third wedding anniversary. We've both always wanted to see the pyramids. It was just a short get-away, a few days, but Will was *so* excited."

The tears continued to stream down her face, and she swiped at them with wet sleeves, as if they shamed her.

"So you have a two year old kid?" Jace asked, putting his hand on her shoulder.

She nodded, and began to cry even harder. "A...a little boy," she sobbed. "Named Stephen."

"Well, Boreas and I just spoke to the Captain. He wanted me to tell you that we'll do whatever we can to help find him."

She looked at him eagerly, and he saw both hope and fear, and for some reason he had a sudden, overwhelming urge to protect her.

He smiled assuringly. "I got to speak to my family today. I can't tell you how happy I was to find out they were safe. But the people on this ship are my family too. And you're part of this crew, at least for now. I'll do whatever I can to help you find your son, I promise."

She thrust her arms around him, squeezing so hard that it almost hurt. "Thank you," she said, her weeping beginning to subside. Her breath was infused with short gasps as she let go of him. "Thank you. I just had to get off that ship. The Claymore, I mean. I was so scared, I knew they'd kill me if I got caught, but I had to try to get to my son, that's why I helped you escape."

"I understand," he said. "I can tell you love him very much. But it doesn't matter why you helped us. We're all in this together."

She nodded, pulling her knees up to her chest and locking her arms around her legs. "I thought," she began timidly, "I thought I was going to have to steal a shuttle or take an escape pod back to the surface. I never expected to have someone willing to help."

Jace rose to his feet and held out his hand to her. "Well, like I said, you're with *us* now." He pulled her to her feet, and wiped away her remaining tears with his own shirtsleeve. It may have been presumptuous, but she didn't seem to mind. "The Captain and Ulrick should be getting back any time now, let's head to the landing bay to meet them."

She smiled and nodded, and followed him back up the ladder.

Galin stood with his crew at the foot of the high, desert mesa, which sheltered the Katara. The area was isolated and inhospitable, and served as the perfect rendezvous point. He had coordinates set up on all the planets they frequented just to be safe. In this line of work, you never knew when you might need to make a fast getaway.

A light, cool breeze swept over the desert sands, and Galin looked up to see a group of buzzards gliding in a circle overhead, eying them cryptically. It felt good to get fresh air again, thought Galin. But he immediately felt guilty for it. How could he enjoy anything while his friends and children might be suffering?

"Alright everyone, so that's what happened. We need to decide how to proceed from here." He'd been watching Boreas throughout his story, trying to gauge the reptilian's reaction to what they'd found. "Boreas, what can you tell us about that hole? Is it true that the Draconians have some kind of elaborate network of tunnels?"

Boreas looked fascinated. "There are stories about my people establishing colonies in other star systems long ago, but I was not much more than a hatchling when my planet was taken over by the Nazerazi. I didn't grow up on Draconia, and did not receive any formal education about the history of my planet or our people."

"The Nazerazi took you off Draconia?" Galin asked him.

"Yes. That is their way. Once a planet is conquered, the Alliance moves the majority of its indigenous population out of the system. Many are used as slaves, and the young are taken to be trained up as an army to conquer other star systems. As far as I know, the Nazerazi do no fighting themselves. I have never seen one of them, nor do I know of anyone else who claims to have seen them. They control their empire through fear and psychological intimidation, plotting one race against another to expand their empire."

"These stories you've heard about your people colonizing other planets, do you think what Mrs. Ponte's uncle said about the tunnels could be true?"

"It certainly sounds possible. It would also explain why we haven't seen any Draconians around on the surface. My people would much prefer operating from beneath the Earth. Especially during winter."

Galin took a long deep breath. He'd hoped that Boreas would have more information than just some old wives tales he'd heard as a kid.

"Captain," said the reptilian, stepping out of the way of a passing tumbleweed, "since the invasion efforts appear to have been coordinated from this tunnel system, there is a good chance that if we explore it, we may find an access point to the Nazerazi network. The probability of success for this approach could be more likely than attempting to gain access from a mother ship."

"Maybe," Galin nodded. "We don't know that for sure, but *that's* the way my kids were taken, so let's get going and see where it leads us." His eyes fell on Hero, who'd been listening in anticipation. "Boreas, Ulrick and I will go back to Mexico City in the Katara. Jace, you and Hero take the Shiv and head to Phoenix. I know that splitting up is a dangerous decision, but we're working against the clock, and I don't see much of a choice."

Jace nodded. He had a more determined look than Galin had ever seen on him.

"I'm going to land the ship on the football field behind this school," he said, throwing Jace a data-pad with the coordinates. "If we lose contact and don't come back out of that hole within a week, take the Katara and get yourselves out of here."

Jace frowned. *Not likely,* he thought, although he didn't say it out loud.

"Alright people, let's kick this pig, we're burnin' daylight." Galin jogged back up into the ship's landing bay.

Ulrick turned to Jace. "Come with me, I've got some guns and equipment you might find useful."

"Thanks," Jace said. He suddenly realized what kind of trouble he might be walking into, and his stomach turned just a bit. Then he looked over again at Hero. She looked so nervous, and so grateful. Jace took a quick breath and nodded to Ulrick. "Okay, lets do it."

Galin took the data-pad out of his pocket and punched in some commands. "Alright, I've activated the Global Positioning program. Hero modified it to run off a sub-space frequency. She's a pretty smart little gal. If it works right we should be able to keep an accurate map of wherever we go."

"All right," Ulrick said, lowering his night-vision goggles, "let's go find something to shoot."

Boreas looked at Galin as if to ask how unstable Ulrick might be. Galin squinted his nose and shook his head, telling him not to worry about it.

They walked off into the darkness. Boreas had a small flashlight that barely lit up the cavern around them.

"I think you need a new battery for that thing," Galin told him.

Boreas flicked his tongue and hissed out a laugh. "My people see much better in the dark than yours do. I will enjoy getting out of your planet's bright sunlight for a while."

The path took them along for a short while before coming to a fork. Another passage broke off to their right, in the same direction they'd come from.

"I'd be willing to bet that this leads up to the

elementary school," Galin told them. "Let's keep heading straight."

They walked for a little over twenty-three minutes, according to Galin's watch, before the tunnel broke into another, slightly larger passageway. The ground remained level for over an hour, passing a few more of the smaller tunnels like the one they'd come out of, before reaching a noticeable incline. Galin knew they were heading further down into the earth, although at times his mind played tricks on him, and it looked as though they were walking uphill. It was a strange sensation.

"Now I know what the life of a gopher must be like," Ulrick told them.

They continued to walk along, mostly in silence, for another few hours, until something familiar caught Galin's eye. He reached down and picked up a boy's tennis shoe, setting off the blinking red lights at the bottom, which seemed surprisingly bright as the cavern walls lit up around them. Boreas cocked his head curiously as Galin gently put the shoe back down. After a few seconds the lights went off.

"Looks like we're on the right path," Boreas said cheerfully as they continued.

They hadn't gotten far before the path leveled off once again and opened up into a much larger corridor.

Galin couldn't believe what he was seeing. The tunnel was about twenty feet across with a twelve-foot high clearance, and appeared to be designed as a major thoroughfare. A beaten stone road vanished off into the darkness in both directions. As the two men and Draconian stepped in, a pale yellow glow began to illuminate the road from bars along the floor and the stone ceiling above them. The lights continued for a few dozen feet in both directions.

Galin and Ulrick dodged back from where they'd just come, supposing it to be an ambush.

"Do not fear," Boreas hissed. "The lights come on automatically. These tunnels were indeed constructed by Draconians, this is similar workmanship to what I have seen on other worlds."

"It's going to be a little hard to sneak up on anyone with automatic lights popping on," Ulrick growled. "Why didn't you warn us about this?"

Boreas ran clawed fingers along his scaly, green face. "This is actually a good sign. It means we're close to something, an outpost or settlement, or perhaps even a city."

"A *city*?" asked Galin, peaking out and taking another look down the tunnel. "You've got to be kidding me."

Boreas walked across the road to examine a large stone in the opposite wall. Galin followed. The stone looked as if it had been clawed on by a grizzly bear.

"Yes, good," Boreas told him. "There is a Pneuma-Tal monastery just a few miles from here, down the path on our right."

"The Pneuma-Tal?" repeated Galin. "Who are they?"

"An ancient order of Draconian warrior-monks," Boreas told them. "I was not aware that any of them resided on Earth."

"What is this thing," asked Ulrick, pointing his rifle at the stone, "some kind of street sign?"

"Yeess," hissed Boreas gleefully. "And we have been very lucky. The Pneuma-Tal might be able to assist us. They are no friends of the Nazerazi Alliance, and hold no allegiance to the Draconian legions. But their fortress will be well protected, and they may already know of our presence here."

Ulrick looked skeptical. "Will these guys have access to the Nazerazi network? Why would they if they're not part of the Alliance?"

Boreas shook his head. "No, I doubt very much that they would have access to Nazerazi systems, but they may still have information that could aid us. They see much that others do not."

Galin took a drink from his canteen. "What's that supposed to mean? Kinda sounds like some weird, lizard-religion mumbo-jumbo to me." He immediately realized that he might have offended the reptilian. "Uh, no offense or anything."

"None taken, Captain. I do not know how the Pneuma-Tal see what they do. I've never met any of them, I just know that they are highly respected among my people, and their skills are legendary."

Galin considered it. The reptilian seemed earnest enough in what he was saying, and hadn't given them any reason to doubt them. "Alright then," Galin told him. "If you think this is the best move, then let's get going."

"Wait," Ulrick said, pointing his finger up to the sign again. "Does it tell you what lies in the other direction?"

Boreas nodded. "Yes, it says that there is a supply station roughly fifteen miles away, and after that there are no services until you reach Hot Rocks Springs, another thirty miles ahead."

"Oh," Ulrick said dumbly. "All right then."

They proceeded, and the road continued to light up as they walked along. They neither heard nor saw anything unusual, and time passed slowly until a few miles had been put behind them.

Eventually, the road ended abruptly at a solid stone wall, which blocked the tunnel from the ground to the roof. Galin saw that more of the strange scratched on writing was engraved upon certain sections of the wall, much lighter than the marks they'd seen before. He stooped to take a closer look. These markings looked old- very old. He made an educated guess that there must be some hidden door or passageway, but could find no clue as to how he might open it, and hoped the reptilian standing behind him might already know the answer. Perhaps he was even amused at Galin's attempt to figure it out.

"Well?" he asked Boreas, who had been standing and watching in silence.

The creature just cocked his head inquisitively.

"Well?" Galin repeated more slowly. "Do you know how to get past this thing or what?"

"There is no getting past *this* wall Captain, not on our own. If the Pneuma-Tal decide to speak to us, they will let us in themselves."

Jace hadn't been to Phoenix in years, not since he was a little kid. But even if he had, he knew he wouldn't recognize it now. Gazing out at the destruction below, he wondered if all the big cities had been hit this hard. He guided the Shiv over the ruins of the once great city, moving toward the coordinates that Hero had given him, while the young woman sat in the seat beside him and wept quietly, taking in the horrors below. The only signs of life were an occasional scavenger or small group of marauders, but such sightings were few and far between. Most of the people they spotted were just lifeless bodies, but even the number of those was lower than Jace expected. He hoped that most people had been able to evacuate safely.

Few buildings remained undamaged, and as they approached their destination it was clear that the area had been just as devastated as the other areas they'd flown over. Jace's heart sank as he listened to Hero's cries grow louder. She pointed to the large house belonging to her parents, which had been reduced to a heap of charred rubble.

"Let me find a place to set down, and we'll go take a look, okay?"

Hero said nothing, but nodded as tears continued to stream down her face.

They found a clear spot of grass in a park a short distance from the house, and Jace made a quick scan for human or draconian life forms to ensure no one would get the jump on them. He landed, cloaked the ship, and followed Hero out the hatch. She sped toward the ruined building, and Jace tore after her, afraid that she might end up hurting herself. He caught her by the arm just before she could spring into the ruins.

"WAIT," he urged her. "Let's go slow, this place is dangerous."

"I know," she said, trembling. "I'm sorry, I just…"

"Don't worry about it, I understand. I just don't want you to get hurt." He smiled warmly. "We'll go together, okay. Take a few deep breaths first, you look like you're about to hyperventilate." He took her hand, and she grinned appreciatively through her tears, staring into his eyes and trying to calm down.

A few moments later he was leading her through the threshold of the front door. It appeared that the place had exploded from within. Most of the roof was missing, along with large sections of the walls. Jace figured that a mortar shell must have come right through the roof. He watched the young woman attentively as she scanned the debris, looking for evidence of her family's survival or demise. They made their way through what was left of the house, but some rooms were too dangerous to enter. Jace scanned the charred ruins as they went, searching for any trace of human remains, and was relieved to see that nothing turned up.

Hero began sobbing again when they entered the nursery. She picked up a stuffed Orca Whale, which had somehow remained undamaged, and squeezed it tightly. "Will bought this for Steven a few months ago when we went to San Diego. He picked it up in a gift shop and wouldn't let go of it." She smiled through her tears. "He really loved this thing."

Jace nodded. He stooped to pick up a picture that had fallen face down in the ash. The glass was broken, but the photo remained intact. It was Hero, her husband, and the baby-sitting on a park bench in front of a tiered fountain. They all wore cheerful smiles, and the baby looked like he was about to reach up and grab Hero's dangling earring. Jace shook off the broken glass and handed her the picture. "It's a great looking family," he said.

She gazed at the image for a few moments before placing it into a side pocket. "I grew up in this house. I can't believe it's all gone. But at least…."

Jace nodded his head in agreement. "I'm not seeing

any signs of human remains on the scanners. At least you know they made it out of here."

Hero gathered a few more things, and they returned to the front entrance. Jace put the scanner back in his pocket. He could see relief in Hero's face, but it was quickly replaced with a renewed sense of worry.

She turned back to stare blankly into the ruins. "How am I ever going to find them? What if I never see my son again?"

Jace wished he could say something to make her feel better. "Maybe Captain Winchester will be able to get some answers. I mean, if all the children *were* taken off world, chances are they all ended up at the same place. Right?"

"I, I don't know. Maybe." The young woman suddenly looked pale. Thinking she might collapse, Jace put his arm around her.

"Come on, we need to get you back to the ship. You don't look so good."

"Okay. You're right." She allowed him to lead her, continuing to stare blankly ahead as they made their way to the Shiv.

Jace could only imagine what she was going through. She'd lost her husband and had no idea where her son was, or even if he was still alive. It was amazing that she was able to cope at all. He just hoped that the Captain was having better luck.

The gears inside Galin's head kept spinning. If there was any possibility that these Pneuma-Tal characters could be of help, he was going to figure out a way to get through this wall, whether they wanted to speak to him or not.

He crossed his arms and frowned up at Ulrick. "You bring along the plastic explosives?"

"Does a bear crap in the woods?"

Boreas gawked at them in confusion, but it was clear that the mention of explosives had given him a start.

"Captain, it would be extremely unwise to show any signs of aggression. In fact, I would advise you to guard even your words more carefully, as I'm sure they are already monitoring us."

"You think so?" Galin gave him a whimsical grin and turned back toward the wall. "If anyone's in there," he said politely, "we'd appreciate you letting us in to talk. Besides, we'd never dream of blowing up your nice, fancy wall."

He hadn't even finished speaking before the earth started to vibrate around them. A low rumble began to emanate from the wall, and then it split right down the middle and each part drew aside.

Galin grinned apologetically over his shoulder at Boreas, who had an amazed and eager expression across his scaled face. Ulrick raised his rifle and took a few steps back, bracing himself for whatever or whoever might be coming through the door.

"Easy, big guy. We don't want to do anything to ruin our first impression."

Two Draconians, noticeably larger than Boreas, and even General Soth, stepped out of the shadows to greet them. They wore thick robes, which blended with the darkness behind them, and upon coming to a stop they nearly faded into the background, and might have vanished altogether if not for the scaly faces protruding out beneath their hoods. The creatures each had their arms crossed before them, and stood quietly and statuesque.

"Uh, I'm Galin Winchester, and this is—"

"We know who you are, Captain, and why you are here," the one on the right told him. "We are the Guardians of the Gate. My name is Prism, and this is Assassin. We have come to escort you to Nicodemus. He wishes to speak with you about your quest. And may be able to help provide answers."

"Excellent." Galin nodded at Ulrick, who in turn lowered his rifle. He could tell that his friend was just as weary as he was about being escorted through the shadows by someone called "Assassin." He leaned over to Ulrick and whispered, "*They look like nice enough guys-for eight foot tall lizards that is.*"

"You are required to leave your weapons with us," Prism told him.

Ulrick growled suspiciously.

"Knock it off, you big baby," Galin said while handing over his blaster. He reached down to retrieve his knife. "Besides, I don't think we're going to need them here. If they wanted us dead, we would be."

Assassin smiled.

It took Ulrick several long moments to disarm. He handed over each weapon with an accentuated frown.

"Do not forget about the plasma disrupter in your right boot," Prism told him stoically.

"Nor the throwing knives in your left," hissed Assassin.

Ulrick looked crestfallen as he handed over these last few pieces. He looked like someone had just made him take all his clothes off.

"Come, follow us," Prism said, and turned to head off down the tunnel.

As they proceeded, Galin soon noticed that the air had changed. It seemed warmer, moister, and had a strange, otherworldly smell that he could not quite place. It was so dark that he could barely make out the forms of the guardians striding before him.

"OUCH," he cried as he slammed his shin against a rock. Everyone stopped.

"The humans' eyes are not as adaptable to the darkness as our own," Boreas told them. "They will require more light."

"Proceed," came a voice from the darkness.

Galin fished for the flashlight he'd dropped in one of

his pockets. Finding it, he took it out and clicked it on about the same time Ulrick did his.

The passage they found themselves in looked much more primitive than the tunnel from which they'd just emerged. In fact, it appeared to be a natural cavern. For a while it was narrow, but before long the cavern opened up before them, eventually becoming so vast that Galin could no longer detect the ceiling or walls, even when he shone his light directly toward them.

They walked for several hours before arriving at a small supply depot where they decided to camp. The temple of the Pneuma-Tal and its surrounding village was still about a seven-hour walk ahead, Prism had told them. Galin knew they all needed rest, as eager as he was to keep moving.

In the morning, the journey resumed. The winding path led them through narrowed passages and open caverns, always taking them deeper into the earth. Galin passed most of the time thinking of his children, and hoping this was not some kind of wild goose chase.

Another vast cave opened up around them. Humungous stalagmites and stalactites decorated the place in a way that was both threatening and beautiful.

All of a sudden, a loud screech rang out overhead, followed by the sound of flapping wings and a stream of rushing air. Ulrick dodged aside and reached for guns that were no longer there, grunting in frustration as his instincts to attack were left wanting.

"I've never seen one of them do that before," Prism hissed to his companion.

"I have," responded Assassin. "Once, long ago."

"And are the old sayings true?"

"We will speak more of these matters later."

Galin looked at Boreas expectantly. "What was that thing?" he whispered. "And what are those two talking about?"

"I do not know, but perhaps—"

"Hey, look at that," Ulrick urged them, pointing ahead.

Off in the distance, a beam of light shone down from the roof of the cavern. It was exceedingly bright, and fell upon the center of a high, underground mountain. Although their immediate surroundings were still dark, Galin could see that the area ahead was well lit.

"What is that place?" Ulrick asked.

"That is the temple of the Pneuma-Tal," Prism answered. "That is where we will find Nicodemus."

Jace landed the Shiv in the docking bay of the Katara, re-closed the bay doors and re-cloaked the ship. He got out and walked to the intercom panel near the door leading off to the cockpit, checking to see if anyone had left a message for them, but no one had. Jace hadn't been able to reach Captain Winchester or the others, but they knew that any signals might be blocked by the

Nazerazi. Only two days had passed since they'd separated, but Jace could only hope that his friends hadn't gotten into something more than they could handle.

Hero came up from behind and touched his arm. "Do you think they'll be alright?"

"Yeah, I think so."

She looked him over as if trying to determine how much he really meant it. He knew the worry must be showing on his face.

"At least, I hope so. The captain is a really resourceful guy, and Ulrick is…well, Ulrick is Ulrick. And from what I've seen, I think we can trust Boreas." He looked at her for confirmation, and to his satisfaction she nodded confidently.

All of a sudden, she pulled him in, kissed his cheek, and embraced him tightly. "Thank you," she said. "For going with me, I mean. Taking me to Phoenix and helping me search. You didn't have to do that."

Jace felt himself go flush. "Don't mention it," he stuttered. "I'm just…I'm sorry we didn't find anything."

"I'm sorry too, but at least I know Stephen wasn't killed during the attack. I don't know where he is, but I really feel like he's out there somewhere. I feel like he's still alive. Does that make sense? Or am I just being stupid?"

"No," he assured her. "It's not stupid. I think you should listen to your motherly instincts. If you really feel like he's safe, then I'm sure he is, now we just need to find him."

She smiled and gave him another squeeze before letting go.

"You look a lot better than you did last night. I was really getting worried about you."

Hero nodded. "So…what are we going to do now? While we wait for the others to get back, I mean." She smiled at him warmly, and pushed her blonde, shoulder-length hair out of her face.

Jace stared at her dumbly. She really was one of the most gorgeous women he'd ever met, and now that he was getting to know her, she seemed even more beautiful. A few thoughts ran through his head that he wasn't about to suggest out loud, and he felt immediately guilty for even thinking them. Hero was hurting and vulnerable, and this definitely wasn't the right time to make a move on her. *You should be ashamed of yourself,* he thought.

"Hey," said Hero, almost coyly. "I've got an idea, but it's a little bit …naughty." She eyed him playfully and bit her lip.

He suddenly felt way too hot, and stuck his finger into his shirt, pulling at the collar to let some air in. "Oh yeah, what's that?"

"How about we open up that crate and take a look at the T3038?"

He laughed nervously in response, breathing out a

sigh of relief. *You're an idiot,* he told himself. Jace had told Hero all about the robot on the return trip from Phoenix the night before, trying to make small talk and get her mind off of her troubles for a while. She hadn't seemed all that interested at the time, and he couldn't blame her. He'd just kept on talking, because every time he'd stopped she seemed to cry harder. Now, her eyes were lit up almost as if it were Christmas.

"Sure, I mean, it's not like the thing's worth anything now. Starla said the thing wouldn't go for much on the off-Earth market, other than it's face value that is. It was worth so much because of its historical significance, but I don't think that means a whole lot now."

She nodded and smiled. "The thing could still be sold for a small fortune to someone needing a robot with that thing's capabilities, but I've been thinking, and it might be just what *we* need right now." She turned and began heading toward the crate. "Ever since you told me about this bot, I've been working it all out in my head. We might be able to reprogram it to help us." She seemed almost giddy. "That is, if you don't mind tampering with an invaluable historical artifact."

"Heck no, I don't care. I hated history class, let's tamper away," he smiled back. "But ...how do you suppose this thing can help us?"

"Well, if my memory serves me correctly, this robot was specifically designed to stealthily gather information, and survive at all costs while doing it. It's kind of like the ultimate super-spy robot, sent to scope out the galaxy."

"Yeah, that's pretty much what Starla said, more or less. But she said it had some kind of virus. That's why it never deployed in the first place. You think you can fix it?"

"With a little research, I bet I can get ahold of the code to delete the virus. It's probably available in Earth's historical files. After that's done, I can reprogram it to retrieve the location of our families, and any other information we want from the Nazerazi." She looked like she could barely contain herself.

"If you can do all that, then you'll be my—"

"I'll be your *hero*? Like I've never heard *that* one before."

"Actually," Jace laughed, "that joke never occurred to me till you brought it up."

She ran her hands hungrily along the crate. "Help me get this thing down to the engine room so I can get started on it, okay?"

Jace scratched his head. He wasn't sure how much the thing weighed, but figured it wasn't light. "Okay, just let me grab a hover cart. You get to work on those straps."

She smiled excitedly at him, and he smiled back as he turned to retrieve the cart. He didn't know if she could really pull this off or not, but at least the prospect gave her hope, and it was nice to see her smiling.

The temple of the Pneuma-Tal rose up in the distance like some gigantic black stalagmite. As they got closer, Galin saw that it looked something like the pictures he'd seen of ancient Aztec pyramids, except of course for the curious way it was lit up. A bright beam of light came down from the roof of the cavern far above, which was redirected throughout the structure, causing windows to glow as if sunlight were being generated from within. Everything around the temple was lit up as well, and the surrounding structures could be seen as long as you avoided looking directly into the bright beam of light.

Along the cavern wall on either side of the temple, hundreds of smaller lights emanated from carved out sections that most likely served as dwellings.

The thing that surprised Galin the most was the amount of vegetation they passed as they neared the buildings. Before long he found himself in a low, dense subterranean jungle. He'd never seen such plant life on earth before. It seemed to glow from within, casting a greenish-blue light. It was faint, but allowed them to navigate without the use of the flashlights.

As dozens, and then tens of dozens of Draconians began to appear all around them, Galin suddenly felt just as alien as he had on any of the distant planets he'd visited. It was strange. Here he was on Earth feeling farther away from home than ever.

Most of the reptilians they saw were nearly naked, except for a beaded kilt-like garment that hung loosely from the waist. Ulrick nudged him and pointed out a group of three that were a bit smaller and looked more feminine than the others. Galin grinned at him. He'd been wondering if the female Draconians would look noticeably different than the males. He'd found that with some alien species, that wasn't always the case. Many of the creatures simply stared as they passed, but some began to follow, and before long they had a sizable group in tow.

"The natives look restless," Ulrick whispered.

"They mean you no harm," came the voice of Assassin from behind him. "They are merely curious. Most of them have never seen a human before."

"They need to get out more," Galin jested.

"Why?" asked the guardian.

"Never mind. Are all of these Draconians members of the Pneuma-Tal?"

"No," Prism answered. "There are only three Pneuma-Tal paladins walking this planet, and Nicodemus is one of them. Most of the Draconians living here are simple citizens; descendants of a colony that arrived on this world long ago."

Galin continued to take in his surroundings until they arrived at the base of the temple, where their escorts stopped them. The crowd of curious reptilians gathered around, and all waited expectantly in an eerie silence.

Ulrick crossed his arms and frowned indignantly. Galin glanced at Boreas, who shrugged back unknowingly.

After several moments of waiting, and scanning the temple and the crowds in anticipation, Galin turned once again to the guardians. "So, what happens now?"

"Now, impatient one," came a raspy voice from somewhere above, "You must go inside the temple, and if you are worthy, then perhaps you will find answers for the questions you seek."

Galin scanned the surface of the temple, eager to find the source of the voice. "Are you Nicodemus?" he asked. "Is it true you can help us?"

"Yes, I am Nicodemus. And yes, I will try to help you, but whether or not that is possible remains to be seen."

Galin could hear the voice clearly, but despite straining his eyes could not locate it's owner. It was almost as if the temple itself were speaking.

"Is your eyesight so poor, human?"

Without warning, a strange streak of light, or perhaps a shadow, came zipping toward them. Before Galin's eyes could focus, the tall form of another Draconian was standing before him. His robes shimmered strangely, blending in so well with rock of the temple behind, that were it not for his face and hands and the staff he bore, he might have faded away completely.

"Do not let his words discourage you, Captain," Boreas told him. "The Pneuma-Tal are seen only when they wish to be. Not even my eyes could detect him."

"Ah," breathed Nicodemus, "this Draconian speaks respectfully to you, Galin Winchester. That is good. Perhaps the universe will find you worthy. Are you ready to begin your quest?"

"I thought I already had," Galin answered. He frowned and eyed the Draconian doubtfully. He'd come to get answers, not some fracking hippie talk about speaking to the universe.

"Yes, you have. But so far you've been fighting to find your way. Now you must go down a path less traveled. You must cease your struggling for a while, and allow the answers to find you. Do you understand?"

"Uh, no. Not really." Galin pursed his lips and sighed. He didn't like the way this was turning out. It all sounded like a bunch of mystical nonsense. But he was desperate. He needed to do something. "But, I'm willing to try, if there's any chance at all it might help."

Nicodemus eyed him approvingly. "That is something." He turned and strode toward the temple entrance. "Come, we shall soon discover how well you listen."

The T3038 lied on top of the steel table in the engine room like an unconscious surgical patient. Getting the thing down here by himself hadn't been an easy task, and Jace felt whipped. He put his hands on his knees and took a couple of long deep breaths. Taking the baseball cap off his head, he tossed it to the floor and looked up just in time to see Hero lean over the robot. *You have got to be kidding me,* he thought. *Look at that behind!* He suddenly didn't feel so tired.

"Isn't it beautiful?" Hero asked him.

"It's the most beautiful thing I've ever seen," he answered dreamily.

She turned her head and raised an eyebrow at him.

Jace felt his face go red again. "Er, it's amazing…I just, um…. Yes, it's a beautiful robot."

She gave him a funny grin and turned back to what she was doing.

Jace found himself sneaking another look before moving to the other side of the table.

"So, what are you looking for anyway?"

"This." She touched a nearly undetectable panel on the bot's forehead, which popped open. A number of soft tones rang out as she pressed a series of buttons. "I'm entering an access code so I can program him remotely."

Jace looked the robot over from head to toe. He couldn't believe something like this was actually considered an antique- it was one of the most impressive androids he'd ever laid eyes on. It was roughly the same size and shape as a tall male human, and much about it's appearance reminded him of a medieval suit of armor. It's arm, legs and torso were square with rounded corners, and it's visored eyes and strong jaw conveyed nobility.

"Starla said these bots were sent out to explore the stars, to find inhabitable planets and return with the information. It was pretty important for them to survive. They must be able to take a lot of punishment."

Hero nodded excitedly. "This thing's body is constructed of crystalized tritanium, so yeah, you could say that. It actually has a highly advanced weapon system too, and runs off a compressed nuclear fusion power core."

"That's pretty much what Starla said, except I don't remember her saying anything about weapons. I thought this thing was supposed to be a peaceful explorer."

"It was." She punched in the robot's access code on her data pad. Its eyes immediately came to life, casting a sapphire light out of the long slit on its knightly face. "The weapons weren't meant to be used against any form of life, in fact, that was against it's programing. They were only supposed to be used as tools, to help navigate through dangerous areas of space or free itself if it got trapped or caught. Things like that."

"Yeah, I guess that makes sense. It's hard to believe that this thing has just been floating around in space for the last few hundred years. It's seen so much, but doesn't even know about any of it. He slept right through it all. It's kind of sad, in a way."

Hero grinned at him as if she thought it had been an

adorable thought. He wasn't so sure that he liked being thought of as adorable.

"So were you able to find the cure for the virus in the historical archives?"

"Yup." Hero waived her data-pad around in the air and laughed at his choice of words. "I've got it right here." She began punching something in. "I'm also going to upload the information on my son and Captain Winchester's kids- their names, images, fingerprints, and DNA sequences, and if he finds any information on your other friends, he'll transmit that to us too. With a little luck, this 3038 will be able to track them down."

"But how's it going to do that? I mean, are you going to program it to break into the Nazerazi network or something?"

"That's exactly what I'm going to do." Her fingers danced furiously across the data-pad. "I'm also going to lift the restrictions on its weapon system, so that if any Nazerazi try to interfere with its mission, they'll be sorry." Her eyes gleamed menacingly, as if it was something she hoped for.

Jace shrugged. "Sounds good to me. Is it really tough enough to go up again those jerks head-on though?"

"Oh yeah, it's going to take a lot more than a few Draconians to take this thing out. Anyway, it's programmed to move stealthily, so it'll avoid confrontation whenever possible."

Jace ran his fingers down the smooth robotic arm. It felt cold and lifeless.

"So, what happens if it actually tracks one of the kids down? It's not like it can just pick them up and fly back home."

"I'm programing it to send us a distress signal. It'll find a secure position and guard whichever child it finds until we can get there to retrieve them."

Jace smiled at her encouragingly.

"I'm downloading a program used in search and rescue bots. That way, it'll be able to build shelter, hunt for food, even perform first aid."

It sounded like she'd thought of just about everything, and from the way her fingers were flying across the data-pad, this wasn't her first time to the rodeo when it came to computer programming. *Who knows,* Jace thought, *this plan might just be crazy enough to work*.

"I think he needs a name," Hero told him. "After all, he's special. Even more so than the other T3038s. He's going to help me find my son, I just know it! Captain Winchester's kids too."

Jace shrugged. "Well, I think he looks kind of like a knight. How about Lancelot or something like that?"

"Naw, Lancelot was a jerk. He cuckolded Arthur."

"Yeah, I guess you're right," Jace agreed, having no idea what she was talking about. He felt his face going red again.

"He had an affair with Guinevere, Arthur's wife," she

explained. "I'd hate to name him after a traitor. That might be bad luck." Hero gazed down into the robot's sapphire eyes. "But you're right, he does look knightly. And we're sending him out as a knight-errant, with a very important mission. Why don't we call him...William Marshal. He was a real knight- one of the greatest who ever lived."

Jace pinched his chin. "William Marshal? Kind of a weird name for a robot, but...sure, that seems to fit somehow."

Hero gave him a toothy smile, and then bent over to kiss William Marshal on the cheek.

"We christen thee, Sir William Marshal." She swung her data pad down on each side of his head. "And we charge thee with this sacred mission, to find our children and return them to us safely."

Jace chuckled nervously, and despite trying, he couldn't control the look on his face. He didn't want Hero to think he was laughing at her, but he'd started to wonder if all the stress was finally making her crack.

She let out a sigh and placed her hand over his. "I'm not going crazy," she assured him. "I'm just excited. I want this plan to work, and feel like we should send this robot off with as much good luck as possible."

"I understand. I think it's a great plan, and I don't think you're crazy, just a little weird. But it's a good weird," he added quickly.

She beamed back at him. "All that's left to do now is

delete the virus and download his new orders, and then we can send him on his way." She crossed her fingers, and entered the command.

Galin followed Nicodemus through the corridors of the Pneuma-Tal temple. Ulrick and Boreas followed them. Torches hanging off the walls lit up their path, and the air smelled damp and smoky. Small, green geckos scurried along the walls, and some seemed to be following them. Galin wondered what had happened to the beam of light they'd seen shining down into the temple. He expected the place to be teeming with light, but instead he felt like he was even deeper in the bowels of the earth than before.

"How did you know my name?" Galin asked. He was curious to find out exactly how much information this strange being might have about them, and how he'd gotten it.

"I have seen your coming. The universe has shown it to me, just as it has shown me other things. Your spirit is strong, Galin Winchester, but it is conflicted. It has never been easy for you to find your path, and the decisions before you will be no easier than those behind."

"Do you know where the Nazerazi have taken my children, or our friends?" Galin pressed him.

"I have seen where the Alliance has taken many of its human captives. But as to the specific location of those you speak of, I do not know, except that they are no longer on Earth. Perhaps *you* will be given those answers. We are nearly to the observation chamber."

After a few minutes they came to a sealed stone door, and Galin noticed the same scratched writing they'd seen before. Nicodemus pressed a stone on the adjacent wall, and the door opened. They entered a large but unremarkable chamber. Like the rest of the place, the walls were stone, and the room was empty. Nicodemus led them toward the center, where he waved his hand above his head as though he were drawing open some imaginary window. A panel in the ceiling immediately began to slide open, and a blinding ray of light came streaming in.

Galin shielded his eyes, but even when he looked away he couldn't open them.

"What's the point of *this*?" Ulrick growled.

"The light is only blinding because you believe it to be so. Open your eyes and allow yourself to see."

Galin tried to force open his eyes, but it felt as though he were staring into the sun. "We're not like you," he told Nicodemus. "Our eyes aren't meant to see things like this."

"I cannot open mine either," Boreas called. "Even with my eyes closed and covered I can barely stand the light."

"Your physical limitations play no part in this," the paladin told them. "Open your eyes, and look upon the universe with your spirit, only then will you be able to search for the answers you seek."

Galin tried again, but the light was too blinding. Either this old reptilian was out of his mind, or he was playing some kind of horrible joke on them.

"This is a waste of time," Galin scowled. "Just close that fracking window so we can get out of here. I've had enough."

After a few moments, the panel in the roof closed. When Galin's eyes adjusted, he saw Nicodemus standing before him. The reptilian's eyes weren't even constricted. Boreas was sitting on the floor looking stunned, and Ulrick just looked angry.

"What was *that* all about?" Galin huffed. "You can't tell me we were really supposed to see something in there."

"Supposed to? I never said you were *supposed* to see anything. Perhaps I was wrong about you, Captain Winchester. You whine like a hatchling. Perhaps you are unworthy after all."

Galin was frustrated and angry. He suddenly felt like punching the Draconian's sharp, crooked teeth out. Instead, he closed his eyes and took some long, deep breaths. They hadn't come all this way for nothing, he just needed to calm down and do what needed to be done. "Maybe you're right," Galin told him. "Can I try again?"

"What?" Ulrick spat. "We need to get out of here.

This nonsense isn't going to help us find anyone. If these people can't assist us, then we need to get back to searching on our own."

"No. I want to try again." Galin took Ulrick's arm and pulled him aside. "You can wait outside if you want, but I'm not going to leave until I get some answers. If there's a chance, any chance at all of this working, then I need to try."

Ulrick let out a discouraged sigh, conceded a nod, and headed for the door.

Boreas followed. "I'll wait outside as well, perhaps you'll be able to concentrate better that way. Good luck, Captain."

Once his companions were gone, Galin turned again to Nicodemus. "Alright, tell me what to do."

The piercing light came bursting into the room once more. It seemed even brighter this time than it had before, and Galin struggled in vain to shield his eyes. Suddenly, he realized something- he'd been so preoccupied with the light's intensity that he'd only now noticed the lack of heat. He'd assumed that the light was a magnified ray from the sun, but if that were true they should all have been incinerated where they stood.

"What is this?" Galin asked. "This light, I mean. Where does it come from?"

"Ah, yes. Very observant of you, Captain. I know

what you are thinking, and you are partially correct. This light is the light of the galaxy. It is the light of hundreds of billions of stars, every star from what your people call the Milky Way, one of which is your very own Sun."

"What?" Galin stuttered. Was he really supposed to believe that light from every star in the galaxy was being reflected into this chamber? "That's impossible. It's madness."

"You are still trying to understand through your human eyes, Captain Winchester. It is time to learn to see with your spirit. You must open your eyes."

Every instinct he had told Galin that if he opened his eyes, they would be burned right out of his head, but he lowered his hands and slowly forced them open. He expected pain, but it didn't come. Still, he could see nothing but a brilliant glow, and the sensation was just short of maddening.

"You're doing well," the Draconian assured him. "I know how disorienting this can be. Just continue to relax. The feeling will pass."

After what seemed like a very long while, the tall reptilian began to take form in front of him. Galin forced himself to relax, to adjust to what he was seeing. A few moments later he could see Nicodemus clearly, and the light melted away all around him, leaving a background of twinkling stars. Even the floor was gone. It was like standing in space, as Galin had done so many times before, but without the need for a spacesuit.

"What is this?"

"I'm impressed," Nicodemus told him. "You learned rather quickly. Faster than most do. It seems that you've done this before, although perhaps you didn't realize it at the time."

Galin looked at him doubtfully.

"This, Captain, is the galaxy. Your people have always been fond of looking at the stars, but few have been interested in listening to them."

"Listening to them? How do I do that?"

"You're doing it now. We shall soon find out if they have anything important to say."

As the minutes passed, Galin gazed at the twinkling stars all around them. He suddenly felt calmer than he had in a long time, more at peace. This whole experience still seemed unbelievable and odd, but he could not deny that something important was happening. That much was very clear. A hundred thoughts seemed to bounce through his mind, but he struggled to block them out. It wasn't time to think, it was time to listen. The only sound Galin could hear was that of his own breathing, and after a while, the breathing of his host. Other than that, silence surrounded them, until it was broken by a chilling shriek.

Galin lunged aside, eager to avoid whatever creature might be coming at him. His eyes flew to Nicodemus, whom he saw looking up. A dozen feet above them, a large reptilian bird flapped it's wings before gliding off into the distance.

"That's the same noise we heard before the guardians escorted us into the city. What was that thing?"

The Draconian frowned. "A Thuban Albatross. The creatures travelled as stowaways upon my people's ships when we colonized the stars thousands of years ago. Their call has always been an omen of death for those that hear it."

"An omen of death? So I'm supposed to die?"

"We are *all* going to die," Nicodemus said flatly. "But will it be *your* death soon approaching? Perhaps, perhaps not. The omen could be a sign for someone near to you. Someone that you love."

"My wife was killed in the invasion. I buried her just a few days ago. Could it be speaking of her?"

Nicodemus shook his head. "I'm sorry, but no. The omen speaks of the future, not of the past."

Galin felt sick. The thought of his own death hadn't scared him for quite some time, but the idea of losing those he loved had always terrified him, and everyone he knew was already in terrible danger- his children, his friends, pretty much everyone he'd ever met for that matter.

"You're thinking too much," Nicodemus said. "You cannot listen to the stars if you're listening to yourself. Clear your mind."

Galin steadied his breathing. "Do I need to ask

questions? Or do the, er, stars already know what I want?"

"You need ask nothing," the reptilian assured him. "Just listen."

The stars continued to twinkle for several long minutes before beginning to move. It was subtle at first, but they were soon zipping past him as if he'd just gone to warp. He glanced over to find that Nicodemus was still there beside him.

Before Galin could turn back around everything came to a halt, and there before him hung a bright blue planet. For a moment he thought it was earth, but soon recognized that the continents didn't look right. There was, however, something familiar about the place. Had he been there before? He couldn't quiet place it.

And then the blue, healthy sphere began to turn grey. It seemed to be dying- decaying, right there before his eyes. The continents twisted and shook until eventually the only thing left was a shell that resembled some grotesque human skull. It was one of the most horrifying things that Galin had ever witnessed. He began to feel himself shake, and thought for a moment that the skull might lunge out and bite him in half.

His heart skipped a beat upon feeling a large hand take hold of his shoulder. It was only Nicodemus. He said nothing, but nodded assuringly. Galin felt disgusted with himself for getting so spooked by a stupid vision.

He looked back around just as the stars began flying

past once more. They came to a stop in front of another planet. This one was bright and green, but instead of hanging there, they descended toward its surface. High, icy mountains reached into the sky in every direction, but as they approached the surface, a wide, lush valley surrounded by rolling green hills spread out beneath them. The grass looked fresh and thick, and a light breeze made the blades dance in waves. It was a beautiful place, a bit like the Swedish Alps, Galin thought, but the mountains were even higher, and he couldn't recall ever having been to a place like this on any planet he'd visited.

Seemingly out of nowhere, flowers began to thud down into the grass, almost as if they were being thrown, but each landed upright and immediately took root. These were all flowers that Galin recognized. They were all from Earth. There were roses, tulips, lilies, and sunflowers, and many that he recognized but couldn't name. Hundreds of flowers, and then thousands thudded down around them, making the landscape even more strange and beautiful than it had been before.

After a few moments, the flowers began to wilt and die, eventually crumbling into dust and leaving only the grass behind once more.

"Do you know where this is?" Galin asked. "I've never seen this place before."

"I believe," Nicodemus said softly, "that this is Zeta Reticulan. I visited the planet once when I was an apprentice, many years ago."

"Zeta Reticulan? Boreas said that human prisoners were being taken to the Zeta Reticuli star system to be sold as slaves. I'm not an expert on hippie visions, but I don't like the looks of this."

"No, it does not bode well for your people, if what Boreas said is true."

The planet faded away and stars twinkled in the distance once more. They waited for several long minutes before Nicodemus spoke. "I believe that is all the stars have to tell you for now, Captain."

Galin didn't feel like he knew much more than he had before they started, except that he or someone close to him had some kind of death omen, and he wasn't even sure he was buying that.

"So, Captain, the choice is clear, although I do not envy you. It seems you must decide which destination to choose first. Not even the Pneuma-Tal have discovered a secret for being in two places at once."

Suddenly it came to him, he knew he'd recognized the first planet they'd seen. Although he'd never been there himself, they had studied the place in school. It was the planet Necron.

"Necron," Galin whispered uneasily. "But why would prisoners be taken *there*, unless...." He couldn't finish the thought out-loud, but knew from Nicodemus' look that he understood. If prisoners were being taken to Necron, they would be dumped on the planet's surface and left for the zombies. It was a fate far crueler than any execution.

The sound of grinding stone broke through the silence, and the shimmering stars faded away as if a curtain of heavy clouds had rolled in, leaving only the solid brick walls of the temple around them.

"Well, that was...enlightening," Galin said, feeling a bit disoriented. "But I guess I have someplace to start, or two places, rather."

"Before you go, Captain, there are a few more things you should know. Things you failed to hear."

"Didn't we both see and hear the same things?"

"In a way, but remember, I've been doing this a lot longer than you have. The stars have shown that you will soon confront someone from the past, someone who was lost to you long ago. However, this person will only be an empty shell of what they were before. Life without life, that is what the stars have shown."

"Okay, life without life. That makes sense." Galin let out a long sigh. Was this all a bunch of nonsense? Normally he'd of thought so, but perhaps he was too tired to argue with his own sense of reason.

"Secondly, there will be a changing of life."

Galin raised his eyebrows. "What exactly is that supposed to mean?"

The Draconian looked off thoughtfully into the distance. "The answer is ...unclear."

"A changing of life, and life without life. Got it. And

all of this helps me, *how*?"

"Helps you? That is for you to determine, Captain. You came here seeking for answers, and that's what you have received."

Nicodemus led Galin and the others back through the temple.

"After you've rested, the Guardians of the Gate will escort you back. Good luck on your journey. I hope you find your loved ones."

Galin thanked him for his help. "Just one more question, before we go," he said softly. "What would you do, if you were me? Where would you go first?"

"The Pneuma-Tal see much," Nicodemus answered. "And we know much. But we do not know everything. I cannot say where I would go, the decision must be yours. Farewell."

The reptilian led them through the door and disappeared back into the temple.

"Did you get any answers in there?" Ulrick asked him as they walked down the steps outside the temple.

Galin was tired. The death omen had him worried, but he felt hopeful as well. At least they had someplace to start. "I guess we'll find out soon enough."

The trek back from the Pneuma-Tal temple took less time than the journey there, although it didn't seem that way to Galin. He was so eager to get back to the Katara that he felt his heart might leap from his chest. Luckily, Nicodemus had sent out some scouts to make sure the way was clear, and they'd made their way through the tunnels without any trouble.

When they got back to the school basement, Galin expected Mrs. Ponte to be waiting for them, but she was nowhere to be seen. The place was dark and empty. He thought it odd that she wasn't at her post, and hoped she hadn't run into any trouble.

After taking a quick look around, they made their way to the gym and Galin pushed open the double doors and looked back out into the world. He had to cover his eyes. After four days under ground, he wasn't expecting the sun to seem so bright. Ulrick came up behind him, blaster rifle at the ready just in case. He had to cover his eyes as well.

Finally, Boreas stepped up behind them. "That's odd," he said matter-of-factly. "The ship is uncloaked."

"WHAT?" Galin barked, squinting toward the football field. The reptilian was right. "That's not a good sign." He clicked on his wrist-com. "Jace, this is Winchester, come in." There was no response. He waited a minute and then tried again. Still, there was nothing.

Ulrick cocked his rifle. "They should be back by now. Something must be wrong."

"If it were the Nazerazi, they would have taken the ship. We need to move quickly."

Galin and Ulrick moved in toward the ship, and Boreas followed. There wasn't much in the way of cover, but they moved as stealthily as they could. Galin dodged behind a large recycling bin next to the fence by the bleachers, and his heart skipped a beat to see a crouching Mrs. Ponte with her blaster pistol pointed at his face.

"Oh, it's you!" she said, lowering the gun. "I nearly blew your brains out. You shouldn't sneak up on an old woman like that."

"Mrs. Ponte, what are you doing out here? What's going on with my ship?"

She grimaced at him and shrugged. "I was walking along the east side of the building over there when I heard that terrible racket, and then that ship of yours de-cloaked. I thought I'd better try to get a closer look."

Galin sneaked a peak around the corner at the Katara. He still couldn't see anyone around. "You didn't' see anything else?"

She shook her head. "Nothing."

"All right. Stay here. We've got to get over there quick. Try to give us some cover fire if things go bad."

She nodded. "Okay, but be careful. I don't know what happened over there, but judging by the noise I heard it couldn't be anything good."

Galin gave her a gentle pat on the shoulder, looked around again, and sprung out. He didn't see any signs of an ambush, but they crept along carefully just in case. It didn't take them long to reach the ship.

"What in the world is THAT?" Ulrick growled as they reached the side of the Katara. A large hole had been torn through the hull.

"It looks like something shot through from the inside," Boreas commented, examining the outward way the steel was bent. "However, I don't see any signs of an explosion."

While Ulrick stood cover, Galin walked up beside the reptilian to get a better look. "This is right beneath the engine room. We'd better get in there quick."

Galin ran to the docking bay and punched in the security code. He ducked in beneath the door as it was raising, and found the Shiv resting peacefully within. It looked like Jace and Hero had made it back after all. He shot off toward the engine room, keeping his gun raised and his eyes peeled for any sign of an enemy.

Scooting down the ladder as if it were a fireman's pole with rungs, he landed hard on his feet and slipped on something wet. Before he knew what was happening, he was down on his back gasping for breath with the wind knocked out of him. His hands slid out from under him as he struggled to sit up. He grabbed a rung from the ladder, and pulled himself up to his knees.

There on the floor in front of him was the body of Jace. He wasn't moving, and was resting in a pool of blood. Hero was crumpled in a heap near the hole they'd seen outside the ship. She slowly opened her eyes and lifted her hand to him.

"Cap...Captain?" she moaned.

He scooted over and lifted up her head, which was matted with blood. "What happened here?" he asked gently.

She blinked, as if trying to keep herself from drifting off. *"The...the T30...I tried to, to repair it."*

"The T3038? *That's* what did this?"

She nodded. *"It, it's going after our kids...."* Tears began to stream down her face. *"And...if, if it finds them....I'm afraid it's going to...to..."*

Galin looked at her in horror. "You're afraid it's going to kill them?"

Book 4

The Queen of the Black Veil

—THE PLANET NECRON—

Peter Cervantes stretched out his bruised body and gazed up at the twin moons of Necron. They lit up the surrounding world with a soft light, giving the jungle a warm, blue glow. The light tonight was just a little bit brighter than that of Earth's full moon, he thought. He gazed out toward the edge of the jungle, which for now seemed particularly quiet, except for the sounds of tree-frogs, some unidentified insects- possibly crickets, and the occasional breeze that shuffled through the canopy of leaves and vines up above.

Tonight, Peter could see the snow-covered mountains

far off in the distance. They were breathtaking, but from what he'd been told, were also a sure death sentence for anyone who tried to cross them on foot. None of the others had proof to back this theory up, but anyone with half a brain could tell it was true just by looking at them.

Off to the North, and to the West was ocean. Rumor had it that there were clean continents out there somewhere, devoid of human life, and also free of zombies. Peter had never studied the geography of this planet, which was something he now regretted, and neither had most of the people he'd gotten a chance to talk to. Those who had were still schoolchildren at the time, and the only thing they remembered was being fascinated and horrified by the planet's dark history.

Off to the south was a vast desert, which was generally agreed to be the best chance of survival for those with a mind to escape. This too was a theory that no one could verify, as once a person left the jungle they never came back, and Peter couldn't blame them. What awaited the lucky traveler on the other side? Whatever it was must be a paradise compared to the tortuous life of this jungle.

After experiencing it for himself over the last few weeks, Peter had made up his mind that he needed to get out. The only reason he'd stayed so long was to try and find Chief Joe, but with every day that passed, the prospect of that happening grew smaller and smaller. It was time to go, but it still seemed that a heaping buffet of death lay before him. All he needed to do now was select the dish he feared the least, and then hope for the best. Any death he might meet in the wilderness beyond the jungle would be better than getting eaten alive, and having any chance of escape and survival, however small, was what truly drove him.

Tom Kaiser snored softly from a short distance away. The sound was soon answered with the thud of a small stone, a tool employed by those sleeping nearby to encourage him to change positions and quiet down. Tom was an old-timer around these parts. He'd been living in the jungle for about eight months now by his own count, without managing to get himself eaten. Peter had not yet met anyone who'd survived longer, although he'd heard there were a few who'd made it for several years. That also gave him hope.

Peter yawned as he watched the moonlight shimmer in the pooled up water of the clearing down below. Even on dark nights the pools had worked well as a primitive security system, making the outskirts of the jungle one of the safest places to sleep. This place, and others like it, was where he'd been coming to bed down lately. Survival in the jungle meant becoming familiar with the best places to sleep, unless you wanted to end up as someone or something's late night snack. The thick tree-branches were an obvious choice, providing a bit of camouflage and safety from the creatures that lurked around below. Others had discovered some of these places before him, and had constructed makeshift padding or roofing to obtain what little shelter they could from the violent rainstorms, which swept through at least every other evening. Such shelters weren't too difficult to find, and Peter liked to imagine that their builders had moved on to safer territory, though he knew he was probably fooling himself.

He closed his eyes and breathed the cool night air into his lungs. It smelled earthy and wet. He was exhausted, yet his mind was racing. He found himself wondering, once again, why he'd never found a good woman and settled down. His mother had told him a million times if she'd told him once- family was the most important thing. Now he knew she was right, and although the crew of the Katara had become like family- he promised himself that once he got out of this, if he ever did- he would find a good woman and start a real family of his own. He suddenly longed for children, especially a son- someone to whom he could pass on the family name, and share stories with. Yes, his mother had always been right, and he would tell her so the next time he saw her. All that really mattered was family.

After a while, his mind began to calm, and Peter found himself reliving an adventure he'd shared with Galin and the others on the moon of Halos IV. They'd finally tracked down the wreckage of an old Boreian science vessel, and the cargo for which the Boreian government had offered a substantial reward. That was the first time they'd had a run in with Stringbean and Dagget, who'd tried to hustle them out of the find. He and Galin had ended up giving Stringbean's ship a real good whipping before the scoundrel escaped empty-handed. Those were good times.

Peter opened his eyes at the sound of splashing water. Had he been sleeping? Not for long, he knew, because the moons were in about the same place they'd been when he'd first closed his eyes.

The sound came again, a splashing of water. *Oh no,* he thought, shifting his body to look down toward the pools. That's when he saw them. Dozens of lumbering bodies came splashing through the water, headed right for them. He lay back down and hid himself as best he could, praying that no one else would make a sound.

MEXICO CITY, TEXAS- EARTH

Galin Winchester slammed down his fifth cup of coffee. Then he shot down the stairs to the ground below, and bee-lined for Ulrick, who'd been working feverishly to repair the Katara's damaged hull. The blonde hulk of a man lowered his welding torch just as the captain came up behind him.

"How's she coming along?" he asked, standing a safe distance back.

Ulrick raised his visor to better examine his work.

After a few moments he nodded, and gave the hull a loving slap. "She's ready to fly again." He hurriedly stowed his equipment, and took the piping cup of coffee that Galin offered. "How are the kids doing?"

"Jace is doing better, although he's not out of the woods yet. I don't think he'll be doing us any good for at least a few more days. Hero got off a lot easier than he did, but she's still pretty shaken up by the whole experience. She blames herself for what happened."

"Yeah, well...."

"I know, I know," Galin said with a wave of his hand. Ulrick followed him back into the ship. "I'm a bit disgusted with both of them to tell you the truth. But...on the other hand I can't say I blame her. She's a grieving wife and mother, willing to do anything to protect what's left of her family. She had her son's best interests at heart, and my kids too, for that matter."

"So, are they fit enough to travel, or are we going to have to leave them here?"

"The doctor said that Jace needs at least another forty eight hours in the regeneration chamber, but luckily he's giving us a mobile unit for the Katara. There were a few left behind by emergency response teams during the invasion."

Ulrick removed his face shield and gloves, and ran his fingers through matted hair. "It'll be nice to have one of those on board. I can think of a few times we could have used it over the years."

Galin closed the hatch and retracted the stairwell. "I've wanted to get my hands on one for a long time now, but have never been able to afford one. I guess a planetary invasion comes with its blessings after all."

"Well, lucky for those two meatheads that a doctor still lived in the area, and that the crazy old teacher lady knew where to find him. I don't think either of *us* could have saved them. Hero might have made it, but Jace would've been a goner for sure."

Galin patted his friend on the shoulder. "They were both very lucky. We all were." He thought of the death omen he'd seen while with Nicodemus in the Pneuma-Tal temple. It was agonizing knowing that someone close to you might die. Who would have thought it might happen by being shot up by an antique robot. "Well, like I said, he's not quite out of the woods yet, but I think he'll pull through okay." Galin had told himself all morning that he needed to keep a positive outlook. Maybe it would even help Jace recover.

They walked through the door into the cockpit, and Ulrick manned the starboard gun turret while Galin tossed his duster over the back of the pilot's chair. He flung himself down on the seat and hailed Boreas on the intercom. "How does everything look from the engine room?"

"As far as I can tell, Captain, everything is working fine. I must remind you again however, that I'm far from an expert on the workings of human ships."

"Hang in there. Hero and Jace will be down to help before you know it. Just keep an eye on the things I showed you, and you'll do fine. Call if you need me." Galin wasn't happy about operating the Katara with a skeleton crew, but for the time being, he had no other choice. Ulrick was next to useless in the engine room, but was a good enough pilot when the need arose, and Boreas had proven himself a useful mechanic, although he lacked experience with human ship design. They'd be all right though, as long as they managed to keep their heads low and stay out of trouble.

"I'm glad to hear you won't hold it against them," Ulrick said as Galin started up the ship. "It was a stupid thing to do, but Jace is a loyal young man, and the girl seems okay too."

"You're just a big softy," Galin told him. "But I'm glad we see eye to eye."

Ulrick tightened his fists. "I can't wait to get my hands on that robot," he huffed. "I'm going to enjoy slagging that rotten thing."

"If we can get to Necron before it does, you may have to put your revenge on hold for a while. It has a good head-start, but there's no way it can outrun the Katara." Galin lifted off the ship and turned toward the hospital. It would only take them a few minutes to get there. "We can leave this afternoon, after we get Jace and Hero situated. If everything goes as planned, we should arrive at Necron long before the T30."

Ulrick gave him an uncomfortable nod. He could tell from the look on his friend's face that they were thinking the same thing. If any of their people *had* been taken to Necron, then the robot was the least of their worries. They needed to hurry.

—SAN ANTONIO, TEXAS
THIRTEEN YEARS BEFORE—

The parking lot outside of the Jolly Jackass Pub was nearly full. Country music reverberated into the night, shaking the windows of Peter's car as he drove around scanning the vehicles. It sounded like someone was having fun in there, though this type of place was not where he came to have a good time. Ear-piercing music and the company of drunken idiots had never given him anything more than a headache. A year ago he would have said the same was true of his best friend, yet here he was in search of Galin's blue, long-bed pickup truck. He'd just about given up, and was pulled up to the road to move on when he spotted the truck parked in front of a boarded-up hair salon next door.

Pulling up next to the truck, he got out and took a good look around. This wasn't the best neighborhood, though he'd seen worse. At any rate, it was a good thing he'd gotten his buddy Joseph Stormcrow to install a custom security alarm and defense system. Anybody foolish enough to try and mess with this baby would wake up sometime the next day with a terrible headache. He clicked it on and walked toward the bar.

The stench of cigarette smoke and booze met him before he even pushed the door open, and he entered to find that the place wasn't lit up much better than the parking lot. The clacking of hover-pool balls from a room in the back was the only thing audible above the sound of the band. Peter headed straight down the bar, and found Galin sitting in the corner nursing a half empty bottle of whiskey. He sat on the stool beside him and gave an accusative frown. Galin grinned back, somewhat stupidly.

"Starla said I might find you here," he yelled as quietly as he could.

Galin shrugged. "Congratulations. You found me. Care for a drink?" He pushed the whiskey bottle across the bar.

"Thanks, but no," Peter yelled, pushing it back. Starla had tried to tell him how much her fiancé had gone down hill, tried to prepare him for what he might find, but until now he hadn't fully believed it. Galin had been missing for about a week, and he looked like he hadn't changed clothes or shaved in at least as long.

"We need to talk," Peter yelled, getting up and taking his friend by the shoulder. "Come on, this place is giving me a headache."

Galin scowled, but rose to his feet. The bartender

gave them a curt nod as Peter led him out.

Thank you, Lord, Peter thought when they got outside. Just being inside the bar for a few minutes had made his skin crawl. "Come on. I'm going to take you home." Despite Galin's protests, Peter got him in the passenger seat of his car and shut the door behind him.

"You look like crap, man. You're supposed to return to duty in two days."

Galin just stared off into the distance through the windshield.

"Starla's been worried sick about you. Why haven't you called her? This isn't like you."

Galin gave him a warning look, as if he was treading on dangerous ground. "Leave her out of this."

"Leave her out of this? What's that supposed to mean? Are you even hearing yourself?"

Galin jumped out of the car and began marching off toward his truck. Peter followed.

"She said you'd been questioned about Allen Carver's death." He grabbed Galin's shoulder and spun him around. "You got anything you want to tell me?"

Galin stared at him blankly. "Just let me go."

"Not a chance. Look, I wouldn't blame you if you had killed the guy. Couldn't have happened to a nicer man. But one way or the other, you have to let me help you. You've got people depending on you, people who love you."

"I said," Galin jerked away, "LET ME GO!"

"And I said no way." Peter grabbed him again.

Galin lunged away, and then punched Peter across the face, knocking him backward and to the ground.

"You're going to regret that." Peter jumped to his feet and planted two punches in Galin's stomach, then one to the jaw. The man dropped to the ground like a sack of potatoes. "You never could fight when you were drunk."

Peter dragged his unconscious friend to the car and threw him in the backseat, though he was tempted to put him in the trunk. "Time to sober up, whether you want to or not."

He got back in the car and headed toward Galin's apartment. He was going to have to call Starla, but it might be a good idea to get her fiancé cleaned up first. She was a good woman, and didn't deserve this. He only hoped Galin could pull himself together before it was too late for them both.

—NOW—

Tree branches snapped, and vines whipped Peter's face as he dashed across the dark jungle floor. He'd already taken several involuntary dives onto the ground; it was a good thing the dense foliage made for a soft landing. Screams filled the night air all around him, creating a nightmarish symphony from which there was no easy escape. Peter knew from experience that once that horrible music had entered one's head, it was not easily turned off again.

He stopped to help a young woman who had fallen back to her feet. A quick thank you was shrieked at him before she tore off back into the darkness. His tired feet had no more begun to move when another terrified call for help rang out off to his left. Peter pushed through the trees just in time to see a small group of zombies descend on the fallen body of a struggling man. Agonized screams pierced the air as the creatures ripped him to shreds. Peter recognized the man's voice, though he'd never heard it sound like this. It was Tom Kaiser. He rushed to help, but a few moments later the screaming subsided into a flurry of gurgled yelps. It was too late.

Curses of frustration and sorrow escaped as he turned back in the direction from which he'd just come. It was a shame; Tom was a good man, and he hadn't deserved to die like that, not that anyone did. Tom had helped Peter and many others learn to survive the dangers of this jungle. How ironic that the man's snoring had led them all into this massacre.

For several long minutes, Peter ran. He pushed himself until there was barely anything left, and eventually, the screams of those who had fallen faded into the distance. He exchanged glances with those who'd escaped the horror with him, and saw that terror remained in their eyes. Terror, confusion, regret, and sorrow. Too many emotions to name, too many to feel.

A woman stood nearby weeping, and Peter embraced her, attempting to provide a little comfort, for whatever that was worth.

Suddenly, a twinkling light caught his eye off in the distance, and a moment later there were several lights, and then a dozen more. Someone was coming toward them. Peter had been so mesmerized by the lights that he hadn't noticed everyone else slip out of sight. He quickly found a leafy hollow and covered himself as best he could, taking a position to see whoever, or whatever, was coming.

The lights came ever closer. Could it be other people? But why would they be coming toward the danger? Peter knew that the zombie's brains were too animalistic to make and use fire, but it might be the reapers. Tom had told him all about those. Reapers had the virus just like all the others, but for some reason their brains had remained untouched. They lived their lives in agony, with bodies going through a continual process of decay and regeneration. Being captured by the Reapers might be even worse than getting run down by the regular zombies.

"Hello, is anyone there?" came a quiet call when the torches got closer. As the newcomers stepped into view, Peter could see that they were normal humans. Their clothes were ragged and primitive, and their hair unkempt, and it looked like they'd been living off the land for quite some time. Most carried torches and had some type of melee weapon- a club or a spear. The others had bows and arrows. And they all scanned the jungle in a way that showed not only the caution that comes from being hunted, but a determination and hunger found only in the eyes of hunters.

A tall, scrappy man with a long grey beard stepped to the front. "If anyone's out there, come on out and show yourself. We won't hurt you, and you'd be much safer with us than you are out here on your own."

Before the man had finished speaking, Peter stepped out with his hands in the air. He saw that several others had done the same.

"That's right, come on out, you're going to be alright now."

Peter got to them first. The man nodded to him kindly, but the two women standing guard behind him were stone-faced, arrows drawn and ready. They looked him over from head to toe, as if trying to ascertain whether or not he posed any threat.

"I'm Andrew Heston," the man told him. He looked back and forth between Peter and the others. "We heard the attack, and came to try and help. I'm just sorry we didn't get here sooner."

Others continued to trickle out, until a few dozen people had gathered around the group with the torches.

"Our people are staying in a system of caves, not far from here," the man went on. "You're all welcome to come with us, and —"

"WATCH YOUR FIVE," called a woman with long black hair, which was tied up into a ponytail. Her bow twanged as she hopped a few steps back, and a zombie crumpled to the ground at her feet.

All hell broke loose as dozens of the decaying creatures came stumbling out of the trees, moaning and grunting. They lunged for those standing closest, but the castaways had been ready, and several more dropped before they could claim victims.

"FOLLOW ME IF YOU WANT TO LIVE," called a man from the opposite side of the crowd. All those who had come out of hiding tore off after him, while the rest of the group stayed to hold off the attackers.

Peter stood firm, and the man who'd been speaking threw him a spear. "Go for the brain if you can. It's the only thing that doesn't regenerate."

Peter nodded, and rushed to join the others. He threw himself between one of the creatures and a young woman who'd just released another arrow, driving the spear up through the monster's head just before it could bite her.

"Thanks," she told him. He looked up to see that it was the woman who'd fired the first arrow. She returned the favor by sending another missile into the brain of a zombie that was coming up swiftly behind him. "Come on," she said, pulling him along by the arm. "We need to circle the wagons."

Together, they ran in to regroup with the others. The

zombies continued to come, but the castaways managed to hold them back. It was clear to Peter that these were experienced fighters. They had a system and worked together as a team, guarding each other's backs and picking off their attackers as they came in one by one. By the time it was over, only one man had managed to get himself bitten.

"You'll be all right," a fellow with red hair told him. "The Doc will patch you up once we get back. You got all your shots as a kid, right?"

The bitten man assured them all that he had, and together, they headed back toward the caves.

"You fought pretty well back there," the woman told Peter. Now that he was getting a good look at her, he saw just how beautiful she was.

"Uh, yeah. Thanks. You did too. Thanks for saving my skin."

"I think you saved me first," she grinned.

He shook his head. "You saved us all, made the first kill as I recall." He held out his hand. "I'm Peter. Peter Cervantes."

She shook it. "Angelica Garcia Ramirez."

"It's a pleasure," he told her. "So, how long have you lived here?"

She laughed. "It always comes down to that, doesn't it?"

He lifted her eyebrows at her.

"I'm sorry," she said, touching his shoulder. "But

that's always the first question anyone asks. Sometimes even before names are exchanged." Her smile was a warm one. "I've been here for two years now. So have some of the others in my group. How about you?"

"I only got here a few weeks ago."

"I figured as much," she told him. "Dropped off by the Nazerazi? We heard about what those frackers did to Earth. These zombies have had a lot more to eat lately. It's made them stronger and feistier than ever."

"That's right. But why...I mean, how did *you* get here?"

"Well, contrary to popular belief, the United Earth Government *has* been dropping prisoners off here for years. I guess it's a lot cheaper to serve people up as food than it is to feed them."

Peter shook his head and cursed. "Sounds about right. I wouldn't put anything past the UEG anymore. So, uh, what are you *in* for?"

She looked him over apprehensively. "Piracy. Our crew was detained for seizing a UEG supply ship. We were going to sell the cargo off world. It was the biggest haul we'd ever attempted. We would have made a killing if we'd actually been able to pull it off."

Peter gazed back at her, not really knowing what to say.

She sighed. "I've had a lot of time to repent for the things I've done, not that anyone cares. Most of our crew was slaughtered a long time ago, there's only a few of us left now."

"I'm sorry to hear that," Peter told her.

"I am too. Most of them were good people. For pirates, that is. We weren't the killing and raping type, just thieves. But we were definitely guilty of that! The punishment doesn't exactly fit the crime if you ask me."

"Well, just think," Peter smiled. "If only you'd lived a good clean life, you might have —"

"What, ended up like you?"

Peter chuckled and nodded. "If you were lucky."

After a few hours of walking, they came to the edge of a steep cliff. The twin moons shone brightly overhead, and Peter could make out the forms of those in front of him disappearing over some hidden path through the rocks. Angelica took his arm.

"Come on, the caves are just up ahead."

She led him to the edge of the cliff and went down ahead of him. As he prepared to step down, something caught his eye on a higher edge of the cliff up above. It looked like a black figure on a black horse. He rubbed his eyes and looked again, but nothing was there. It had to have been a trick of the moonlight.

"Hey, you coming or what?" Angelica called to him.

"Sorry." He hurried to catch up. "I thought I saw something up there."

"Oh yeah? What?"

He shook his head. "Eh, it's stupid. Thought I saw someone on a horse. It must have been some shadows."

She looked back at him uneasily and took his hand. "Come on, we need to keep up with the others."

—SAN ANTONIO, TEXAS
THIRTEEN YEARS BEFORE—

Peter rolled his eyes as his mother placed another heaping plate of spaghetti onto the table and pushed it over in front of him.

"Enough already. You keep nagging me to find a wife, but every time I come over you try to fatten me up like a Thanksgiving turkey."

His sister Mara laughed. "He's right, you know. Besides, it doesn't help that you're the only Mexican woman in history who cooks more Italian food than the Italians do."

Peter put his finger over his lips. "Hey, you're going to let the cat out of the bag. She thinks she *is* Italian."

The woman ignored their comments, but reached over to pinch Peter's cheek. "I just want to see you get fed right once in a while. You don't take good care of yourself, living off of beer and crackers when I'm not around."

"Come on, I don't do that."

Mara waved her finger in front of him. "She's got a point there. I've seen your fridge. The last time I opened it up all I saw was beer, a jar of pickles, and something in a leftovers box."

"That's right," his mother declared with renewed enthusiasm. "You need to find yourself a wife who's ugly and knows how to cook. Then you'll be happy forever."

Mara laughed. "Is that what Dad did?"

"No, not many women are gorgeous, faithful, and know how to cook. He just got lucky."

"So why don't I find one just like you?" Peter asked.

"I'm one of a kind. No, you find an ugly woman with a nice butt who knows how to cook. Then you'll be a happy man."

"An ugly woman with a nice butt, huh?" Mara laughed. "Let me guess, then he can flip her over and pretend he married a super-model?"

"You've got it! You might not have inherited my beauty, but you sure got my brains."

Peter pushed out his chair. "All right, it's time to get going. You guys are getting wild, and you're starting to give me a headache."

"Nope," said Mara. "You aren't going anywhere until Jose gets here with the kids. They haven't seen you for a month."

Peter pursed his lips and scooted his chair back in. He loved his nieces and nephews, but preferred their company at places like the park. Out in the open where he could tell them to go and scream their heads off someplace else. His brother-in-law once told him that coming over to visit their house was the best form of birth control Peter would ever get.

"Oh, we're embarrassing him," his mother said. "We need to change the subject. Let's talk about your friend Galin. How is it that your best friend managed to find a willing woman but you haven't, hmm? How'd something like that happen? You're more handsome than he is, and you've got Latin charm. Galin doesn't have any Latin charm, and he's getting married. You want to explain me that?"

Mara's face brightened. "Oooh, Galin *is* a hot one, Mama. Peter, you give me his number and watch the kids for me some time. I'll take him out for a one on one bachelor party, okay. Just don't tell Jose."

Their mother burst out laughing. "Or maybe he likes older women." She turned to Peter. "You take your father to the lake and I'll teach Galin everything he needs to know about keeping a woman happy, how's that sound?"

Peter put his hands over his face. *Please, God, make them shut up for a while,* he prayed.

His sister clapped her hands together. "Oh, come on you big baby, we're just kidding. Oh, look how red he is, it's so much fun to embarrass him like this."

"All right," their mother said. "Seriously though, all four of your sisters and your brother have settled down and given us grandchildren. Now it's your turn. No rush or anything, just sometime before we die might be nice, okay?"

Peter just nodded his head and smiled. He knew from experience that it was best not to argue. He *did* want to get married and settle down someday, but he wanted to enjoy his freedom for a while first. What was wrong with that?

"Oh," yipped Mara, looking at their mother as if she'd just remembered something. "You haven't told Peter about your ghost yet!"

Actually she had. Several times.

"You wouldn't believe what I saw up in the attic a few weeks ago. It was like this big, black shadow, but shaped like a human. It looked right at me, and then disappeared behind that old stack of Space Latina magazines."

"I told you there was something supernatural living in this house," Mara told her. "I saw it lots of times when I was a kid. You never believed me then, but I told you so, didn't I?"

"Yes, I suppose you did. Guess I should have listened. That thing sure was freaky Peter, you should have seen it."

"Sounds like the two of you need to cut back on Grandma's special cough syrup," Peter told them with a smart-aleck grin. "Either that, or you've been reading too many story-books to all these kids running around here."

If looks could kill, they both would have slain him. His mother whipped away the untouched plate of spaghetti.

"Fine then, don't believe me." She marched toward the kitchen, looking back just before walking through the door. "You've got a lot of your father in you." She stuck her tongue out at him.

Once she was gone his sister turned to him, pointed her finger in his face, and gave him an immensely over-exaggerated frown. "She's right, you know. Dad never believed me either. Maybe you'll see it for yourself one day. And if you do, I hope it scares the crap out of you." She chuckled.

"I hope so too," he told her seriously, taking a swig of his sweet tea.

Mara picked a stray piece of spaghetti off of the table and threw it at him.

Yup, he thought, *she definitely spends too much time around the kids*.

—NOW—

Morning was breaking as Peter and his new companions reached the entrance to the caves. Two guards stood watching, and waiting to welcome them. They stood upon boulders that Peter knew must give them a pretty good view of the surrounding area. Rocks and boulders were all around, but off to the left there was a green valley that, as far as he could tell, would provide little cover from an attack.

One of the guards nodded to Angelica as they passed. "Looks like you guys were able to gather up quite a few newbies. Good work."

She smiled up at him sadly. "Yeah, but a lot of people died up there before we could get to them."

"It always hurts to lose people," he said, giving her a sympathetic nod. "I know how you feel, I've been there too." He gave Peter a friendly wave. "John Rodgers."

"A pleasure to meet you," Peter said, and introduced himself.

The other guard's name was Hudson Ryan. He was friendly enough, but seemed a bit more serious about his duties, and kept his eyes on a constant scan in the distance.

They walked down a path that led through the middle of the guards, and Angelica led him through a narrow entrance, which looked like no more than a darkened crack in the rock. Peter moved carefully, and had to duck in several spots, but the tunnel soon opened up into a much larger cavern. Torches hung from the walls, and the sound of trickling water echoed through the distance. A small group of people had surrounded the newcomers to greet them, and more were coming out from nooks and passages around the cave as they heard the commotion. These people all looked genuinely happy to meet new survivors.

Angelica introduced Peter to a few of her friends.

"This is Sally Bevins, and Anne Brown. This is Anne's husband Henry. This big lug is Karl Fisher. Ironically, he's probably the best fisherman we've got." They each greeted him warmly. As they all spoke, another man came and pulled Angelica aside. Peter noticed that she said something that caused the man to give him a rather odd look.

"What was that all about," he asked her as they moved on.

"That was James Locke. He's somewhat of the leader here. I told him about what you saw at the top of the cliff, the figure on the horse. He's going to want to talk to you about it later."

"All right," Peter chuckled. He didn't really know what the big deal was about seeing a shadow in the moonlight.

Angelica introduced him to a few more people as they walked, and then she took him through one of the passages in the back wall of the cave.

"Where are we going?" he asked.

"To get you something you've needed for at least a couple of weeks," she told him.

This tunnel led them on for a while, and Peter could feel the air growing warmer and moister. Finally, the path descended sharply and opened up into another cavern with dozens of dark pools. Water poured from the pools in the back into the ones up front, and exited from some hidden place that Peter could not see.

Angelica walked along the wall to the far end of the cave, where it was a little darker, and set her bow and pack down upon a waist high rock. She slipped off her shoes and immediately began to remove her clothing.

"Do you mind?" she insisted, raising an eyebrow at the attentively watching Peter.

"Sorry," he grinned, not meaning it. He turned to face the cavern wall. "So how many people are living down here, anyway?"

"Well, there were sixty two of us before, but about twenty five more came in with your group. I'm assuming most will want to stay, so that brings us in at about eighty seven."

"You've rescued people who've decided to go back out there by themselves?"

"Sure. Usually somebody who has family or friends they've gotten separated from. We have people here willing to help look, but sometimes what we're willing to offer isn't fast enough or good enough. We're always willing to help, but we didn't survive this long by being reckless or stupid."

"That's understandable."

"And then, every once in a while we have to kick someone out of here. That doesn't happen often, but it's not like we can toss anyone in jail. Being crazy or violent is a sure way to get your ticket out of here."

Peter heard her step into the pool and sink down into the water.

"Hot springs," she said. "Temperature holds at about one hundred and four degrees Fahrenheit, it's just like being in a hot tub. You coming in or what?"

By that point, Peter didn't really care what the temperature was. "Do *you* mind?" he asked, unbuttoning his shirt.

She chuckled and turned away.

He quickly undressed and began to walk down into the pool.

"Whoa, hold your horses there, big boy. That's your pool over there." Without turning her head, she pointed to the next one over, which was about four feet away.

"Of course, I knew that. Just wanted to check the temperature was all."

"Sure you did," she laughed back. "So how many people were with you when you got abandoned on the surface?"

He stepped down into the pool. The effect of the hot water relaxed him almost instantly, despite the horrible memory of the drop being brought back to mind. "I don't know for sure. A few thousand I think. I was with a friend on the ship, but we got separated in the confusion. His name's Joseph Stormcrow," he said, looking at her hopefully.

She shook her head. "Never heard of him, I'm sorry."

He shrugged. "I didn't think you would have. We were dropped a long way from here." He splashed some warm water over his face, scrubbing away at the filth.

"It was absolutely horrible. Probably the worst thing I've ever seen. Those creatures were waiting for us when we got there. I've been told that they listen for the planes."

She nodded.

He sank down into the water, so that it came all the way up to his neck. "People scattered in every direction, were dying in every direction, being torn apart by those things. I never saw Joseph after we were dropped from the plane."

"I'm sorry," Angelica said, and he could tell that she truly meant it.

"Thank you. Joseph is a good man. A smart and resourceful man, so who knows? Maybe he's okay." His thoughts wandered to all of his other friends too. He didn't know where any of them were now, whether they were dead or alive. And then there was his family. His parents, brother and sisters, nieces and nephews. Would he ever see any of them again?

The sound of voices came echoing down the passageway, and a small group of people stepped into the chamber, leading newcomers to the baths.

"You look a little disappointed," Angelica laughed. "You didn't think you were getting special treatment, did you? After all, you're sharing a bathtub with eighty six other people now."

He splashed a handful of water at her. "That's what you get for leading me on," he chuckled.

She splashed him back, smiling. "Men! You all have a one track mind, don't you?"

They waved to some of the other bathers on the opposite side of the cavern before turning to give them some privacy.

"Anyway," Angelica said quietly. "Maybe I was leading you on and maybe I wasn't. I haven't really decided yet."

He turned his head just a little too late as she got out to retrieve her clothing. "I can live with that."

Peter wasn't sure how much time had passed by the time he woke up. There was no alarm clock, nor sunlight coming in through a window to tell him he'd slept too long. He'd been sleeping on a moderately comfortable bed of leaves, which was tucked in a hidden corner of a cave containing several other such private nooks. This was Angelica's room, if it could be called that. She insisted that he lay down and rest, and that he use her bed, as humble as it was, while she went out and gathered some more material for him to make his own.

He got to his feet and attempted to rub the sleep out of his eyes. Wandering out into the open, he scanned the primitive possessions that other people had lying around. It appeared that making weapons had become the most popular pass time, obviously through necessity. Peter had to grin despite himself- this place looked like a four star hotel compared to where he'd been staying lately.

When he emerged into the common area, Angelica was nowhere to be seen, but James Locke caught sight of him and walked over to greet him. His long, grey and white beard wiggled as he walked, and with his broad, toothy grin he looked a bit like a skinny, shipwrecked version of Santa Claus.

"Sorry we didn't get to meet earlier," the man said, extending his hand. "Thing's were a bit hectic, though, weren't they?"

Peter nodded. "You could say that. Peter Cervantes."

"Oh, yes. Angelica told me. I thought I'd heard that name before, but it didn't hit me until you were already in there sleeping."

"You know me?" Peter asked, a bit surprised.

"No," James said, shaking his head so that his beard wiggled again. "But I know someone who might. Come with me."

Peter followed. Hope and relief began to build up within him. They must have found Joseph.

"Are you the same Peter Cervantes who served with a man named Winchester, on a ship called the Katana?"

"Yes, that's me. But the ship is called the Katara."

"Ah yes, my apologies. He corrected me on that as well."

"Happens all the time. So, how is Joe? Did he just get here?"

James shook his head. "I'm not talking about your friend Stormcrow. Angelica told me you were looking for him, but this is someone you might not be expecting."

"Oh. Well then, who are you—"

"Over there," James told him, pointing toward the cave entrance. "He's just getting back now from picking fruit."

A dozen or so people had just come in, and were carrying baskets full of apples and pears. Peter's eyes were immediately drawn to the one who looked most out of place. Was it a child? A little boy? Was it....

"DAVID?" Peter yelled, hardly believing his eyes. He took off toward the boy, nearly knocking over a young woman who had also gone to greet one of the fruit-bearers. David Winchester was the last person he'd expected to see.

"Uncle Peter? What—" The boy let out an involuntary humph of air as Peter threw his arms around him. A moment later they were both shedding tears of confusion and joy.

"How long have you been here?" Peter asked, pushing the lad out for re-examination, as if he couldn't believe what he was seeing.

"He arrived about a week and a half ago," James answered, walking up from behind. "We don't see many children around here, next to never actually."

Peter turned back to the boy. "How did you get here?"

"I stowed away. I saw you and Chief Joe, and I snuck into the crowd the Draconians were leading onto the ship. I thought my dad must be on there too."

"But…why were you there in the first place? At the transfer station, I mean. You'd gotten captured, then escaped, then snuck back onto the ship where you'd seen us." He was speaking while working it all out in his head. "Well, I guess it makes sense. What else were you supposed to do?"

"Where's my dad? Have you seen him?"

Peter gazed at him sadly, and shook his head. "I haven't seen him since we were taken off the Claymore. I'm sorry."

"What about Chief Joe, or anyone else?"

"You're the first person I've run into since I got separated from Joe during the drop." He went to one knee and took the boy by the shoulder. "At least we have each other now. And, we were lucky enough to run into these good people." They looked up at James, who gave a smile and a quick nod. "Don't worry, David, we'll get out of here and find your dad. I promise."

The boy nodded confidently, wiping the tears from his eyes. He'd always been a tough kid. He was going to be okay. Peter would make sure of that.

—SEVEN SISTERS ORBITAL OUTPOST, MAIA TWELVE YEARS BEFORE—

Peter Cervantes slammed a fistful of money onto the bar, drawing the attention of the Pleiadian bartender. The giant man trudged over and loomed above him. Pleiadians looked just like humans, but they had chiseled, Nordic features and stood on average about three to four feet taller. Peter had been a little freaked out around them at first, but after a while found that most were pretty mild mannered and kind.

"How about another round for me and my friend here," Peter called up to him, shifting in the oversized stool and pushing away his glass.

"You kids want a man's drink this time, or are you sticking with root-beer?"

"More of the same. If that's okay with you, Tiny."

"You've got it," he replied with a wink, taking their glasses.

"I really *am* doing better, you know," Galin said. "Having a pint of the good stuff wouldn't kill me."

Peter shook his head. "I'm not going to be the one responsible for a relapse." He reached up and rubbed the sides of his head. "You know, this Pleiadian rock music is going to drive me crazy." He jumped down, went to the jukebox, and made a few selections before returning to the bar. "A few more minutes of this, and then we'll hear something more familiar."

"Anything good?"

Peter shrugged. "No, not really, but anything's better than this."

Galin reached for his refill and nodded to the bartender in thanks. "Captain Winters once told me that he thought Pleiadian music sounded like a choir of angels singing while torturing a pond full of ducks."

"Okay," Peter laughed. "That…actually makes sense, somehow. So, how are things going with Melissa?"

"Well, that's kind of what I wanted to talk with you about." He suddenly looked a bit nervous. "She's pregnant."

Peter gave him a kind grin and nod. "Is she really? So what are you two planning to do about it?"

"I've asked her to marry me," Galin came back quickly.

Peter sighed, but continued to smile. "Are you sure that's the best idea? I mean, don't get me wrong; I really like Melissa, always have. But you two haven't exactly had a smooth relationship."

"I know that. But we can work things out." He gave his friend a serious glare. It was the same look Peter had seen a thousand times; the look Galin got whenever he thought his honor was in question.

"Okay, okay. I'm just saying, there *are* other options. You could always give the baby up for adoption, or enlist it in the Space Marines Future Warriors Program. They'd make sure the kid got a fighting chance- literally."

"The baby is my responsibility. So is Melissa." He took a swig of his root beer and broke back into a broad faced grin. "You worry too much. I'm going to be fine. I've always wanted a family, you know that."

Peter was silent for a few moments. "And what about Starla? She's the love of your life. *You* know that."

Galin's smile faded. "She's better off without me."

"But—"

"I can't even look at her without being reminded of what happened to Jamie. I blame her for it." His eyes looked pleading. "God help me, I blame her for it, at least a little. She doesn't deserve that."

"No, she doesn't. And neither do you."

"Me?" He laughed a little. "Of course I do. I'm a hundred times more responsible for it then Starla is. Don't try to tell me otherwise."

"Listen, —"

"NO, YOU listen. She doesn't deserve it. I've hurt her enough, you understand me? I'm moving on."

They were both quiet for a while.

"All right, you bastard. So when's the wedding?" Peter asked, as cheerfully as he could. "I'm going to need to put in for leave."

"I'm not sure yet," Galin said, more calmly. "We have a few dates in May that might work, but...I'll have to let you know. Listen, I wanted to ask you something. I want you to be the kid's godfather."

"Me? I'm, I'm honored, but why *me*? You know how

awkward I am around kids."

"Because I trust you. You're like a brother to me. You'd lay your life down for me, just like I would for you. Heck, both of us already have. I know you'd do the same thing for my children."

Peter nodded. "Yeah, that's true. I would."

"That's why it's got to be you. For this kid, and any others that come along, I want you to be the godfather." He took a swig of root beer. "I thought you Catholics ate up this kind of stuff."

Peter chuckled. "All right. I guess if you got yourself greased and left me with a bunch of kids I could take them over to one of my sisters' houses. They wouldn't even know the difference."

Galin grimaced and nodded. "Thanks, that makes me feel a whole lot better."

Peter called for the bartender. "Another round. Root beer for my friend, but I'll take whiskey."

The Pleiadian poured him a glass.

"Just leave the bottle."

—NOW—

David sat down beside the fire and handed Peter a large, yellow apple.

"Thanks." He took a huge bite. When was the last time he'd had an apple? Couldn't have been more than a few months, but it felt like years.

Light from the fire danced across the cavern walls around them, the air was warm, but not nearly as smoky as Peter had expected. *There must be holes up there in the ceiling,* he thought, *drawing the smoke out and into the night sky above.* He wondered if it might attract the zombies.

"So, not to be rude or anything," Peter whispered, turning to Angelica, "but is it really wise to send a kid out looking for fruit when there are man-eating freaks running around?"

"We have a system," she told him. "We send out scouts, have the route planned out, that kind of stuff. He's just as safe out there as he is in here. Besides, the zombies don't seem to wander down into the valley very often. I think the sunlight hurts their eyes. They stick pretty close to the jungle most of the time."

Peter nodded, though he still wasn't sure he liked the sound of it. James Locke strode up and sat down beside them, then placed several catfish on the rocks inside the fire pit so they could cook.

"Peter, there's something I've been wanting to discuss," he said when he'd finished. "Angelica told me that you thought you saw something last night, as your group was coming in. A black figure on a horse?"

"You've seen her too?" David barked. He looked back at James pleadingly. "I told you guys I wasn't crazy."

"We never said you were," Angelica assured him.

"Her? Who's *her*?" Peter asked, eying the fish hungrily. He hadn't had meat for nearly a month.

James ran his fingers through his beard. "It's kind of a local legend, you might say. She's called the Queen of the Black Veil. Or sometimes the Lich Queen, or the Queen of the dead."

Peter looked up from the fire. "Really? Ghost stories? You people need ghost stories in a place like this? I would think that real life would be enough to fill the need for thrills."

"It's not a ghost story," David insisted. "I've seen her three times. She wears all black clothes, and rides a black horse. Some of the others have seen her too. She just hangs way back in the distance and watches you. It's really creepy."

Peter grimaced at the boy. He'd never been one for ghost stories, and that sort of thing was not what David needed.

"Does that sound like what you saw?" James asked him.

Peter shrugged. It all made him feel ridiculous. "What I saw was…just a shadow really. I couldn't really focus on it. It looked like a black figure on a black horse, and a second later it was gone. That's all."

"It was her, I know it was," David insisted. "You'll see her again someday, and then you'll believe me."

"I never said I didn't believe you, it's just that this all sounds a little hard to swallow. Your imagination can play tricks on you sometimes, especially in a place like this. Have either one of you seen this thing?" he asked James and Angelica.

"No," she told him. "But like David said, a few others have. Their descriptions were more like yours though. David is the only one who's gotten a really good look at her."

Peter watched eagerly as James flipped over the catfish. He'd never been much of a fish eater, but his mouth was starting to water. He lovingly gave David a squeeze on the shoulder. "So tell me more about this Queen of the Black Veil. What's her story anyway?"

"She's the ghost of a mother who was stranded here with her children by pirates," David told him. "The zombies ate them all, and now she wanders around looking for her kids, but she's never been able to find them."

"David's convinced that she's after him because she thinks he's one of her missing sons," Angelica told him.

"But she *is* after me. Why do you think I'm the one who always sees her."

"But you weren't around when Peter saw her," James said, adjusting the fish. "In fact, no other children were around, you're the only kid around here, remember?"

This seemed to stop the boy in his tracks. He got a thoughtful expression and entwined his fingers on his lap.

Peter smiled at him assuringly. "Besides, where'd she

get the horse?"

"What do you mean?" David asked.

"Well, if she's the ghost of a mother dropped onto the planet by pirates, then why does she have a horse? Where'd she get it?"

David looked as though he hadn't thought of that.

"Well, it looks like the catfish are ready," James told them. "Who wants some?"

Peter threw his hand into the air and waved it around, making David laugh. They began to eat, and Angelica changed the subject, asking about how David's bow was coming along.

"Don't worry if your first few attempts don't turn out too good," she told him. "I had to make about five bows before I had one worth keeping. We'll work on it together in the morning, before you go out to gather fruit."

The boy smiled gratefully, pawing through his fish.

Soon after dinner, they sent him off to bed, and Peter wanted to hear a bit more about this ghostly queen of theirs.

"So what do the two of you think about all this?" he asked them.

"I don't know," James responded. "Like you, I've never been one for ghost stories, but it *does* seem interesting that several people have seen the same thing."

"It could be one of the zombies," Angelica suggested. "I've heard that every once in a while, one of those things ends up with an intact brain."

Peter nodded in agreement. "My friend Tom said the same thing. He called them Reapers. If they really do exist, it's amazing that the effects of the virus don't drive them insane."

James brushed through his beard with his fingers, making sure to shake out any remaining pieces of fish. "The idea of any of those creatures being able to think scares me more than anything. The mindless ones are easy enough to deal with if you keep from getting outnumbered, but to have to deal with ones who can reason and plot...."

"If Reapers do exist," frowned Angelica, "do you think they eat humans just like the others?"

"I don't know," James answered. "I just hope none of us ever has to find out."

The twin moons shone brightly overhead. One of them was full, and the other was at about three quarters. The blue light fell upon Angelica's face in a way that almost made her seem like *she* was glowing.

"I can't believe he's here," he told her. "I never expected to find any kids on this planet, much less one that I knew."

"Well, you're lucky you found each other. What are the chances?"

"Sometimes the universe seems like a pretty small

place, doesn't it?"

She smiled back at him. "Yeah, sometimes it does."

"I wonder about what happened to David's father, and the rest of the Katara's crew. Galin Winchester is one of the most slippery little devil's I know. We've gotten out of so many scrapes together; I've nearly lost count. Somehow this all feels different, though. Somehow… it feels like the end."

"I wouldn't worry too much if I was you," Angelica said, taking his hand. "Necron just tends to have a depressing effect on people. I can't imagine why." Her eyes followed his to the moons above. "But, if there's one thing I've learned on this planet, it's that there's always hope. I see it all the time."

"What do you mean?" he asked.

"Well, take you and the boy, for instance. Things like the two of you running into each other don't just happen. You were meant to find him. That *has* to mean something, don't you think?"

He shrugged. "I don't know what it means. I'm just glad it happened. Now I need to find a way to get us all off this stinkin' rock. No matter how pretty of a place it might be."

She laughed. "I've got something you might find interesting." She looked him over with feigned suspicion. "We don't usually show it to people until they've been around for a little while, but you seem trustworthy enough. Follow me."

Gladly, he thought. Following Angelica anywhere had proven to be a pleasure.

She led him back into the cave, and took a couple of fresh torches from a pile by the wall, handing one over. Most everyone was sleeping now, except for a few night owls here and there, who waved as the two went by. The passage they took this time ascended up rather sharply, and wound around like a spiral staircase.

"These caves of yours are really something else," he told her.

"Yes, they are. Maybe finding these caves was another thing that was just meant to be. We're almost there now."

The cave they entered a few moments later was already decently lit from a large window-like opening that let the moonlight in. In the center of the room was a broad table of stone, which looked like it had been carved right out of the rock. A dozen wooden chairs surrounded it.

"What is this place?" Peter asked Angelica, placing his torch in a holder to which she pointed. "A conference room?"

"Something like that. Pull up a seat."

He did. The table was covered with some artistically detailed maps. He pulled over the one on top, and after a few moments, was fairly certain he'd found the entrance to the caves they were in.

"Good work," Angelica told him. "I guess a pilot

needs to be pretty good at navigating his way around."

"It comes in handy. What's this over here?"

"That's an old homestead, ruins from back when this planet was called Bios. As you can imagine, some of the settlers were pretty wealthy people. This orchard outside the ruins is where we gather a lot of our food. And over here," his eyes followed her finger, "is the river where we caught tonight's dinner."

The next map down detailed the layout of the caves, and Peter did a double take when he saw just how extensive they were. A massive cavern, far inside the mountain, caught his eye almost immediately. "Is that a ship?" he nearly yelled.

She put her finger over her lips. "People are trying to sleep, remember? Yes, it is. But it needs a lot of work. A LOT of work, such as an engine, a navigational computer…a fuel source might come in handy."

"I might be able to help with that thing. You know, from this drawing it almost looks like a Dagger class starship, just like the Katara. There weren't many of those, though. It's probably something else. I'd really like to take a look at it and size it up for myself."

"I thought you might say that." She laughed to see him so excited. "Don't worry, you'll get your chance. With the exception of a few genuine *outdoorsmen*, everyone else here is just as eager to get out of this place as you are, believe me."

The next map down was much broader in scope. It

showed the entire jungle and some of the surrounding areas. "What's this over here, on the western outskirts of the jungle? Some kind of compound?"

She nodded. "We think it's an old science station, but the closer you get to it, the more zombies you run into. Nobody has ever been able to get close."

"There could be a lot of parts there we could use. Maybe even an intact ship or two," he told her.

She grinned and looked at him piercingly. "Duh! Believe me, if we ever get the manpower to make a break for that place, we will. But, just imagine the worst zombie attack you've seen so far, and multiply it by about a hundred, that might give you some idea of what that place is like."

"Hmmm," he scratched his chin. "So you're saying this place wouldn't be fit for a second date?"

"Second date? I wasn't aware there had been a first one."

"What do you call this then?"

"I don't know," she laughed, "babysitting?"

"Well, I have to say you're the best looking babysitter I've ever had. The nicest one too. All the others ended up locking me in the closet."

"If only caves had closets," she mused. "But it's past my bedtime, so we'll talk again in the morning. You can stay up here all night studying maps if you want to." She rose to her feet and picked up her torch.

"No, I think I'll turn in, too. I can't believe how

exhausted I am." He rose to his feet as well, and followed her out. "Listen, I want to thank you for how kind you've been to me. Showing me the ropes around here and all. I really do appreciate it."

"Don't mention it. Maybe tomorrow I can show you around a bit more. I'll be busy in the morning, but after that I'm free."

They reached the large common area cave, and she unexpectedly thrust her arms around him. "Sleep tight. I'll see you tomorrow." She let go and gave him a peck on the cheek, and then turned and walked away toward her corner of the cave. He watched her walk for a few seconds before turning toward his own bed.

Thoughts of Angelica drifted through his mind as he nodded off to sleep. She was really something. Something special. He felt happy. For the first time in weeks, he felt peaceful and happy.

The next morning, Peter woke to find that David had already gone out with some others on a fruit run. He'd hoped to check in on him, and make sure he hadn't been worrying about ghosts from their discussion the night before. Tracking down Angelica, he found her working with a few others to replenish the supply of arrows.

They chatted for a while before the subject of David came up. "I don't mean to seem like a pest, but I'm not so sure I feel comfortable with him going out to pick fruit," he told Angelica. "I mean, I believe you when you say that he's safe out there, but I'd feel a little better if I could see it for myself."

"All right. Give me a few more minutes here and then we'll take a little walk together. You can see how we do things first hand. If you're still uncomfortable with it you can keep him closer to home."

He smiled gratefully. "I'll be outside waiting, I could really use some fresh air."

She smiled and nodded, and as Peter walked away, he turned back to see that the two women beside her were watching him, giggling.

The air outside was crisp and cool. He nodded to the guards as he walked by.

"We're going to have to get you out here to take a turn sometime," one of them called down to him.

He smiled. "I'd be happy to pull my own weight."

Climbing to the top of a large boulder a few hundred feet from the entrance, he stood tall and took a good look around. A high cliff of rock rose up behind him, towering above the entrance to the caves. At the top was the edge of the jungle, he knew. He shuddered to remember the last few weeks. Off in the distance before him, a green valley spread out almost as far as the eye could see. Ant sized fruit trees speckled the horizon, and above them, snow capped mountains rose up to meet the sky. He sat down, closed his eyes, and breathed deeply.

"Beautiful, isn't it?"

The voice startled him. He looked down to see Angelica standing at the bottom of the boulder. Her bow and a quiver full of arrows was hanging across her back, and from where he was sitting he had a more than satisfying view of what was in front of her.

He smiled innocently. "Reminds me of home. I've never been to another planet so much like earth. But I guess that's because it was terraformed to be that way."

"Seems like an awful waste, doesn't it?" she said, as he slid back down off the rock. "Could be a nice place to raise a family if the surface wasn't plagued with raving lunatics."

"Speaking of that," he said. "I've been wondering, has anyone tried to have children here?" He was afraid he already knew the answer, and his expression told her so.

"Yeah, or so I've heard. Problem is, babies born here have never been inoculated against the virus. You can guess the result."

"Sorry I asked," he said, seeing the disgusted look on her face. "So, tell me more about yourself. Where are you from? Any family to speak of?"

He climbed off the rock, and they began walking out toward the fruit trees. "I was born in Tucson. As far as family goes, none that I've talked to for a few years now, obviously." She smiled. "I've got a sister and a couple of brothers. They're all good people, but not as adventurous as I am. They all ended up settling down young and having families. That kind of thing always scared me a lot more than blazing through the stars did. I guess I'm kind of weird that way."

Peter couldn't help but smile.

"What?" she asked. "Are you *laughing* at me?"

That did make him laugh. "No," he assured her. "I'm relating, actually. My family's the same way. Let me guess, your mother is always pestering you to settle down and give her more grandkids, as if she needed them."

"Close, she died about five years ago in a hover car accident, but other than that you've hit the nail on the head."

"I'm sorry to hear it. That she died, I mean."

"Thanks. It's been hard. We didn't always see eye to eye, but we really loved each other. At least everyone else gave her grandkids before she died."

Peter told her all about his family as well. There were so many similarities that it felt almost as though he already knew her family and she knew his.

"But all that's gone now, isn't it?" she said sadly. "Our families, our homes. It's always been comforting to know that life was still going on as usual back home, but now...."

Dreams are taken just as easily as they're given here on Necron, James Locke had once told her. She never imagined that even her dreams of home could be stolen.

Peter gazed into her dark brown eyes. "Now you feel lost? Broken? It all seems like some terrible nightmare, and things are never going to be the same again?"

"Yes. I wake up and everything looks different now. It's like a cloud has descended over everything." She reached over to take his hand, and grinned at him sadly. "Thanks for listening. Not many people care to hear about my big, crazy family."

"We'll exchange therapy bills in the mail," he told her.

She chuckled.

"But you know, after all my family's pestering, all the years of being judged for not settling into the same life as the rest of them, I do want a family of my own someday. A beautiful wife, not an ugly one like my mother recommended, and a reasonable amount of kids. It's what I've always wanted. I just wanted to do it when the time was right."

Again she smiled. "Funny how things work out, isn't it. I wonder if either one of us will ever get the chance?"

"Well," he said, giving her hand a squeeze, "you just never know. Life leads to some pretty interesting places."

She nodded. "And to some interesting people."

The breeze that swept over the grass was refreshing and cool, and it was nice to feel sunlight on his face. It was something he didn't get enough of when wandering through the jungle.

"Well, I can see what you mean about this being a pretty safe place," Peter said. "You could see anyone coming from miles away, and those creatures aren't exactly known for their stealth."

Angelica shook her head. "Nope, and like we talked about last night, they don't seem to like being out in the sunlight too much. We *have* run into them down here, but that seems to be pretty rare, and you always have a lot of warning."

The fruit trees in the distance had grown much larger. It wouldn't be long before they were there, but Peter still couldn't see anyone picking fruit.

"So this was an actual orchard?" he asked.

"Yeah, it was. It's gone a bit wild, and the trees have spread out. Other plants and trees have moved in, but the place has been an invaluable source of food, I can tell you that."

They soon arrived at the tree line, and Angelica led him through to the ruins of an old stone building.

"Take a look at this," she told him excitedly.

The place was humungous, and looked somewhat like a castle. Seeing it impressed Peter and depressed him all at the same time. The fortress was a testament to the pioneers who'd come to colonize this planet after it had been terraformed, but it was also a monument to the horrors that mankind was capable of inflicting upon itself.

"Something's wrong," Angelica told him nervously. "A lookout should be positioned up there," she pointed, "on that wall. I don't see anyone. He should have revealed himself to us by now."

She bounded off through the grass, and Peter

struggled to keep up with her as she led him through the ruins, around the overgrowth and onto the stone, climbing up until they finally reached the place to which she had pointed. No guard was there, but a smear of blood remained upon the rock, and trailed off the wall in the other direction.

Angelica ducked down, hid herself behind the rock as best she could, and urged Peter to do the same. They scanned the orchard below. The breeze blowing through the leaves made the whole place swish and flutter like a vast ocean of green, and the overgrowth made it impossible to see through to the ground beneath.

"Over there," Angelica whispered, pointing off beyond the trees toward the base of the mountains. A small group of people had been herded up like sheep, and Peter could make out a boy among them. A black figure on a black horse was before them, and two robed guards stood positioned behind.

—THE STARSHIP KATARA
EN ROUTE TO NECRON—

Galin watched the scanners anxiously as the stars blasted by on the view screen. He flipped on the com.

"All right you guys, I've finally got the slaggin thing in my sights. It's on a direct course for Necron, but we should overtake it in about ten minutes. I'm a bit tempted to intercept it and blast the thing to bits."

Hero's voice came back across the com. "That's not a good idea, Captain. That thing has highly advanced—"

"I know," Galin interrupted. "I know all about how much firepower the damned thing has. I said I was tempted, not that I was going to do it."

Ulrick came in from the door behind him. "I say we swing in behind that thing and send a torpedo right up its—"

"No," Galin told him. "I feel the same way, and maybe we'll get our chance. But first things first, and Hero's right about that thing's defenses. We can't afford to jeopardize our mission."

"Well, if that's the case, you might want to change course a bit and give the thing a wider berth. If it hasn't picked us up yet, it'll do so soon."

Galin looked back at the radar just in time to see the robot change course, headed for a position in front of their bow. "Uh, I think it's already got us. Looks like it's moving to intercept."

"Let him come then," Ulrick growled, hopping into the starboard gun turret.

Galin flipped on the com. "Boreas, Hero, get ready for some action. It looks like the T3038 is making a move for us. I'm changing course to try to avoid him, but get ready just in...hold on a minute. It looks like he's returning to his original trajectory."

Ulrick growled again, this time in disappointment.

"Maybe it just wanted to get a closer look at us," Galin told him, a bit confused.

"I'll bet it sized us up and decided not to try anything," Ulrick laughed. "At least it's smart enough to—"

A series of explosions suddenly rocked the ship. The shields flickered and the power went out as the Katara dropped from warp. A few seconds later the emergency lights kicked on, along with the red alert siren. Galen reached over and flipped the siren off. "WHAT THE FRACK JUST HAPPENED!" he demanded from no one and everyone.

Hero's voice came back over the com. "I was about to ask you the same thing. Did we engage the T30?"

"No," Galin barked. "The thing's been way ahead of us the whole time." He watched as it flew out of range on the radar screen, and then turned to Ulrick. "Keep an eye on things up here. I'm going to the engine room."

Galin fumed as he made his way through the halls of the ship. He racked his brain, trying to figure out what could have gone wrong. Had they been attacked? Or maybe the ship hadn't been repaired correctly in the first place. Maybe Boreas' and Hero's unfamiliarity with the Katara's systems had caused them to overlook something or perform an improper repair. It sure felt like the ship had been *hit* with something though.

As Galin began to descend the ladder into the engine room, it suddenly hit him- EMP caltrops. He'd run over them once before. It had been long ago while serving in the space Navy, while pursuing pirates who'd been harassing civilian supply ships around Saturn. The caltrops had completely knocked out the electrical systems of the fighter he'd been in, including life support. If help hadn't been nearby, he wouldn't have lasted very long. Luckily, the Katara had defenses against such weapons, but that didn't mean the ship had escaped unscathed.

"What's the damage?" he asked as he dropped to the metal grating, where Hero and Boreas awaited.

Hero looked like she was going to start bawling. "We're still trying to assess the damage, but it doesn't look good. At the very least, we won't be going anywhere for a while. What happened up there anyway?"

"I'm pretty sure we were hit with EMP caltrops."

"EMP caltrops?" She said it as if he told her a unicorn had charged the ship. "The T30's spec sheets didn't say anything about being equipped with those."

"Apparently, there were a lot of things that spec sheet didn't warn us about."

She looked back at him as if he'd slapped her.

"Look, I didn't mean anything by that. I know you were only doing what you thought was best by trying to reprogram that thing."

Then she began to bawl. "I, I just don't know what went wrong. I've gone over my work a dozen times, and still can't find any errors."

"This may explain things," Boreas told them, as he pulled something from the processor panel. "It appears that whatever that robot hit us with has destroyed the Katara's C.P.I.C."

Galin and Hero rushed over to take a look.

"This isn't the ship's proper unit," Hero said accusingly. "The Draconian's must have replaced it back on the Claymore."

"Look at this piece of junk." Galin scowled, taking the unit to examine it more closely. "No wonder it got shorted out so easily. The unit I had installed would never have gotten fried by a couple of EMP caltrops. You two didn't know anything about this?"

Boreas began to go over the rest of the processor panel for damage. "No Captain. Someone must have switched the units before Hero and I were sent to make the other repairs."

"Well, it makes sense," Galin told them. "They would have wanted to examine the Katara's C.P.I.C. They'd want to download and scan it to see what they could find, bypass any security overrides, and prevent any remote takeover of the ship. It's a pretty standard procedure to switch units after capturing and detaining an enemy ship, but things got so hectic back there, it never even crossed my mind to check."

Hero grimaced. "I guess we're pretty lucky the Nazerazi didn't try to take remote control of the ship after we'd escaped."

"They may have," Galin said, "but we've got a few tricks up our own sleeve. Me and Chief Joe put in safeguards to prevent that sort of thing a long time ago."

Boreas put his hand on Hero's shoulder. "This must be why the T3038 attacked you and Jace, and why it attacked us again a few moments ago."

Hero looked at him as if he'd just pardoned her from the chair. "Oh my God, you're right. He must have picked up the core's energy signature and thought the Katara was a Nazerazi ship. I programmed him to destroy any Nazerazi that got in his way. It's actually been taking it pretty easy on us."

"Perhaps it's confused," Boreas suggested. "It probably couldn't figure out if we were friends or enemies, that's why it hasn't killed us, but rather has sought to disable us."

Galin took Hero's hand and gave it a pat. "It wasn't your fault after all. And it looks like we don't have to worry about that thing gunning for our kids. It actually *is* going to try and save them."

Hero placed her hand over her stomach and moaned in relief. "So what are we going to do now? We aren't going anywhere without a C.P.I.C. Even after we repair everything else that took damage, we'd still need another four or five experienced crew members to fly the ship safely without that core."

Galin let out a long, deep breath. "Luckily, we have a

spare."

Hero thought he must be joking. "You have a *spare* central processor and intelligence core?" Those cores usually cost about half as much as the entire ship.

"Chief Joe found the ship's original core buried under some old equipment right over there in that storage closet. We haven't had a chance to examine it yet, but it appears to be undamaged."

"Aren't those cores usually taken and destroyed when a vessel gets decommissioned?" Hero asked.

Galin nodded. "Plugging that thing back into the ship could be a risk. We have no idea what kind of information or commands are still loaded on it, and there's no way to wipe it or reprogram it out here in space."

"I could reprogram it," Hero said excitedly, but then her smile weakened. "But not until after it's been installed. That kind of defeats the purpose."

Galin sighed. "Well, it's a chance we'll have to take. But the rest of the damage needs to be repaired first." He flipped on the com so Ulrick could hear him. "All right everyone, here's the plan. Boreas and I are going to take the Shiv and head for Necron. We'll be able to get there in less than a day. Hopefully, that robot does most of our work for us; he's built to track things down, after all. If he finds anyone, we can make a fast pickup and be back within a couple of days. Hero and Jace- when Jace wakes up, will work on repairing the Katara.

Ulrick, you're going to stay here to guard the ship just in case. This section of space is known for pirates, and things might have gotten worse now that Earth has fallen. It looks like the camo shield is still operational, but I'd rather be safe than sorry."

"I don't like the idea of you two going to Necron by yourselves," came Ulrick's voice. "Are you sure that's a good idea?"

"No, in fact I think it's a horrible idea, but I don't see any other way right now. I'm not about to send out an S.O.S. in pirate infested space, and I'm not going to abandon any of our people to the horrors of Necron."

Hero and Boreas just looked at him in silence.

"If anyone has a better idea, I'm willing to hear it."

Nobody spoke. As difficult as the situation seemed, there was nothing else to be done.

"All right, let's get moving," Galin said. "Ulrick, meet me in the docking bay. We're going to need guns. Lots and lots of guns."

The Shiv was all loaded up, and everyone knew what part they had to play. Galin handed Hero the case with the Katara's original C.P.I.C.

"For some reason, the Nazerazi really want this ship. I don't know why, but some of the answers might be on this core. Make sure you put it someplace safe, and don't install it until we get back, unless you have no other choice."

She nodded dutifully and handed over a data pad displaying the completed damage report. "It's not too bad really, but it's going to take me about four days to complete the repairs on my own. If Jace is in any condition to help tomorrow morning when he comes out of the regeneration chamber, then things will move a little quicker."

"Just do your best," he told her. "Who knows, maybe Boreas and I will be back before too long to help." He doubted it though.

"Good luck down there, Captain. I really hope you find your friends."

"I hope so too. And then we can get on with finding our kids. At least wherever they are, they're a lot safer than anyone down on Necron. Take good care of my ship for me. Make sure you patch her up right."

"I will."

Ulrick stood beside her. Galin could tell he was itching to come along.

"I need you here. Make sure you keep your eyes wide open. If things get too hot and you guys have the ship repaired, then don't be afraid to high tail it out of here until you can come back with some extra hands. And don't worry about Boreas and me. We'll keep our heads low, and won't make contact with anyone on Necron until we find some friendly faces. This is all about stealth, we're not going in to launch an attack."

Ulrick's face was red, but he held his tongue and clapped his friend on the shoulder. "Just be careful. If it comes down to it, shoot first and ask questions later."

Galin just smiled. There was no need to tell Ulrick to do the same. He turned and climbed into the Shiv, and closed the hatch behind him. After a few moments the bay doors opened and they headed out into space. He set a course for Necron, and let out an uneasy sigh.

"Don't worry, Captain. We'll be alright."

"For some reason it's not us I'm worried about." He didn't know why, but he had a very bad feeling about leaving the Katara behind. He clicked on the rear camera and watched his ship grow smaller, until it faded into the stars as the camo shield was engaged.

—NECRON—

Peter and Angelica moved through the trees as fast and quietly as they could. Peter hadn't run like this since his days at the Academy, and hoped he wouldn't drop dead before they could get where they were going. The air was cool and fresh, and smelled of the rotting apples that had fallen down all around them. Peter shuttered to think about what fate might be awaiting David and the other captives if they couldn't find a way to help.

"None of them are warriors," Angelica called, as if reading his mind. "The people who come out here to gather fruit are usually the weakest members of our community. They won't be able to help us much in a fight."

By the time they reached the edge of the orchard where they'd seen the group gathered, it had turned and was moving back toward the cliffs. They were probably about a quarter of a mile ahead. The two robed men and the black figure on the horse were ushering the crowd off like cattle.

"It doesn't look like anyone's been hurt yet," Peter observed as he scanned the area. They stopped to catch their breath. "Except for the lookout I mean. I hope he's still alive."

Angelica clenched the quiver of arrows hanging at her side. "Did you happen to bring along any weapons?"

Peter held up his fists. "I was the middle-weight boxing champ for three years straight back in college. These'll have to do for now. But maybe it won't come to that. Let's try the diplomatic approach first."

"The diplomatic approach? Seriously? With those *things*?"

"We're still not exactly sure what those *things* are. Just make sure you're ready with that bow of yours, okay?"

She nodded, but looked like she might be sick. "Let's get going then."

They took off running, and it wasn't long before one of the robed guards saw them. The black figure on the horse stopped the group and waited for the two to approach.

"So much for any element of surprise," Angelica mumbled.

As they got closer, Peter took the lead, and Angelica remained a dozen feet behind him, holding her bow in her left hand and her right hand resting on her quiver.

Now Peter could see the black figure clearly. It was indeed a woman, all dressed in black clothing, which matched the color of pitch, the same as her horse. A black veil covered her face, and not a bit of flesh could be made out beneath her clothes. It was no wonder that people thought she was a ghost, though she looked solid enough now. David was seated in front of her on the horse. The two guards accompanying the woman were fully covered as well, although their robes were grey and tan. They raised blaster rifles as Peter approached.

"UNCLE PETER," David cried when he saw them. The boy attempted to leap from the horse, but the veiled woman grabbed ahold of him. She pulled him in close and held on tightly.

Peter fixed his gaze upon the woman and stared at her unflinchingly, and for a few moments the only sound upon the plain was the wind blowing through the grass.

"I think you're holding something that doesn't belong to you," Peter said.

As the woman behind the veil held his gaze, he heard her chuckle. "Take them," she said softly to her guards.

One of the robed men circled around behind them, his rifle held steady at Angelica's chest. The other came around to the side of Peter.

"Let's go," the man told Peter, motioning toward the other captives with his rifle.

Peter dropped, sweeping the man's legs out from beneath him. A shot from the blaster rifle escaped into the air, headed harmlessly for the clouds above. As soon as the guard hit the ground, Peter was on top of him. He pulled the man over and used him as a shield, just as his partner got a shot off. The blaster bolt landed square in the guards chest, and the smell of sizzling flesh wafted across Peter's nose as he grasped for the dead man's rifle.

The remaining guard took aim at Peter's face, prepared to take his shot, and screeched in pain as a bow came whizzing through the air to crack him across the head. Angelica felt her weapon break, but the sound it made told her that something in the guard's face had broken with it.

Another blaster shot sounded across the valley, echoing off the cliffs as the dead guard fell to join his companion upon the grass.

Peter stood to face the woman sitting upon the horse, the dead guard's blaster rifle in his hands. He could sense what the lady was thinking, how easy it would be to turn and bolt off with the boy. He wouldn't dare shoot her for the risk of hurting him.

"Don't try it," he told her. "I won't shoot at *you*, but

I'll drop that horse. I'd rather see the boy's arm broken than have him eaten alive by freaks."

She slowly turned the horse to face him more directly. "I have no intention of harming this boy. My only desire is to protect him." Her voice was surprisingly soft and motherly. She didn't sound like a ghoul.

All of the other captives began making their way to Peter's side. "If that's the truth, then let him go."

"No," she said coldly. "He belongs to me."

"Who are you?"

She did not answer.

"Are you one of the reapers?" Peter demanded. "A zombie with a working brain?

Again she said nothing, but Peter could feel her eyes scanning him from beneath the black veil.

"You aren't taking the boy, or anyone else either. If you're hungry, go pick yourself some apples."

She remained silent for a few moments before speaking. "If you want the boy, then put the guns down and come get him."

"Do you think I'm stupid?" He lowered his rifle, and motioned for everyone else to move back, which they did. Only Angelica remained beside him, stubbornly holding her ground, as well as the other rifle.

"The girl too," the veiled woman insisted.

"It's all right," Peter told her. "Head over with the others. You can cover me from there."

She looked at him pleadingly, and opened her mouth

to say something, but then decided against it. Reluctantly, she backed up to stand with the others a few dozen feet away.

"Come closer," the woman in black told him, and he did.

"Just give me the boy, and I'll let you ride away unharmed," he said, not sure whether he really would or not. He was a man of his word, but whatever or whoever this woman was would most likely come back with more guns. If she didn't know about the caves already, she could probably find them without too much trouble.

With the boy held firmly in her grasp, the woman slowly dismounted. "I *know* you," she told Peter weakly, almost as if she wasn't sure about it.

Although she stood just a few feet away, he still couldn't make out her features beneath the veil. "Who are you?" he asked her again, more softly.

"Yes, I know you. I remember your face." she was beginning to speak through heavy breaths, as if thinking about it pained her.

"Why do you want the boy?" Peter pressed her. "Let him go, he's only a child."

David gawked at him nervously, but held his tongue.

"I mean the boy no harm. I will make him like me, and he will be my son. He belongs with me."

Peter raised the rifle and pointed it at the woman's head, but something stopped him from pulling the trigger. "Take that veil off your head," he commanded her. "I want to see your face."

She hesitated for a moment, then reached up, and began to pull the black cloth from her head. He imagined what waited underneath- the gruesome, rotting remnants of what had once been a human face. A part of him had pitied those zombies he'd seen in the jungle, their bodies in a constant state of decay and repair. He couldn't imagine the pain it would cause. Their insanity was a blessing. But to live through the disease and know what was happening? He couldn't imagine a fate more horrible.

Peter braced himself as the remaining stretch of cloth slid off the woman's head, and his stomach tightened to see what had been hidden beneath. Her face was beautiful. It was flawless, except that it looked cold and somewhat blue. She stared back at him with soft, worried eyes.

"I...I don't understand." His entire body began to quake, whether through happiness or fear, he could not tell. "J...Jamie?" Here was his best friend's sister, a woman who he'd seen buried almost fifteen years before, standing in front of him. She didn't look a day older than she had the last time he'd seen her. He didn't know whether to shoot her or throw his arms around her, yet he felt the blaster rifle drop to the ground, and his leg take a step toward her. "Why are you...HOW are you here?"

She stared at him through those worried, confused eyes. "Jamie? Yes, that was my name. I knew you then. We were friends. I loved you."

David slipped away and darted to Peter, throwing his arms around the man's waist. Peter squeezed him reassuringly, and dragged him along as he walked toward Jamie. A tear escaped down his cheek as he embraced her.

"I don't understand this, but it's going to be alright now. YOU'RE going to be alright now...." He struggled for words, not knowing what to say, not really grasping what was happening, or why.

He never saw the knife, and only felt it for a moment as it was thrust up beneath his chin and into his brain.

The lifeless body of Peter Cervantes fell to the ground, and Jamie watched as red ribbons began to flow through the green blades of grass.

Christmas colors, she thought. *And I've been given a present, too. Christmas hasn't come for years now, but this feels a bit like it.* She dragged the screaming boy back onto the horse, and sped him off toward the cliffs.

Angelica ran after her, crying out in fury and anguish. She squeezed two shots off before getting herself back under control.

"NO!" shouted an old man from behind her. "They're too far, you might hit the boy."

She had realized that before he'd said it, and dropped the rifle to the ground. Sobbing as she approached the body, Angelica knew what awaited her. She'd seen it happen, seen him fall, but she didn't want to believe it. Out of all the friends she'd lost, all the people she'd seen die on this miserable planet, this one felt the worst.

Dreams are taken just as easily as they're given here on Necron, James Locke had once told her. As she stooped over the body of this man she'd just met, this man she had already started to love, she knew that her friend had been right, and she hated him for it.

Book 5

The Wrath of

Black-backed Jack

—THE STARSHIP KATARA—

Ulrick spun the ship around to confront the two vessels coming up behind him. They were fast, but he was faster, and a few moments later they'd each been reduced to stardust. He engaged his thrusters and flew through the asteroid belt, launching a frontal assault upon the mothership as it continued to spew out fighters. It was a bold move, especially since he'd missed the last weapons upgrade, which had bounced across the screen.

"SLAG IT ALL," he shouted as a laser zipped from the mothership's starboard cannon, sending his final vessel careening into a nearby asteroid where it was incinerated in a rather unrealistic, yet impressive explosion.

Ulrick tossed the data-pad down into the co-pilot's chair. It had only been about six hours since Galin and the Draconian had left for Necron, but he was already bored out of his wits. He gazed out at the stars, and with two fingers combed out his thick, yellow mustache.

If he couldn't shoot something, maybe he'd try to get a little sleep. Closing his eyes and leaning back in the pilot's chair, he tucked his hands beneath his head like a pillow, and tried to clear and calm his mind. It was only then that he realized just how tired he actually was. Sleep was nearly upon him when Hero's voice came over the com, startling him back to reality.

"Ulrick, you still awake up there?"

"Yeah," he growled in annoyance. "What is it, kid?"

"I'm almost done repairing the environmental control system, but I'm going to need to divert power from the camo shield for a few minutes. Is that alright?"

Ulrick looked over the radar and scanner panels. Everything looked just as peaceful and calm as it had for the last few hours; they appeared to be all by themselves.

"Now's as good a time as any. We aren't going to have to drop the main shields are we?"

"No, just the cloak. That should give me the juice I need to finish this up. I'm going to need about ten minutes."

Ulrick reached up and disengaged the camo shield. "Alright, the ship is de-cloaked. After this we should both try to get some sleep. Just let me know when you're finished, okay?"

"I will. Thanks."

Ulrick leaned back in the chair, assuming the same position he had before, and gazed out into the stars again. For a moment, he thought about picking the game back up, he'd been trying to beat his high score for hours now, but then he decided against it. He'd had his tail kicked enough for one night, and it would only get him all wound up again. Maybe it would be a nice change to just sit and watch the stars twinkle for a while. Perhaps it would be 'relaxing', just like Galin always said it was.

At first, it was a little too relaxing, and Ulrick felt his eyelids begin to drop, but then they shot back open when the stars began to shimmer and shift in a way that could only mean one thing. Ulrick sat up in his seat and gawked as the much larger ship de-cloaked before him. It was a pirate ship. This particular vessel was one of a kind, designed to look something like the old sailing ships from Earth's past. It even had solar sails, which was an outdated and semi-useful technology, and bore the figurehead of a big-busted wench with an eye patch and coy smile. Some of these space pirates took the title a bit more seriously than others.

Ulrick felt his heart skip a beat. He'd never seen this ship in person, although he recognized it almost instantly. He'd heard tales about the thing from one end of space to the other. It was called *The One-eyed Whore,* and its captain was the infamous Black-backed Jack, who claimed to be a direct descendant of Blackbeard the pirate.

The communicator began to ring and blink, and Ulrick reached over to click it on. The image of a red-faced, black-bearded man popped onto the view screen. His face was jolly and maniacal, and dark smoke rose up from his beard, immersing his face in a greasy fog. The only thing missing was a big, black hat.

"Captain Galin Winchester, I presume?" he asked in a calculated voice.

"That's right," Ulrick told him. "And who, may I ask, are you?"

The pirate laughed. "You're a terrible liar, Ulrick von Liechtenstein. And I can tell by the look on your face that you already know who I am. So much time is wasted with introductions, don't you think?"

The ship quaked, and Ulrick knew a tractor beam had snagged them. A few moments later, Hero came over the com.

"Ulrick, did you just feel something? Some kind of turbulence?"

"I'll get right back to you. Hold on." He clicked off the com.

"That's right, Sweetcheeks. You and that little boat of yours are coming with me. The Nazerazi Alliance has put quite a price on your heads. I don't know why, but they sure want that little pisspot you call a starship."

"I thought you were a pirate, Jack, not a bounty-hunter. You want to risk your reputation to get a paycheck?"

Again he laughed. "You're bold, I like that. You'd make a good pirate. You *would* have anyway, but now you'll probably rot in some Nazerazi prison for the rest of your miserable life."

"Get slagged."

The pirate chuckled, but this time Ulrick could see the fury hidden behind his smoky, contorted face.

"As much as I love a good fight, I'd appreciate you coming along quietly. I'll make you a deal. You and whoever else is on there, abandon ship, and I'll let you go quietly."

"You're not a very good liar either," Ulrick grunted. "You want this ship? Then you're going to have to work for it. That boat of yours may be big, but you don't have the muscle to drag us all the way home if we resist. Besides, your reputation precedes you. Rape the woman and drink the wine. Leave no prisoners. Those things sound familiar, don't they, you lice-covered freak?"

Black-backed Jack just sneered at him. "All right then. We'll do things the hard way. I'm coming for *you* personally. Prepare to be boarded."

His image disappeared from the view screen, leaving the busty, one-eyed wench smiling back at him from the front of the other ship.

Ulrick got back on the battle com. "Hero, you need to find a good place to hide, RIGHT FRACKING NOW!"

William Marshal alighted on the grass to examine the DNA sample, which his long range scanners had located. He'd been able to find the sample remarkably fast, and supposed that the humans might call such a thing 'being lucky'. William wasn't sure how much damage he'd inflicted on the starship that was chasing him, but the attack would only delay them, and then they would most likely resume their pursuit.

He still didn't know why he had been re-activated on a ship that emitted both Earth and Nazerazi energy signatures, although he had searched for answers among his data files. This confused him, and he hoped to investigate the situation further, but for now, his mission was clear- to locate the missing Earthlings and contact a ship called the Katara in order to report his findings.

DNA analysis was confirmed. This was the blood of Peter Cervantes. William scanned the horizon in all directions. Not far away, he picked up another, smaller sample, close to a large cluster of apple trees, and further down and amidst the trees, another. These were just little drops of blood, but they were enough to form a trail.

The robot strode through the grass, continuing to scan the area as he went. It was remarkable to see so many of Earth's species on a foreign planet. He scanned his database to find out why. Terraforming. Interesting. His original programing had directed him and the other T3038s to go out and search for inhabitable planets, or those that might be suitable for terraforming, although the process had not yet been perfected. Apparently, that had changed since the day of his original programming. He still had much to integrate into his memory banks.

The trail led through the apple trees and into the ruins of an old human structure. Another large sample of blood was detected upon one of the walls, but this belonged to some other human, not one of those he was looking for. The drips of Peter Cervantes' blood continued through the ruins and out the other side, eventually ending close to a willow tree beside a small river.

William Marshal heard the sound of the water flowing across the rocks, and the breeze blowing through the trees. He watched the sunlight sparkle across the bubbling waves, and observed the fish swimming about. One of them charged up and caught a water spider that was skating around the reeds. It was all very fascinating. William had never been to a river before, and could easily spend hours here observing the hundreds of forms of life he'd already seen. Unfortunately, he had other matters to attend to first.

Walking to the place where the last bit of blood had fallen, the android observed a patch of recently disturbed earth. That was odd. Scouring his memory banks, he quickly deduced that this must be a grave, and scanned the area beneath the surface. The body of a human male had been buried approximately five and three fourths feet below. Identity confirmed. This was the body of Peter Cervantes. Perhaps he should dig up the body and take it with him. No, he decided after reviewing the data on human burial customs, this would not be an acceptable thing to do. He would catalog his findings and report the location of the remains, nothing more.

With one requirement of his mission completed, he would now need to move on to the next. Upon the discovery of Peter Cervantes, the probability of finding Joseph Stormcrow on this planet had just gone up by 23.78 percent. Perhaps he had even been the one who'd buried his friend. William scanned the area once more, doing a thorough search for any sign of the man's DNA. He could find none, but there were a few other samples nearby. The most prominent was that of a human female, approximately thirty-four years of age. He knelt down and picked up a strand of her hair. Perhaps she might know where to find Joseph Stormcrow. Locating the woman would be a good place to start, statistically speaking. He ran her DNA structure through a search of all databases, and a moment later her image came up.

-Angelica Garcia Ramirez-

-Arrested and convicted of piracy and other high crimes against the United Earth Government- June 17 2386-

-Details classified-

Now he had a face and a name as well. That might make the search easier if he happened to run into living humans.

William soon found a trail composed of footprints and damaged blades of grass, and began to follow it across the plain. Before long, a rocky cliff rose up in the distance, and above it, his sensors picked up a jungle. He had never been to a jungle before. Perhaps if he were lucky the trail would lead there. He might even get to see a panther.

The One-Eyed Whore had come about sideways, and Ulrick watched as a long line of hatches opened up along its midsection. A dozen plasma cannons slowly emerged, and then charged up with a bright aqua colored light. As much as he was itching to attack, Ulrick knew there were other things he had to do. The Katara could have put up a good fight if it was fully manned and operational, but firing on the pirates now would only be a waste of time. The ship was a sitting duck, and Black-backed Jack knew it. Ulrick rushed from the cockpit, and charged down to the docking bay, where the regeneration chamber awaited.

Jace was supposed to stay in the thing for another

five hours, but if the pirates found him like this they'd drag him out and use him for target practice, and that was if he got lucky. Ulrick reached up and powered down the chamber, then he opened it up and lifted out the unconscious young man, flinging him over a shoulder and heading for a hidden storage compartment under the floor behind the stairs. The room began to rumble and shake as plasma balls bombarded the shields.

"Slag it all," Ulrick mumbled as he struggled to stay on his feet. Reaching the compartment, he lifted up the grating and reached for a stack of moving blankets. Soon, he'd fashioned what looked like a make-shift cradle, and he lowered Jace down into the hole. "Hang in there, kid." With any luck, the kid would sleep through the whole thing; after all, he still had plenty of sedatives running through his body. When everything was over, Ulrick could put him back in the chamber to finish his treatment.

Now it was time to check on Hero. Bounding up the stairs, Ulrick charged through the hallway that led to the kitchen and into the common rooms. When he reached the lounge, the ship rocked so hard that he was thrown across the coffee table, which flipped over and crashed back down on top of him. His head was pounding as he got back to his feet and stumbled to the service passage that led to the engine room.

"The shields are down to seventy six percent," Hero cried as he came bolting down the ladder.

"I thought I told you to find a place to hide."

"I can't do that," she protested. "If I don't stay down here to —"

"They don't want to destroy the ship, they need to take it in one piece, but they may not have the same intentions for us. Once our shields are down they're going to come on board, and believe me, you don't want these guys to find you."

He picked her up under one arm and carried her away from the shield generator circuits. Where was he going to hide her? No place in here would conceal her well enough.

"PUT ME DOWN," she demanded in a scared voice.

"Shush, girl. I'm trying to think." If anyone knew how to search a ship, it was pirates, and he didn't have much time to hide her. Jack had already heard the girl's voice, and knew she was onboard. He and his men would stop at nothing to find her so they could have a little fun. These were the worst kind of outlaws, Ulrick knew. If Hero survived a run-in with them, she would probably end up wishing she hadn't. Where could he possibly hide her where they might not look?

Then, an idea struck him. He wasn't sure it was a good idea, in fact it terrified him, but it might be the only way. He ran back to the shield generators and ejected the camo shield unit.

"What are you doing?" she squealed helplessly from beneath his arm.

He scanned the room frantically as the ship continued to rock beneath them. "I need a portable power supply. Do you have one?"

"Over there," she pointed to an equipment bench in the corner. "But what are you—"

"You'll see. It's a little trick Galin taught me." He grabbed the power supply in mid-air as the ship rumbled from another blast. "Now get your butt to the docking bay," he told her, and set her back down to her feet near the ladder. "We don't have much time."

As he pulled the space-suit helmet down over his head, Ulrick felt the Katara shake beneath his feet again, this time more roughly than it had done before. He'd learned long ago what it felt like when shields collapsed, and he also knew that the last plasma ball had been fired. The next time the vessel shook it would only be seconds before they had unwanted visitors.

The final piece of his barricade, an empty steel crate, was pushed into position before Ulrick ducked down behind it and lifted his favorite heavy-repeating blaster rifle onto his shoulder. "It's just you and me now, Sally," he said to the gun. "If they want to take our ride, they're going to have to bleed for it."

He lied there waiting, watching the docking bay door like a hawk and refusing to scratch an increasingly itchy trigger finger.

Only a few moments passed before a harpoon came ripping through the bay door. Once inside, the head of the missile split apart and spread out in every direction, fastening to the door and creating an airtight seal. Where the unmolested bay door once stood, an open corridor now connected the two ships.

Smoke began to pour from the opening, and Ulrick growled out a chuckle. A lot of pirates employed such tactics to make themselves look evil and sinister, and strike fear into the hearts of their victims. The only thing all these stupid pirate tricks did to Ulrick was make him laugh. He already knew just how evil these scum were; he didn't need any black smoke to tell him that.

A concussion grenade came rolling out of the passage, and Ulrick shot it before it could stop. The explosion had no effect on him through the helmet. *Amateurs*, he told himself, although he knew they weren't.

Pirates came charging out of the hole as if someone had turned on a faucet, and Ulrick's repeater fire flew to greet them. He wasn't expecting so many men, and it was clear that they hadn't expected to meet such resistance. He cut through the assailants as easily as he might chop through vegetables, and a few minutes later, as the red mist cleared, Ulrick counted the bodies of nearly two dozen men, which littered the bay floor. They were strewn from the entrance to the edge of his barricade, but he knew that this had only been the first wave. Checking the power source on his repeater, he saw that it was still three quarters of the way full.

Moments later, another horde of pirates came charging through the corridor. These had personal shield devices, which flashed and flickered as Ulrick unleashed everything he had upon them. Most were able to return fire as they dodged over the bodies of their comrades, though some slipped and fell upon the blood covered floor. One man slipped and hit the ground so hard that Ulrick heard his neck snap; his bulky body and legs bent over on top of him like a pretzel.

Ulrick's body shook gently at first, as a few of the pirates' shots found their mark. His space suit's shielding flashed furiously as more and more of his attackers locked onto him.

Wait for it, Ulrick told himself as a line of the men advanced. *Wait for it, wait for it....* He stopped firing and entered a sequence of numbers into the control pad on his left wrist. The blaster bolts and lasers continued to land, and his forehead began to drip with sweat from the heat building up in his suit. His shields couldn't take much more of this. *Wait for it,* he thought, as the pirates advanced.

Ulrick engaged the command, and a sizzling, blue force field appeared from the floor to the roof, cutting another six pirates in half. Ulrick jumped to his feet and whipped off the space helmet, drawing a deep breath of the cooler air into his lungs.

He looked over to see Black-backed Jack staring at

him from the entrance to the passageway. Lit fuses burned from his beard, and a broad grin revealed grimy, yellow teeth. He stood with his hands on his hips, eying Ulrick as though trying to determine if he was merely an amusement or a real threat.

He's probably faced much better resistance than this, Ulrick thought, gathering his rifle and heading up the stairs for his first fallback location. *I'm only one man, they've taken on a lot more, but not many enjoy playing these games like I do.*

He knew that the men who'd fallen meant nothing to a fellow like Jack, who would spend other men's lives as freely as the coins in his pocket.

Ulrick turned to face him before heading through the door. "Good luck," he called, and then he was gone.

Black-backed Jack nodded his head and laughed. "This one's going to be slippery, lads. One gold bar to the man who brings me his head. Two gold bars if you bring him to me alive."

Hero turned her head and tried not to retch from the horrific smells that filled the Katara's docking bay. Blood, sweat, grime, and burning flesh all wafted around her like the aromas that might arise from some kitchen that was run by ghouls. The sounds of blaster fire pierced the air, causing her head to pound and the rest of her body to shake. *'Stay in the corner,'* came Ulrick's words in her head. *'Keep hidden behind this crate of food rations until Black-backed Jack comes out. He'll be the last one through.'*

'But how will I know which one he is,' she'd asked.

'Believe me, you'll know him.'

And when he came through the hole, she did. He looked twice as vicious and bloodthirsty as any of the others, and was even bigger than Ulrick. His black hair and beard sizzled and smoked as if he'd just clawed his way out of hell.

Hero watched as Ulrick set the force field and climbed the stairs. He turned around to face the pirate. "Good luck," he called, but she knew he was talking to her. Then he was gone.

Black-backed Jack nodded his head and laughed. "This one's going to be slippery, lads. One gold bar to the one who brings me his head. Two gold bars if you bring him to me alive."

Hero suddenly envisioned Ulrick standing at the top of the stairs, but it was the pirate who'd lost his head, and her friend held it up to her as if he were presenting a bouquet of flowers. *You creeps don't know who you're up against,* she thought while glaring at them. Jace and Galin had told her stories about some of the things they'd seen Ulrick do. He was a man of honor, but he was built for war. Until now, Hero had been a bit afraid of him, but now her heart had sank to watch him go.

"Cease fire," commanded a particularly ugly pirate with a bald head and braided beard.

"Cease fire, cease fire," repeated the thing sitting upon his shoulder. It looked like the spawn of a house cat and a turkey, with large wings, short tabby colored fur, pointed ears, a blue face, and a long red wattle. "Cease fire! Rip out their eyes, drink their wine, tickle their bellies with blazing steel." Its voice was screechy and gave Hero the chills.

"Turtle Top," whined the mangy looking fellow beside him, "can't you keep that thing quiet for a change?"

Turtle Top smacked the man hard, and he spun all the way around before falling with a crack upon his rear. "Mind your tongue, else you might find yourself without it."

"HAR!" the bird thing laughed mockingly.

"Shut it, you," Turtle Top barked, punching at the creature as it snapped back at him. "Come on, lads. Look lively," he called to the men. "This bloody force field ain't going to short itself." He picked up the body of one of his fallen comrades, and tossed it through the air like a sack of flour. It landed upon the force field and stuck in place as if it had been glued, where it sizzled and burned and sparked until there was nothing left but smoke and ash.

Other pirates began to do the same thing, casting their fallen comrades into the field as Turtle Top egged them on. Hero turned her eyes away from the horror and quietly stepped out from her hiding place, praying that her cloaking shield would hold. Gerry-rigging a ship's camo shield to a portable power supply and using it as a personal cloaking device was not something that would have occurred to her. It was a good idea, or at least it would be as long as the power-supply held up.

Hero crept along the wall, nearly slipping several times on the blood splattered grating, until she came to the corridor. Black-backed Jack stood just a few feet in front of the hole, but took no notice of her as he was barking commands at his bald lieutenant, who in turn passed them on to lesser men.

The smells and sounds faded as Hero made her way through the dark metal tunnel. It bounced beneath her feet, and she could hear places where air was escaping through small damaged sections due to neglect. It made her nervous, and she rushed through to the other side.

Only after emerging did she see the man standing guard beside the entrance to the tunnel. She jumped, thinking he had seen her, but he was only raising his hand over his mouth in a yawn. She took a few slow, deep breaths, and her heart began to beat once more.

She took a look around, and found herself on the deck that contained the plasma cannons. A few gruff looking men unenthusiastically serviced the machinery. They didn't look like the other pirates, in fact, they seemed more like slaves. These were no fighters, yet they were none to be trifled with either, Hero decided.

She proceeded gingerly across the deck to a place where a ladder ascended and descended. Next stop was the engine room, and that meant going down. The rungs of the latter felt cold and grimy as she fumbled invisible fingers across them; it was strange to be looking at her hands without being able to see them. Hero wondered how long she might have before the shield's energy supply dwindled, and then she gasped as her hands flickered in and out of view. Ulrick had warned her that the battery wouldn't last long, but that was a fact she already knew. Her hands disappeared once again. She needed to move fast, or this would all be for nothing.

Here I go, she thought, and began to climb. Hopefully she had enough juice to make it to the engine room and finish her work without being seen. All she needed now was a little bit of energy, and a whole lot of luck.

Black-backed Jack sneered in satisfaction as the force field flickered for the last time and collapsed. He made a final survey of the carnage around him. Over twenty of his men had fallen so far, and that was a lot more than he usually lost on a job like this, but men such as these were easy enough to come by. The ship wasn't his yet, but it was only a matter of time now.

All the bodies but three had been used to short circuit the force field, but the floor was still covered with blood. They would have been standing in a pool of it if not for the steel grating.

"Ha, ha," laughed Thumbkin, a dwarf with a yellow,

braided beard, which nearly touched the floor. "There are times when I find it a blessing to be a dwarf. When the bullets start flying is one of them." He performed a cartwheel and then wiggled his bloody fingers in front of his comrades, who laughed at him encouragingly.

Jack stooped down to the floor, taking up a bit of blood and smearing it around between his thumb and index finger. "Turtle Top, prepare the men. We need to catch that rat before he crawls too far back into his hole."

"All right, you scrubs," Turtle Top called to the men, "you were lucky enough to make it this far, and if you keep your heads about you, you've nothing to worry about. He's only one man, after all, so take a piss, wet yer whistles, lock and load, and prepare to press on."

Jack rose back up to his feet, yawned deeply, and rested his right hand upon his repeater pistol. This Ulrick fellow was going to give him a run for his money. In truth, it was a refreshing change from some of the weaklings he'd come up against lately. The pirate turned his torso to enjoy a good stretch, and happened to gaze back toward the corridor where something a bit out of place caught his eye. He moved closer to take a look, and sure enough, a pair of footprints, painted in blood, went leading off through the corridor back to his ship. *Well, well, well. What have we here?* Did he have a yellow-bellied deserter amongst his men? If so, he'd rip the coward's head off with his bare hands. He retraced the last few minutes in his mind, and realized that nobody could have gotten past him without being seen. Looking down at the prints once again, Jack suddenly realized how small they were. Perhaps they belonged to a woman or older child. He smiled in irritation, annoyed and impressed that someone had been able to sneak past him. But how had they done it? As much as he wanted to get his hands around the throat of that little freedom fighter, he did love a good mystery. So someone actually thought they could stow-away on his own ship, did they. *What kind of captain would I be,* he asked himself, *if I didn't give our guest a warm, friendly welcome.* He turned to face his men.

"Turtle Top, Thumbkin, take the others and press ahead. John Saber, you stay here and guard the bay. I'll be back as soon as I finish...looking into something." He ran his fingers through his greasy, smoking beard and followed the bloody footprints. This was turning into an interesting job indeed!

The rocky outcrops and scattered boulders weren't nearly as interesting as the landscape down by the river, but they did provide more than adequate cover for one not wishing to be seen. William Marshal peeked up and scanned the two men who appeared to be standing guard on the rocks up ahead. What could they be guarding? William wasn't aware of any reason men would be guarding such rocks. He hadn't picked up more than a few insignificant traces of any precious gems or minerals nearby. At any rate, perhaps these fellows were associates of the female he was looking for.

A search for information on the weapons they carried revealed them to be of no threat. Primitive weapons such as spears and bows were incapable of damaging the crystalized tritanium body of a T3038.

Striding off toward the guards, William continued to scan the surrounding area for signs of life. Even rocky terrain such as this contained an abundance of life forms. Thousands of creatures were picked up as he strode along. Snakes, spiders, worms, rats, even a den full of coyotes. The different kinds of animals were so intriguing that before he knew what was happening, the guards were calling out frantically to one another, and by the time William reached them, the two men had been joined by a few dozen more. He identified expressions of curiosity and fear as he strode up to them.

"Greetings. I am William Marshal," he said. "I mean you no harm. Do any of you know where I might find the human male that has been designated Joseph Stormcrow, or the female with the designation Angelica Garcia Ramirez?" Using the projector in his optic circuits, William displayed a small holographic image of each of them.

A slender man with a long grey and white beard took a step toward him. "My name is James Locke. Where did you come from? Why are you looking for these two?"

"I have been reprogramed to locate Joseph Stormcrow, aid him if I can, and report my findings back to Captain Galin Winchester or one of his crew mates. I have also been directed to investigate the locations of three children. Their designations are Sarah Winchester, David Winchester, and Stephen Anderson." James and the others listened intently while William went on to explain the rest of his mission, and how he had obtained Angelica's DNA samples from Peter's gravesite.

"Well, that's quite an amazing story," James told him when he was finished. "I can tell you that Angelica doesn't have any information on Joseph Stormcrow, but we do know some things about that Winchester boy you're looking for. He lived here for a while, but was carried away by some cryptic woman on a black horse. In fact, Angelica and a few others left just yesterday to try and track them down. I'm sure they'd more than appreciate your help. Go back to the other side of the apple orchard where you picked up the trail of Peter's blood. You should be able to track them pretty easily from there."

"Thank you for your assistance," the android told them. He noted that the looks on their faces had changed, and searched his database for what these new looks might mean. Relief, hope, and happiness were some of the possibilities. He must have done well while communicating with them. He was pleased.

"Once you get back to your ship, tell your friends

about us. Tell them we need help, if they're able to give it."

William thought about James' words. Were the people on the Katara his friends? He wasn't sure about that, but maybe they would be if he asked them nicely, or if he did a good job of communicating with them. "I shall deliver a complete record of our encounter." He fired up his boosters, waved goodbye, and rocketed off toward the orchard. "Farewell."

It was unexpected to learn that David Winchester had been brought to Necron. That had not been a statistical probability, but according to his orders, the recovery of the three children was his utmost priority. He now needed to hurry more than ever; he needed to get there before the Nazerazi vessel arrived.

Nothing tastes as good as cold beer while killing pirates, Ulrick thought as he slammed one down before closing the door to the refrigerator. The charges had been set, and the pirates would be along shortly. He took a quick look around. It was going to be a real shame seeing all this stuff sucked out into space. About three months back, Starla had finally convinced Galin to let her refurbish the kitchen and dining area, and in a small way Ulrick felt like he was betraying her, but it couldn't be helped. Hopefully, he'd get to make it up to her one day, but that meant making it out of this with his life, and with the ship.

The gleeful shouts of the pirates came echoing up from the landing bay and through the hallways as the force field collapsed. *Here we go again*, he thought, begrudgingly locking his space helmet back onto his suit. Raising his blaster rifle, Ulrick waited as the men rushed up into the hall and approached the door to the cockpit, where they assumed he'd gone.

He picked off four of them using shield piercing charges, and the rest momentarily retreated in confusion. Checking his ammo, he saw that only three of the charges remained, but he'd definitely gotten their attention. Clicking the rifle back over to regular charges, he fell back as the pirates regrouped and began to gush into the dining area.

Thumbkin darted in beneath the legs of one of the men in the vanguard. "Come on, you slugs. Let's slag this filthy rat before he bites us again."

Blaster bolts lit up the room as Ulrick's shields flickered and fizzled, struggling to keep up with the amount of energy being bombarded at him. At this rate, they wouldn't hold up for long, but if everything went according to plan he wouldn't need them to. He reached the back of the room and magnetized his boots, locking himself firmly to the floor. There were twenty pirates in the room if there was one, and although a few were still trying to push their way in, Ulrick punched the code into his wrist-pad and remotely closed the door.

A sharp pain pierced his foot, and he looked down to see that Thumbkin had stabbed him with a dagger. Ulrick swung his rifle like a golf club, knocking the dwarf through the air until he crashed against the opposite wall, landing on the counter and knocking the coffee pot to the floor.

Thumbkin growled like a wolverine, and reached out to brace himself against the wall as he rose to his feet. Feeling something wet, he examined his hand, and then the wall, and finally looked back at Ulrick in horror.

"FALL BACK, LADS," he squealed. "WE NEED TO GET BACK THROUGH THAT DOOR, NOW!"

Here goes nothing. Sorry about this, Starla. Ulrick executed another command into his wrist-pad, and the explosive foam, which he had sprayed upon the wall a few minutes before, detonated. A rectangular section of the ship's hull ripped off and was drawn into space, and the terrified, wounded dwarf wasn't far behind it. Ulrick reached for a nearby rail, gritted his teeth, and struggled to hold on as he watched the contents of the room being sucked through the hole. For an instant, the pirates looked horrified, realizing there was no way to avoid their fate. And then they were gone.

Everything became still. Ulrick de-gravitized his boots, and pushed himself off the ground toward the hole. Another sharp surge of pain ran through his foot where the dwarf had stabbed him. He growled out in irritation, and stopped himself on the wall where the refrigerator had once stood. Lamenting the cold beer that had been claimed by space, he looked through the hole to examine the warped remains of the Katara's kitchen and dining room, as well as the twenty or so piratesicles that now had permanent looks of horror frozen on their faces. Thumbkin's head flew off like a slow, spinning football amidst the other pieces of his filthy little body.

"Yuck," Ulrick grunted. He couldn't help but feel a bit sorry for all of them as he placed the force field generators along the outskirts of the hole. When he was finished, he clicked the force field on, and then re-pressurized the room and removed his helmet. The kitchen now had that window that Starla had suggested. Too bad all the appliances and furniture were gone.

Ulrick clicked his rifle back over to shield-piercing rounds, knelt down toward the back of the room, and paced his breathing. He could hear the remaining pirates pounding on the door, demanding that their companions let them in. It wouldn't take them too long to get through once they put their minds to it, and when that happened they were sure to head for the engine room. That would be where he'd make his last stand. That would be where the fate of the Katara would be decided.

Ulrick didn't know how many of the pirates were left; he just hoped his shields would last long enough to deal with them. Getting back to his feet, he headed for the ladder leading down to the engine room.

The floor grating clacked just a little too loudly as Hero dropped off the ladder in the engine room. She cursed herself silently. That was a stupid thing to do. It had become force of habit to drop from the last few rungs of a ladder whenever she was in a hurry, and she sure was in a hurry.

A large pirate, holding a steel pike with a crackling electric prod on the end, eyed the area suspiciously for a few moments before returning his attention to the other men working in the room.

"Hey, you," he called to a man who'd stopped his work to look toward the ladder. "Back to work, you slug." He shook the prod threateningly before leaning back lazily against the wall.

The man who'd been threatened returned to his task, but looked back suspiciously a few times right where she was standing. Had he seen her? She needed to get hidden and set the explosives before the camo shield collapsed. Ulrick had urged her to plant the charges in the hopes that he could hold off the pirates trying to take the Katara. Disabling the One-Eyed Whore might be their only chance at limping away to safety, but that was a long shot. He'd also told her that if he got killed and the Katara was taken, the only thing she could do was find a safe place to hide until an opportunity arose to escape. Her chances were small, but at least that was something. It was a sad thing to think, but she had grown tired of fighting, tired of hurting, and if sacrificing herself was what it took to save Jace and Ulrick.... The only thing that kept her from blowing up this ship either way was the hope of finding Stephen.

Snapping out of her thoughts, Hero looked around the room and counted three men performing various tasks. Two of them looked to be performing routine maintenance, but the third man, the one who she thought had seen her, was performing a much more delicate repair upon the ship's warp engines.

Hero pounced gingerly toward the warp core. Planting the charges near the core would take out the whole ship if the right time came to detonate them. She glanced at the slaves and her stomach fluttered with sadness. Why was it that the actions of evil men always led to the suffering of innocents? That was a lesson she'd learnt long ago.

She sank to her knees and planted the charges, hiding them in places where they would not easily be found, then rose to her feet and scanned the area for a good place to hide. The engine room wouldn't be the ideal place to hold up for the long haul, but her camo shield wasn't going to last much longer, of that much she was certain.

Hurriedly, she crept back over to the ladder and began to climb down. Her foot hadn't touched the second rung before someone yanked her back up by the scruff of her shirt.

"You don't want to go wandering around down there." It was the man she'd seen working on the engine. She looked down to see what she already knew, that her body had become clearly visible.

"What's going on here?" demanded the pirate with the electric prod, stumbling over to have a look. "Who the 'ell are YOU?" he asked, getting uncomfortably close to Hero's face. He smelled like a still.

The pirate's face suddenly jerked back before clanking down with a hard crash into the ladder. He crumpled to the floor at their feet, and the prod clacked down after him.

Hero looked up in shock at the man who'd saved her.

He shrugged. "Long Rob isn't so bad, really," he said, looking down at the unconscious man. "Not compared to the rest of these scoundrels anyway. *You* sure don't look like a pirate."

"What?" she said, shaking her head. "No, I'm...of course I'm no pirate. I'm Hero."

"A hero? Our hero? You came to rescue us?"

"No," she said with a moan, trying to recover from the scare. "I'm not a hero. My *name* is Hero. Hero Anderson."

"Oh, sorry about the confusion." The man held out his hand. "Joseph Stormcrow."

Hero's jaw dropped. "You've got to be kidding me. *You're* Joseph Stormcrow? *The* Joseph Stormcrow?"

He raised an eyebrow at her. "Didn't know I was famous. As far as I know, I'm the only Joe Stormcrow there is."

"Listen," she said, grabbing him. "I don't know how you got here, but the ship that these pirates are assaulting right now- it's the Katara."

"WHAT? The Katara? You came here with Galin Winchester?"

She nodded. "Yes, but he's not on the ship now, he went to Necron to search for you and Peter. The only people on that ship right now are Ulrick and Jace."

He just gawked at her in disbelief.

"Ulrick is trying to hold off the pirates, and Jace is hurt. We stashed him in a hidden compartment in the cargo bay."

"Well, why did you come over here?"

"Ulrick sent me here to hide, and to plant explosives just in case we got the opportunity to escape."

"Nobody has ever escaped once Black-backed Jack got his claws into them," he said, looking down again at the unconscious pirate at their feet. "At least that's what I've heard." He smiled at her. "But there's a first time for everything. If we move quickly, maybe we can secure this ship while Jack and his thugs are away. He only left a few men to guard the slaves. And, if I know Ulrick, he's probably managed to grease the majority of those raiders. He can't hold out forever though."

"We'll help, if we can," one of the other workers told

them.

"This is Dave, and that's Jerry," Joseph said. "We were all taken off Necron together. That's one of the places where Jack gets reinforcements for his crew. It's also where he gets the zombies he keeps down below."

"You mean...."

"Yup. It's a good thing for you that camo shield ran out of juice when it did. You didn't know what you were headed toward down there. One wrong step and you end up as zombie chow."

"That's how the pirates 'convince' us to work for them," Dave said, shifting uncomfortably. "Well, one of the ways they do it, anyway."

"You bring any weapons?" Joseph asked, turning to Hero.

She pulled out two blaster pistols, which had been stowed in her cargo pockets, and handed him one.

"Well, it's a start. Jerry, you tie up Long Rob and keep an eye on things down here. If any more pirates come down the ladder, stick that prod into their butts, that should do the trick."

Jerry looked nervous, but nodded in agreement.

"We need to head back up to the deck with the cannons, where you came in," Joseph said to Hero. "There are a few men up there who can help us, and from there we can try to take the bridge. But first...." He ran over to an equipment cabinet and took out a fresh power supply. "We need *you* to get invisible again."

Jace ran his fingers along the android's smooth, cold arm. It sure was an impressive bot.

"Okay, here goes nothing," Hero said, giving him a smile. She entered the command and William Marshal sat up and looked at them. Hero squealed in excitement. It had really worked, the android was functioning normally.

Hero took a few steps back, stood near the ship's engine, and stared at the robot proudly. "Well, are you ready to get to work?" she asked him.

Jace watched as her joy turned to confusion, and finally fear as the android stood up and extended his arm blasters.

He lunged across the room as the android began to shoot, catching the girl around the waist and knocking her away from the line of fire. He gawked at their attacker as time seemed to slow, felt the blaster bolts sear his side and back, and felt his body crumple on top of hers as a horrible realization came to him. The robot hadn't been firing at Hero, he'd aimed for the engine.

I knocked her into the line of fire, Jace remembered in horror, and woke up with a start. Everything was black. He tried to sit up, but struck something hard and fell back down. Pain shot through his head and down his spine, and fear took hold of him. Panicking, he felt all around, hoping to find anything that might help him. Was he dead? Had he been buried alive? Had Hero been killed too, all because of him?

Whatever he'd struck his head upon was just a few

feet above. It felt cold, but budged a little when he shoved on it. With all the strength he could muster, he pushed against the cold steel, and to his relief it raised up and a bit and light came streaming in. He closed his eyes and turned away, and the covering fell back down. After taking a few short breaths, he pushed up again, lifting up and pushing the lid off to the side. He covered his eyes, moving his hand a little at a time to let them adjust, until finally, he could leave them open. A sense of nausea overtook him, and it seemed as though the whole world was spinning like a merry-go-round. He measured his breathing for a few moments, and reached up again to the sides of his grave, drawing his hands back when he felt something wet. A thick, red liquid dripped from his fingers. He looked at them in horror, and as the plethora of horrid smells caught up to him, he vomited all over his bare chest.

"What was that? Who's there?" came a voice he did not recognize.

Jace reached up once again, and carefully pulled himself to a sitting position. He could just see over the grating of the floor, and finally realized for sure where he was, but he couldn't grasp what was happening. Had someone stashed him in one of the hidden cargo compartments? Why would anyone do that?

"Hey, what the frack happened to you?" came the same voice.

Jace looked up to see the face of a grimy young man

who couldn't have been much older than him.

"Who are you?" the young man asked. "You aren't one of us."

"One of wh...who?" Jace stuttered before coughing.

"You really look like crap, you know that?" the man laughed. "Oh, I get it, you must have been in that regeneration chamber over there. Your buddy pulled you out to hide you so Jack wouldn't find out. That was nice of him, kind of a stupid plan though."

"Jack?" Jace coughed again. He suddenly felt very cold, though his head was dripping with sweat. "Who's Jack? Who are you?"

The man laughed again. It was an unkind laugh, as if he relished knowing something that Jace did not. "My name's John Saber. And Black-backed Jack is the one who's taken over your ship. All your friends are dead by now, I'd imagine. If they aren't yet, they will be soon."

Jace's heart sank. This all had to be some hellish nightmare. How could pirates have taken the ship? The last thing he knew, they were all still on Earth.

"Maybe if you beg for your life," John Saber told him, stooping down, "then Jack will show mercy and let you join the crew. As you can probably tell from all this blood, we lost some men after coming aboard. The boss likes to keep plenty of hands around."

"Why would *I* want to be some slaggin pirate?" Jace barked, trying to keep himself from throwing up again.

John Saber sneered. "Oh, come on, it's not all bad.

If you can figure out how to keep yourself alive, there's plenty of reward involved- lots of food, money, and even women to be had, whether they want to be or not." Again he laughed, and stood up straight, crossing his arms in front of his chest.

Jace didn't know what to do. He wasn't strong enough to fight; in fact it was taking all his willpower to stay upright and awake. For now, he just needed to keep this guy talking, and he seemed to be fond enough of that. "Why do they call you John Saber?" he asked.

John's face suddenly lit up with a maniacal grin. "Because of *this*." He whipped the handle of a laser sword out from somewhere beneath his baggy clothes. Clicking it on, the brilliant, crackling blue blade shot out and lit up the room around them. John Saber began to swing the blade around over his head and back and forth through the air, hacking through enemies who weren't there. He nodded knowingly at Jace, whose eyes had grown big. "That's right, I've been practicing with this sword for over eight years now. Even though I'm one of the youngest members of the crew, I've earned Jack's respect. I haven't come across anyone yet who can defeat me in melee combat." He cut the rails of the nearby staircase as easily as if he were slicing through butter, and smoldering drops of molten steel were scattered to the floor. "I've even defeated six other men who were wielding laser swords just like this."

The blade swept past Jace's face a few times, coming

much closer than he would have liked.

"Do you know how many men I've killed?" John asked rhetorically. "How many woman I've spoiled since joining up with this crew? I fracking LOVE being a pirate." He passed the sword from hand to hand behind his back, and whipped it back around the front. It vroomed through the air in a display so impressive that Jace nearly forgot about his pain, and how tired he was.

"I'm going to have my own ship someday, too," John went on, twirling the blade. "Black-backed Jack said that if I work really hard, wha...WHOA," he yelped, as his foot slipped across a wet section of the bloody grating.

Before Jace could blink, the head of John Saber came plopping down into his lap. The young man's body crumpled, and the laser sword went skidding across the floor, slamming to a stop at the foot of the steps and clicking off.

Jace looked down at the young man's decapitated head, and tossed it away just before spewing vomit all over himself once more.

"What the 'ell do you want?" Solomon Tandy snorted as Joseph stepped off the ladder onto his deck.

"Just need to borrow a monkey wrench. Long Robb said I could come up and get one."

The pirate sneered. "You idiots misplacing your tools

again? Turtle Top is going to hear of this. 'E'll feed you to the zombies and get some slaves who know how to keep their equipment straight, if there's such a thing as justice."

"I certainly hope so." Joseph agreed with a smile, walking to the toolbox.

Solomon Tandy shot toward him, grinding his teeth. "You 'ittle smar'-ass. I'll rip your bloody 'ead off and toss it back down to the engine room where it belongs." He lifted up his electric prod with one arm as if it were a spear, but turned with a look of confusion upon feeling a hand tap his shoulder. No one was there.

Joseph hit him fast and hard, and a moment later two of the man's teeth were clanking across the floor like a bloody pair of dice.

Solomon turned back to his attacker with a look of surprise and fury. "OOUUCH! 'Ose were gold teef you 'irty 'ittle—."

This time Joseph hit him with the wrench, and he went down like a ton of bricks.

Hero reappeared, wearing a pained frown as she looked down at the pirate.

"Don't feel sorry for that one," Joseph told her. "He would have gutted us both without a second thought, and then gone to bed tonight to sleep like a baby. Besides," he gave the body a few nudges with his foot, "he's not dead. We'd better tie him up nice and tight like we did Long Robb."

The three gruff looking men whom Hero had noticed upon coming in were now gathered around them with hopeful, hungry looks- like the dinner bell had just been rung.

"It's a mutiny," Joseph told them. "There's only a handful of pirates left on the ship. You men work on barricading this passageway."

"Why don't we just retract the thing and leave those fracking savages over there?" asked a short man with a blossoming yellow beard.

Joseph shook his head. "We've got friends over there, Jeremy. Really good people. And if I'm right, those pirates are going to have their hands pretty full. Black-backed Jack might be a living legend, but Ulrick will do his best to make him a dead one."

"Okay. Come on, guys, let's get to work," one of the other men chimed, and sprinted off dutifully toward some crates. The others followed.

Joseph turned to Hero. "We need to take the bridge. Follow me." He hurried to another ladder, which only went up, and began to climb.

Hero followed him. They went up three levels before Joseph turned and whispered down to her. "We're nearly there. Turn on the cloak, and follow my lead. There should only be two men up here, possibly three. I'll get close to one of them, you sneak to the other, and then we'll take both out at the same time. As soon as my guy drops, you blast yours, okay?"

"Alright."

"You okay? You ready for this?"

"As ready as I'll ever be." She turned the cloak on and flickered out of sight.

They continued up the ladder and emerged onto the bridge, and it was like no bridge that Hero had ever seen. Instead of metal, the floor was made out of wood planks, at least that's what they looked like. She gathered that the walls and ceiling must be constructed of transparent aluminum, because she could see the stars twinkling all around them, almost as if she were standing on solid ground looking into the night sky. It was beautiful. Three thick masts rose up toward the stars, holding the retracted solar sails. Hero was so fascinated that she nearly forgot what they'd come for, but one of the pirate's voices startled her back to her senses.

"What are you doing here?" asked the rough voice of the man in front of Joseph.

She quickly scanned the bridge as he made up an answer. The only other man she saw was standing near the helm, some fifty feet away. Drawing the blaster pistol out of her pocket, she scurried off toward him, as quietly as she could, praying that Joseph would give her enough time to get into position.

The pirate yawned as she approached. He was gazing off into the stars as if he might drift off to sleep at any moment. This had to be the first mate.

A voice came over the ships com, making both Hero

and the pirate jump.

"Walter, you there? This is Turtle Top."

"Yeah, go on then."

"We've finally got this rat cornered in the engine room. It won't be long now. We've lost a lot of men though, most of them, actually. It wouldn't surprise me if the Captain turns us back toward Necron."

Walter growled in frustration. "I've not seen my bloody wives for five months now. At least *they'll* be happy about another delay."

"Just thought you'd like a heads up," Turtle Top said.

"Alright. Put a few extra holes in that frakker for *me*, would ya?"

"My pleasure."

A few moments of silence passed before the sound of a blaster pistol rang through the air. Hero turned to see the pirate next to Joseph drop to the deck.

"WHAT?" growled Walter. Hero blasted him as he turned to charge off, and his body skidded across the floor and tumbled down the small set of stairs that led to the main deck.

And then Hero heard something she didn't expect. The sound of clapping hands came echoing across the bridge. Slow, heavy, and deliberately the hands banged together. CLAP. CLAP. CLAP.

"Very good. Very impressive." Black-backed Jack seemed to step out of nowhere out from behind Joseph, who raised the blaster and squeezed off a shot into the pirate's belly. Jack's shield flickered as the bolt was absorbed, and he laughed all the harder, lunging toward Joseph and punching him so hard in the stomach that his feet left the ground. He fell to his knees, and the pirate kicked him in the head as if it were a football. Hero half expected to see it go sailing through the air, but it didn't, and Joseph landed with a thud, where he remained motionless upon the deck.

"Come out, come out, wherever you are...." sang the pirate. "I know you're here, girl, don't you want to come out and play?"

Hero moved away from him as quickly and quietly as she could, hoping that her panicked breathing wouldn't betray her position, and looking for some way of escape.

"I've locked down the bridge. You aren't getting out of here now," Jack called to her happily. "Why don't you shoot me? Come on... play the game."

She wasn't stupid. Shooting at the beast would only reveal her position. What was she going to do? What could she do, but hide and wait.

Ulrick had barely made it down the ladder and into the engine room before falling to his knees. Was the heat from the suit getting to him, or had that nasty little dwarf poisoned him with something when he'd stabbed his foot? Everything began to go black, and the big man growled and shook his head, refusing to be overcome by whatever was trying to take him. Yup, it was definitely some kind of drug or poison, but hopefully it had just been meant to knock him out, not to kill him. Only time would tell.

Dragging himself toward the wall, he found a place to lean up alongside a toolbox, which provided a bit of cover and a clear view of the entrance. He placed the rifle across his legs, and removed the gravity boot to get a better look at his injured foot. The blade had gone deep, but the wound looked clean. That was a good sign. The air felt dry and heavy, and breathing seemed to become more of a chore with each passing minute. Ulrick smacked himself across the face, struggling to stay conscious.

Loud noises suddenly filled the room above, letting him know that the pirates had broken through. He pulled his helmet back on, and gritted his teeth while drawing the boot onto his foot. When that was done, he reactivated his shield. They would be upon him soon. He lifted his rifle, which seemed twice as heavy as it had before, and took aim at the top of the ladder.

Before long, a pirate came sliding down the outer rails. He landed much too hard, and Ulrick heard a crack, followed by an agonizing squeal of pain. The poor man must have broken his ankle. Ulrick ended his suffering by squeezing off a shield piercing round. Two more pirates were right behind the first, and they received shield-piercing rounds as well. A red light flashed on from the side of the rifle, telling Ulrick what he already knew- that he was out of shield piercing rounds. Regular charges weren't going to be much help against another bunch of these guys, not if their shields were worth anything. He wondered how many were left.

Two more assailants rushed down the ladder. Ulrick lit the first one up with blaster bolts, and his shields flickered for several moments before collapsing. That was an unexpected, but welcomed surprise. After a few more bolts landed, the man dropped to the floor. His partner was now firmly planted on one knee, with his own gun, a heavy repeating blaster, firing off rounds at Ulrick.

Another man, who was bald and had an ugly bird-like creature perched on his shoulder, stepped down from the ladder and strode toward him, carrying an energy buckler. Ulrick kept his fire on the man who was shooting at him, intent on giving every last bit of effort before passing out. He felt like he was being roasted inside the space suit, which heated up a little bit more with every shot that landed. Finally, his shield collapsed, and his fingers slipped from the rifle as the last few bolts hit his suit. One shot took him in the right arm and the other in the upper, right chest. Without the suit, he would have been dead for sure.

With much pain and effort, he lifted his head. Why had the pirate stopped firing? Ulrick laughed to see the man sprawled out on the ground beside his companion.

His shield must have collapsed the same time mine did. You couldn't get much luckier than that.

His eyes were nearly closed when the force of the bald pirate's kick startled him back into consciousness, and he felt the weight of his rifle leave him before hearing it clank across the floor.

The pirate turned off his buckler, which collapsed in a swirl of crackling light, and knelt down in front of his fallen enemy. "I've got to give it to you, scum, we haven't had a fight like this in a long, long time. Those are my last two men lying dead on the ground over there."

"Lying dead, lying dead," the bird thing squawked.

Turtle Top reached down and removed Ulrick's helmet. He looked him over with contempt, and a hint of respect. "Got any last words before I turn out your lights for the last time?"

With effort, Ulrick lifted his head to better meet the pirate's gaze. He met the man in a mad-dog stare for several moments, and then looked over at the creature on his shoulder.

"Yeah," Ulrick grunted. "That's the ugliest slaggin' chicken I've ever seen in my life."

"CHICKEN?" screeched the bird. "CHIIICKEEEN!" The look taking form on the creature's face was unlike anything he'd seen on an animal before. Even a rabid wolf looked of fear and rage, but this thing's eyes shone with malice.

"Shut yer mouth," Turtle Top commanded, punching at the bird that'd just screamed in his ear. The creature beat its wings franticly, and its wattle vibrated with anger below its contorted face as it continued to shriek. "Shut up, damn you. Yer givin' me a headache!"

The pirate took the bird by the neck, and began to squeeze, but it only seemed to make things worse. It ripped its talons into his shoulder and jerked back and forth, attempting to get away, and turning its rage on its owner.

"I'LL BLOW YOUR SLAGGING HEAD OFF," Turtle Top screamed back at him, drawing a blaster pistol from his belt and pointing it at the thing's head. It finally tore free and lunged for his face, taking the nose off with one quick bite. The brigand screamed and reached for his wound, dropping the blaster in Ulrick's lap. He grasped for the bird with both hands, ringing its neck and twisting until he held the thing before him in two separate pieces.

Ulrick smiled. Over dinner last Thanksgiving, Peter had told him how Frommerian chickens become enraged when you called them by that name, but until now he'd never really believed it. He'd really thought his friend was pulling his leg. Ulrick tried to remember what the proper name for the species was, but couldn't. The ridiculousness of it all made him chuckle.

Turtle Top shot him a hateful look, as if just now remembering he was there. Blood streamed down his face from the place his nose had once been. "What the 'ell are you laughin' about?" he demanded angrily.

"This," Ulrick mumbled, shooting the man with his own blaster pistol. He crumpled to the floor on top of his bird.

Everything was quiet then, and after a while the only sound Ulrick could hear was the whir of equipment fans and the pumping of his own blood. His wounds throbbed in time with the beats; it was like some tortuous music. His eyes slid shut. He couldn't keep them open any longer, couldn't stay awake. He wondered if he was falling asleep or dying, and then everything faded to black.

Rain poured from the sky as if some legion of unknown gods were casting their fury upon the jungle. Angelica bit her lip as the last bit of flame vanished from her torch. This was going to be a miserable night. None of the party was familiar with this part of the jungle, and they'd not been able to find adequate shelter before the rainclouds unleashed their wrath.

Angelica's mind wandered back to when she was a girl, living in the hot, dry desert. She used to get so excited at seeing even the smallest hint of rain. At this moment, she longed for a hot, desert atmosphere. She was cold and tired, and wanted nothing more than to lie down in some warm, dry place and go to sleep. In the jungle, sleep was always a danger, but the irony was that these cold, heavy rainstorms seemed to keep the zombies away. The very thing that made sleeping safer would keep you awake anyway.

Peter's image popped into her head, just as it had many times that day. Angelica had been thinking about him a lot, about how this place had robbed her of him, stolen away their future together even before it began. Then again, she'd barely known the man. Perhaps the dream of what might have been was nothing more than that, just another false hope that was given, only to be snatched away by the hungry jaws of this planet. *Dreams are taken just as easily as they're given here on Necron,* came James Locke's voice in her head again.

Whatever she might have felt, or would have felt for Peter didn't really matter now. All that mattered was getting David back. It was her fault the boy had been taken, Peter had told her that he hadn't liked the idea of him being sent out to gather fruit, but she hadn't listened. None of this would have happened if only she'd listened. But it was too late to change any of that now; all she could do was try to get David back, even if it meant she might not return herself.

"Come on, we need to huddle up, try and stay warm," Carl said to her and their other companions. Carl was a good man, and a good friend. He'd lived in the caves for over a year now, and had even gotten married to another castaway. She'd ended up dying from an infection from a broken leg a few months before; more proof that the planet Necron was just as bloodthirsty as it was beautiful.

Angelica huddled up back to back with the rest of the search party. Sammy, April, Kenny, and Roger- all of them good people, all of them so damaged from life on this planet that they would welcome almost any release, even death. None of them spoke of it, but none of them needed to. It was something they all shared. Every member of this group had volunteered to go after David, not only because it was the right thing to do, but because the fear of death had been stomped out of each of them by the losses they'd suffered.

Pulling her knees to her chest and lowering her head, Angelica closed her eyes and without even thinking of what she was doing, began to pray. *God, if you really are listening, please help us. Help me, whatever that means. I'm just…I'm tired. I'm tired of being broken. Please give me something. Something that makes me feel like wanting to be alive again.* Her mind was numb, and even the cold water flowing down her body was soon forgotten. She began to drift off into something that was a little bit like sleep.

"Hey," April's voice chattered nervously. "Hey, what…what the heck is *that*?" She pointed off into the distance, where a strange blue glow could be seen coming toward them. Was it a flashlight?

Perhaps they were all too cold or tired to move, or maybe it was curiosity that froze them in place, but nobody budged.

A tall, silver form appeared through the trees and torrent. It was an android, coming toward them like some ethereal medieval knight in the moonlight. Its eye-slot was what they'd seen glowing. After getting a good look at them, the robot retracted the guns on its arms and lowered them down to its sides. Angelica didn't think she was sleeping, but this had to be a dream. Maybe she was hallucinating.

The thing walked right up to them, as if it were scalping concert tickets. "Greetings, Angelica Garcia Ramirez. My designation is William Marshal. I have come to ask you about the location of the human, male child David Winchester."

Angelica just stared at him, and her companions gawked at them both.

William Marshal gazed at her for a few moments, before looking up into the sky. "Does it rain here often? I've never been in the rain before tonight."

"Uh, yeah, it rains here a lot," April blurted nervously. Now everyone was staring at her. She shrugged.

"I didn't think humans enjoyed sitting out in the rain," the robot mused. "Clearly, I still have much to learn about human behavior. Is this a social event? Perhaps some kind of social bathing? Or religious baptism?"

"I'm sorry," Angelica snapped, gathering her wits. "Did you say you were here looking for David

Winchester? Why…I mean, do you want to explain that a little further?"

"Affirmative. I was programmed to determine the location of several human beings. I arrived on this planet because research indicated a seventy eight point three percent chance that two of them were brought to this planet. I succeeded in finding one- Peter Cervantes, the man whom you buried. I have not yet determined the location of Joseph Stormcrow, though your associates at the cave insisted you knew nothing about him. They informed me, however, that one of the children I was instructed to find- David Winchester, was also on this planet, and that your party had gone off to find him. That is when I tracked you here."

"What happens when you find the kid?" Carl asked, unsuccessfully attempting to wipe the water from his eyes. "You aren't going to hurt him are you?"

"Negative. I have been instructed to keep the boy safe until the starship Katara arrives to pick him up."

"He was taken," Angelica told him. "By a woman on a black horse."

"Yes, your associate James Locke related that information. But this rain will make him more difficult to track. Can you tell me where the woman has taken him?"

"There's an old research facility, a few miles north of here," Angelica told him. "That's where they have to be heading."

William fired up his boosters. "Then that is where I shall go. When I find the boy, I will return back to your caves with him." He rose into the air. "When your bathing ceremony is complete, there is an abandoned cottage approximately ninety eight meters to the south west. It would provide better shelter than this canopy of trees. You will find a cache of phaser rifles buried beneath the floor in the kitchen. They might come in useful against the humans with the Solanum virus."

"Uh, thanks," Angelica said, still struggling for words.

"Good luck," April shouted and waved as he blasted off through the trees.

Angelica watched as the android disappeared from sight. She thought she might be crying, but couldn't tell for sure. Maybe hope could still be found on Necron after all. Maybe David was going to be okay. Maybe they all would.

"Well," Carl said. "Shall we take a vote? Who's up for a night in an old cottage and some blaster rifles?"

The terrified young woman continued to make her way around the outskirts of the bridge, staying as far away from the hulking pirate as she could. The mere sight of him frightened her, and Hero knew she was running out of time. The cloaking devise was drinking away its battery the way a thirsty man guzzles water, and she'd already noticed herself flicker back into sight a time or two, luckily, Jack hadn't noticed.

They were looking right at each other the third time it happened.

"Peek-a-boo," the pirate yelled while charging. "I see you, girl."

All she could do was continue to move, and cover her mouth with her hand to help muffle the sobs. Her body flickered back out of sight. A hundred thoughts of what this man might do to her ran through Hero's head, and she didn't like any of them. How many women had this man, if you could call him that, terrorized over the years? She wished she had a knife so she could sneak up from behind and cut off his manhood. That way, he would end his miserable life knowing a little bit more what it was like to be a woman.

She approached Joseph's body, and looked down at him pleadingly. He hadn't moved since he'd fallen, but Hero kept hoping he would spring up to help her. It was a fool's hope, she knew. Even if the man was still alive, he was in no shape to help himself, much less her.

Black-backed Jack danced around the deck like a child in the schoolyard, checking every possible hiding place as he went. It was clear he was enjoying himself. *The man might claim to live off of bread, meat and wine,* Hero thought, *but it's terror that really feeds him.*

Hero heard a small electric crackle, and knew the camo shield had finally exhausted its power source. She successfully ducked behind the captain's chair just before the pirate turned his head, but what use would it do her? She crawled up into the chair and curled into a ball. There was no escape, he *was* going to catch her, and then....

He came into sight around the corner, and a moment later disappeared near the wall behind the chair. Had he seen her? Everything was quiet, except for the faint sounds of her own breath, and the tears that dropped with a soft pat upon the dirty, leather chair. She held her breath.

And then, the chair spun around so fast that her body was hurled to the ground.

"GOTCHA!" Jack yelled.

Before she could get away, the pirate was on top of her, squeezing so hard that things began to go dark. She screamed. Or rather, she was screaming, she didn't know when she'd started.

The pirate laughed and pinned her against the deck. He backhanded her so hard that her head bounced off the floor, and Hero watched as a stream of blood shot from her mouth into the air.

"Stop that screeching, you're giving me a headache," the beast spat at her. His face and voice had changed. He was no longer smiling, at least not in a playful way. Now his lips had curled into something much more sinister, more demonic. With one hand, he ripped her shirt away.

"Now you be quiet and cooperate," he told her,

turning her face toward his and looking into her eyes, "and I just might let you live when I'm through with you. Understand?"

She didn't answer. Her body felt cold and rigid, as if she might break in half at any moment, and her face was pounding. *Think of Stephen,* she told herself, closing her eyes. *Think of Stephen. Think of Stephen.* She could feel the pirate's horrible, intrusive fingers running all over her, he moved them down her stomach and seized her pants. She sobbed quietly as he ripped them from her. She wanted to scream, wanted to kick, punch, and fight, but all she could think of was her son. She was all he had, and she needed to find him. She needed to live, had to endure anything that meant getting back to him.

"That's a good lass," Jack said soothingly. "Please me, and I might even keep you around for a while."

As the huge man forced her over onto her stomach, Hero found herself in the park near her parents' house, where she'd sometimes taken her son to play. Stephen smiled at her as she tossed him a ball. He never caught it, he hadn't learned that yet, but he laughed every time it bounced off his chest.

The pirate yanked her toward him. It hurt. Her whole body hurt, and she knew that things were about to get much worse. She gritted her teeth, and cringed as her undergarments were torn away. How could she escape? How could she stop this? She couldn't. *Think of Stephen. Think of your son.*

A sound she did not recognize came buzzing through the air, and the monster on top of her screeched out in pain. He fell off to the side, and she turned her head to see him writhing in agony.

Hero scrambled away from him, hiding against the captain's chair before looking up to see Jace Chang standing over her attacker's body, holding a laser sword. He looked like death warmed over, looked like he could barely stand, and appeared to be nearly as afraid as she was. She scrambled for her clothes, eager to cover her nakedness.

"Are you okay?" Jace asked her. He sounded as miserable as he looked.

"I am now," she told him, but it was something of a lie. Tears streamed down her face, and her heart was thumping so hard that she feared it might leap from her chest and bound off across the floor.

She looked at Black-backed Jack, who was whimpering, and convulsing in pain. A black, iron plate had been grafted into his back; it looked like some kind of exoskeleton. The charred cut that the laser sword had given him ran diagonally across its length.

Jace raised his weapon into the air, preparing to bring it down upon the pirate's head.

"Wait," Hero said quietly, raising her hand. "Don't kill him. I have a better idea."

The light of the twin moons shone down upon the compound as William circled overhead. It seemed that the light and sound of his boosters had drawn the attention of several hundred wild humans. That was unfortunate. His programing forbid him to intentionally harm humans, even those who had been infected with the Solanum virus. Hopefully they would not interfere with his mission like those on the Nazerazi ship had. That incident still disturbed and confused him. Why had humans been on the ship in the first place, much less jump in front of his line of fire? He had only sought to disable the engines.

Angelica told him that the compound below was some kind of old scientific research facility, but as he scanned the place, he saw that it was much more than that. This place had the same features as some of the human military bases in his data files, though any military presence had abandoned the area long ago.

A blaster bolt came sailing passed him, and a moment later it was followed by several more. William looked down to see a group of six robed figures standing in the yard by one of the large buildings, pointing up at him with blaster rifles. He felt a slight fluctuation in his shields, and saw that another man aimed a sniper rifle at him from a guard tower at the edge of the perimeter. A piercing siren went off and rang through the night air, and then several spotlights shot up through the darkness to follow him.

This was a curious development. Humans infected with the Solanum virus, as these were, were supposed to be incapable of rational action and thought. He would have to research this further when time allowed for it.

Continuing to circle the skies, William scanned each building thoroughly before going on to the next. Hundreds of infected humans were showing up throughout the compound, but then something much more interesting showed up. Two signatures were unlike the others. These weren't infected like the rest of the humans in the area, but they didn't look quite normal either. One belonged to an adult female, and the other to a boy, the only child he'd detected so far. An infected adult male was in the room as well.

He turned toward the building, where another of the robed guards had taken position on the roof and begun to fire at him. William landed just in front of the man, snatched away the blaster rifle, and snapped it in half.

"Greetings. My designation is William Marshal. I don't suppose you could direct me to the best path for reaching the fourth floor, room 453 of this facility, could you?"

The robed man drew a blaster pistol, and squeezed off several rounds into the android's face.

"Very well, I shall find it myself." He scanned the rooftop, and each level below him more thoroughly, mapping out the best route to the boy's location.

"Curious. None of the doors in this facility appear to

be locked- a questionable approach to security." William glanced around at the dozens of guards who had taken position in the towers at the compound's perimeter, and noted the multitudes of infected humans beyond its fences. "I suppose you don't have to worry about many intruders, though, do you?"

He strode toward the door to the stairs as dozens of shots found their marks on him. None of these weapons could hurt him. It would take approximately three million two hundred thousand and fifty-seven shots from such rifles to collapse his shields, and even then the weapons could do little to damage his tritanium chassis. They did tickle a bit though, or at least what William imagined tickling must feel like.

The shots followed him as he walked through the door, and he could hear the guards scrambling overhead while descending the stairs. Down three flights he went, before opening the door on the fourth floor and walking into the hallway. Everything was quiet for a while as he strode down the hall, but as he turned a corner, two more of the robed men came charging toward him. He extended his arm phasers and stunned them, sending both men crashing to the floor. Perhaps that was bending the rules about not harming humans, but it was clear that these men had no intention of letting him carry out his mission in a timely manner.

William reached the end of the hall and turned another corner. Room 453 was just up ahead and to the left. He began to run another scan, but stopped when something very strange caught his eye, and it took a moment for him to process what he was seeing. Standing in front of the door to room 453, looking in through the glass window, was the figure of a young boy. William scanned him, but the boy had no material form. He matched the pictures of David Winchester; it certainly looked like him, but there was no DNA to confirm his identity.

The boy looked at him. "Is that me in there?"

William walked up beside him, and gazed through the window. The body of a boy rested on the bed inside. He scanned it, confirming that it was indeed David Winchester, but the body was dead; its energy signature had expired.

"They killed me, didn't they?" the boy asked him. "I thought they might. They kept telling me not to worry, but I didn't believe them." He sounded sad, and William thought that he might begin to cry. He'd never heard a child cry before, not in person. Then again, the boy had no tear ducts, or eyes for that matter. He was obviously composed from some type of energy, though William couldn't say what it was. Nothing like it existed in his data files.

"I am William Marshall," the android told him.

"David Winchester," the boy responded.

"I was sent to find you. I've been programmed to return you to Galin Winchester, your father."

The boy looked at him blankly. "I wish you'd gotten here a few minutes ago."

Out of nowhere, a series of flashes shot from the window, and something not unlike lightning filled the room.

William watched in fascination. "What's happening in there?"

"I don't know, but someone's coming. Are they with you?"

William followed the child's stare, turning his head to look back down the hallway. "I don't see anyone."

"I don't want to go with them." The boy sounded scared. "Will you take me away from here? Please?"

William nodded his head, though he wasn't sure how he might do it. He reached out to touch the boy, but his hand went right through. At almost the same time, David jumped toward him, and his face turned to shock as he passed through the robot's chassis and into his body. It tickled a lot more than any of the blaster bolts had.

"Now I need to get you back to the Katara."

"I don't want to go there," David told him, but William heard himself say the words. "I want to go find Sarah first. Will you take me to my sister instead?"

William thought for a moment. His orders were to locate each individual, and then protect them until the Katara came for retrieval. But what if he went to find the girl first? That wouldn't be against his orders, not strictly speaking. He *was* supposed to find both children, after all. "That would be acceptable."

"Good, now get us out of here before they get me!"

William didn't know who "they" were, but he jumped into the air and rocketed through the roof. It was almost as if he couldn't help himself.

"What about your body?" William asked him.

"No!" David insisted. "We need to get out of here, NOW! Besides, I told you they killed me. What good is my body going to do me now?"

"Perhaps your program could be re-downloaded," William suggested as he crashed through the outside roof. Rubble went flying in all directions.

"I don't think that would work," David told him. "That woman and the doctor are evil. They were doing weird things to me, I watched them through the window before you showed up."

The guards in the towers scrambled to resume fire, and the boy cried out in fear as blaster bolts flew passed them from every direction.

"You do not need to fear them," William told him. "You are with me now, and they can not harm me."

The android rocketed up toward the smaller moon almost faster than the guards' eyes could follow.

"Do you know where my sister is?"

"It is believed that many human prisoners, especially young females, were taken to the Zeta Reticuli star system to be sold as slaves."

"Do you have a ship that can take us there?"

"I will take us there, but the journey will take many days." William wondered what they might talk about along the way. "Have you ever been rained on?" he asked.

Hero felt like she'd been run over by a truck, but things might have been much worse. Despite her bruises, she had escaped with her honor, and more importantly, her life. They had all escaped with their lives. They'd found Joseph, and had been able to free dozens of other slaves. Hero wondered if she should feel happy about it all. She wanted to, but most of all, she just felt numb.

She brushed the dirty, yellow hair from her eyes and examined the control panel. As it turned out, one regeneration chamber was not enough to go around. Jace had been taken out of his cycle a bit too soon, and Joseph and Ulrick had each taken significant wounds. Luckily, one of the slaves on the pirate ship had been a doctor, and he was more than willing to help get everyone patched up.

As beaten and wounded as the rest of the crew was, they'd all agreed on one thing- Black-backed Jack should have the honor of being the first patient in the regeneration chamber. Revenge was a dish best served cold, and this particular pirate had a lot of people waiting in line to serve it up for him.

Hero felt no joy as she programmed the chamber.

Species -Human-
Approximate Age -40 years old-
Gender -Female-

"Rest well," she told the man who'd tried to violate her, though he couldn't hear. "When you wake up, you won't be the man you used to be."

She began the regeneration cycle, and trudged up the metal steps toward the cockpit. Her legs each felt like they weighed a ton.

Ulrick and Jace were sitting in the captain's and co-pilot's chairs. Ulrick had his feet up and was snoring peacefully. A large bandage covered his right foot, and only his toes stuck out.

Jace turned and smiled at her.

"You look a little better," she told him, touching his neck. "Just a little."

"Thanks. I expect you to fill me in on everything, just as soon as we've both had a good, long nap."

"I will. Joseph is in the engine room, says he'll be there if you need him for anything. He seems really happy to be back down there."

"I'll bet he is," Jace agreed. "For lots of reasons."

A voice came over the com. "Hey, Jace, this is Daniel. Matt and I are ready to engage the tractor beam and move out. Is everything ready on your end?"

"Yup, everything's good to go over here. Thanks again for the lift."

"Are you kidding me?" Daniel laughed. "Thanks to you guys we have our lives back, not to mention a ship. The least we can do is give you a tow. I just hope it's not too late for our friends back on Necron. I hope we make it in time to save them."

"I hope so too. But you haven't been gone long, I'm sure you'll find everyone right where you left them. Listen, I'll be on watch if you need anything."

"Okay, same goes for us. Talk to you later."

The com clicked off, and Jace and Hero gazed out at the pirate ship. A thick green tractor beam shot out and the Katara shook gently as it struck them.

"Those two *are* experienced pilots, right?" Hero asked nervously as she felt the beam take hold.

Jace looked up at her and shrugged. "No, they're Amish barn makers. But they said they could drive a buggy pretty good. I told them that piloting a starship wasn't that much different." He winked at her, and she laughed.

"Sorry, I'm just…still a bit on edge."

Stars began to move past them as the ships picked up speed.

Jace stood up, and embraced her gently. "You've

been through a *lot* lately, and you don't have *anything* to apologize for." He looked deep into her eyes. "I'm really proud of you. What you did, sneaking over onto that ship... it saved us all. If Jack hadn't gone back to find you, we'd probably all be dead now."

"I'm just glad you showed up when you did. A minute longer, and ... and...."

"Me too." He kissed her on the forehead. "You want to hang around up here with us for a while? You can have the chair. Join Ulrick in a little shut-eye while I keep an eye out?"

She considered it. "I think I'll rest better in my own bed. But I wouldn't mind you checking in on me after the big guy wakes up."

"I will," he promised. "Go take a hot shower and get some sleep. You'll feel better."

She nodded, and turned to leave.

"Hey, Hero, hold on a sec." He reached into his right cargo pocket. "Could you throw this in the garbage compactor for me?" he asked, dropping the laser sword into her hands.

"I thought you said you've always wanted one of these."

He cringed. "Yeah, I did. But...I think I'll just stick with a blaster pistol from now on."

She shrugged. "Okay. But maybe Ulrick would like it, or—"

"No. Just get rid of it for me. Please."

She squeezed his shoulder. "All right. I will."

"Thanks," he said, sounding relieved.

The door slid shut behind her, and Hero made her way toward Starla's quarters. She quivered upon seeing what was left of the kitchen, and imagined what Ulrick must have gone through dealing with the invaders. He was right though; the place did look nice with a window. She wondered if they might install one there, and opened up the trash compactor chute. Tossing the sword in, she felt a little sad. After all, Jace had used the thing to save her. But the sword was extremely dangerous, and she was glad that he'd decided to get rid of it. It clanked down the chute and out of sight.

Thank God that he came when he did. Jace was a good man; a good friend. And maybe even something more, but she couldn't think about that now. Her dead husband's face popped into her head, and it felt too much like betrayal.

Upon reaching her room, Hero carefully undressed and examined herself in the mirror. Her body hurt all over, and it was littered with fresh bruises. Her face looked like it'd been kicked by a horse. But did she look as bad as she felt? Probably not. Tears began to run down her face again. It seemed that she'd spent more time crying lately than not. *You need to be strong,* she told herself. *Think of Stephen, just focus on getting him back safely.* At least she wasn't alone. She had friends now; friends that cared about her, friends that were willing to *help* her.

But would they still be her friends, and willing to help if they knew who she really was? If they knew why she'd really come? Hopefully she'd never have to find out.

ABOUT THE AUTHOR

Ethan Russell Erway, author of the ADVENTURES OF MICHAEL BELMONT fantasy series, and THE BLEEDING STAR CHRONICLES adult novellas, has been a life long fan of the fantasy and science fiction genres. His third book, MICHAEL BELMONT AND THE CURSE OF THE THUNDERBIRD, is due for release in late 2013. Ethan has a Bachelor of Sacred Literature degree from Summit Theological Seminary, and is the Minister at Agua Fria Christian Church in Humboldt, AZ where he lives with his wife Kara and sons Gabriel and Caleb.

Connect with Me Online:

http://www.EthanRussellErway.com

http://twitter.com/@ethanerway

http://www.Facebook.com/EthanRussellErway